Gitana
Life Plan

Beth M James

Written by Beth M James

Copyright © 2013 Beth M James

ISBN 978-0-9889428-1-3

Cover Photography: Peter Veiler

This book is dedicated to:

My husband, Mike, who helped me in a million ways to get this story published.

My children, Willow and Hans, my love for them will always run deep.

My mom and sisters, Deb and Pam, for they introduced me to romance books.

And last but not least, to my stepdaughter Lisa.

Lesson #1
Good-byes open doors.

Gitana Sothers caught sight of the baby blue Mercedes as it turned into the gravel parking lot near the houseboats. Her first instinct was to run.

That son of a bitch.

Doctor *GQ* with the sun-bleached hair and golfer's tan. He inched his convertible forward as if on parade. When he stopped near her side, she lifted her chin and gave him a cold, unwelcoming stare. Sausalito was not his territory.

"And why are you here, Doctor John?" She drawled his name, letting him know she didn't think too much of his status now that they were divorced. He continued to show up at her place with an excuse to see her, and it was getting old. She hated how he observed her like a case study—an object versus a human with feelings. "Don't you have more important things to do?"

"Nice to see you too," he said, shifting into park.

Gitana stepped back to provide a little more distance from the car. She rested her hand on her hip and watched him scrutinize her attire without words. She wore form-fitting jeans and a scoop top where cleavage met the edge of purple fabric. Her black lacy bra peeked from underneath. Inappropriate wear in her ex's eyes. The bastard. He had no right to stare at her like she was trash.

She leaned forward and put her hands on the top edge of the passenger door, purposely touching his precious car. His nostrils flared and his jaw tightened, but he didn't comment. He showed restraint—so unlike him.

Gitana smiled like the Grinch would after a bad deed. Poor thing would have to polish his baby again.

She stepped away, and the sun must have caught the small diamond stud in her nose. John looked at her recent piercing with disgust. "That can cause a serious infection, you know."

So typical. He was good at pointing out what he didn't like. If one eyebrow hair were out of line, he would have the tweezers ready. If a dress made her appear "thick," he would choose another for her to wear. The diamond in her nose must have curled the hairs on his ass.

"Is that what you came here for? To give me some doctorly advice?"

She waited for an insult to slide from his mouth, but he bit his lip instead.

With no makeup, she knew her dark brown eyes didn't have the sophisticated appearance he liked. She had no need for mascara though; her lashes were already black and thick. John used to make her put it on anyway. Back then, she had to be his model-perfect wife.

Gitana stared at him, challenging him to a duel. He had plenty to slam her with, as he had high expectations of her appearance in public. *But to hell with him.* She looked better now, more Californian and fresh. She had gained weight since their split, toned her muscles with weights and exercise. She was no longer pale or rail thin.

John flicked his head up as if to say "whatever" to her challenge. He reached over to open his glove compartment and pulled out an eight-by-ten padded envelope for her. He said, "Here, you could use it."

"Hand-delivered. Nice." How appropriate for him to give her the final monthly check that kept her finances in the black. She would miss the settlement payments, and he knew she would struggle without them. The envelope bulged with something else, but she refrained from asking.

He stayed to watch her reaction.

She wondered if he thought she'd get all excited. Gitana rolled her eyes, ready to get rid of him. "What do you want? A signature?"

"Not this time. I included a gift you can probably use." He threw the gear shift into first.

She hated his smugness in that perfect smile. She had the urge to slap him for showing no remorse about wanting the divorce. No guilt for leaving her for his pregnant mistress.

"Bye-bye," she said and tapped the hood of his car with the palm of her hand. Gitana dragged her fingers along the shiny surface to make sure he would have to polish more than just the one spot on his precious baby.

"Make it last," he said as she walked away. The car's wheels pushed against the gravel as he drove off. Rocks kicked up from the back tires and bounced near her feet.

"Asshole," she mumbled under her breath.

Gitana held her chin high and refused to watch him leave. She walked to the small park at the end of the peninsula, nestled between the houseboats and the marina. The air tasted saltier as the wind picked up. A few white caps waved across the water and sparkled in the sun. She stopped when the sidewalk ended and enjoyed the bay instead of thinking about her ex.

The day could turn around. She had a good morning. The afternoon started fine but then turned to crap after she left work. So what if she left her keys at the winery and now couldn't get inside her boat. Or that John, in all his smugness, decided to bring her the last payment in person. Her neighbor Layne would be home soon; he had a spare key to her place. Her ex had left. The sky was blue and the sun felt great. She lifted her head to capture the bright warmth on her skin. The sailboats seemed to do the same with their silver masts pointed high.

Breathe in. Breathe out.

Don't let him get to you.

Did he think she couldn't get on with her life? Is that why he came around so much? At first she thought it was because of their history. For many years they tried having a baby. She left her marketing career and her art to concentrate on getting pregnant. And each time she tested, the result came back negative. He had always been supportive, sharing tears when the fertility treatments failed. She thought he would continue to care for her, but the mistress won. Now she had to find a new plan. A yellow cigarette boat idled toward the marina and tied up at the gas pumps. She admired the sleek form and wondered if she could match on canvas how the sun danced against the silver-flecked sides of the boat. The wind changed direction and a strand of her hair blew across her cheek. She brushed it aside. Gitana looked over at her rented houseboat on the other side of the inlet. The steel-hulled boat needed a good coat of paint and some character. The owner dismissed the idea of being unique and in good condition like the surrounding boats, splashed with brilliant shades of pinks, reds, blues, and greens. Each one had personality that matched its owner. Many floated on steady hulls made from cement, while her tattered wooden boat rocked with the slightest wave.

Maybe this afternoon, when she could get back into her home, she would try painting the yellow boat. Her oils and acrylics were out, ready to go. Or she could go out and find a permanent job. Working at the winery was temporary. Living on the boat was temporary. Gitana needed stability. Plain and simple. The divorce crushed her, and now she had to get her life back in order. But not today. Bad days like this one were not good times to start.

Gitana turned her attention to the envelope and took a deep breath. Enough worrying. She opened the flap so not to tear the check inside. She pulled out the familiar crisp white envelope with *Singhauser and Breck, Attorneys at Law,* printed in the corner. A seagull squawked overhead, distracting her for a moment. It flapped its wings, waiting for a morsel to drop from her hands, though with the smell of fish surrounding the bay, the bird had better sources to prey on than her.

Gitana dug into the envelope again and this time pulled out a small plastic container. Diazepam. The sound of disgust came from her throat. Pop a pill. Mask the pain and all the worries. Take one tablet. Maybe two. But do not come back. Her ex had given her a fucking prescription to calm her nerves. Her blood boiled.

She glanced toward the parking lot. No baby blue Mercedes waited to see her reaction. She pictured the smirk on John's face as he drove off; the twisted grin that said he was better than her. That she was nothing in his eyes. A castoff.

The hurt swelled. Tears threatened, but she kept both in control. He was not going to get to her.

Gitana tucked the padded envelope under one arm and held the bottle of pills in her other hand. She used her pinky to open the white envelope, half expecting a bill instead of a check. *Yes, a check*. The amount was ten dollars less than what she normally received—he'd charged her for the pills!

A wind gust came up and would have ripped the check from her fingers if she hadn't tightened her grip. She tried stuffing the flimsy paper back into the small envelope, but the corner got stuck. She opened it wider. Another gust whipped across the peninsula, and this time the check slipped from her fingers.

Wide-eyed, Gitana watched as the paper twirled above the peninsula like a kite, but without the string to reel it back in.

'No!" Her throat tightened as the money waved good-bye. She ran to follow the white flutter. She stretched her hand upward, but the gap was too great.

I need that check!

The thought of calling John's lawyer and telling him how she lost it was not an option. He would immediately call her ex, and they would enjoy a good laugh at her expense. Who knows when they'd cut her a new check.

Even the seagull seemed to laugh. It swooped near her head, then caught the check in its beak. Gitana ran after the bird.

"Give it back!"

She gripped the bottle of pills in her hand, ready to throw them at the gull. Her aim had limits. The vial? Not heavy enough. Neither would do her any good. But maybe the damn thing would go for a pill, wanting food. Gitana struggled to twist the cap off, pressing and turning hard with her palm. She kept her eye on the seagull.

The cap popped off and tumbled to the ground. Shaking a pill into her hand, Gitana twirled the powdery tablet between her fingers, then flung it at the bird.

Go after the pill. Drop the check!

The gull ignored the white dot. The check, in its beak, flapped like a second set of wings.

Drop it!

She tipped the vial and let a few more of the tablets fall into her hand, ready to tempt the gull with them.

Her nose itched and then tickled. She lifted her hand, feeling a sneeze come on.

***

Cade DeVerine left the small gallery with fists clenched and steam shooting from his nose. Rumor had it that one of his exclusive artists was selling her work at different shops around the city. He flipped his cell phone out of his pocket and called his assistant.

"She's done. I want her paintings out of there today." He ended the call.

As a gallery owner and sculptor, he knew both sides of the fence. He treated his artists with respect and demanded the same. He took pride in his galleries and offered his clients the best. They wanted unique art and would pay the price. That artist now stamped out her oils as cookie-cutter prints, selling them in every gift shop for a quick buck.

He breathed in, allowing his broad chest to expand as he walked off his anger. Two women passed by and smiled coyly at him. He ignored them. The last thing he needed now was a female to rile him up some more.

Cade took longer strides as he passed the little shops and the restaurants. Along the bay, a community of houseboats popped into view. He decided to check them out, aware that many artists tried to capture the beauty of the boats in their paintings. Most failed to show the sparkling water or paint in the sensation of waves lapping against the hulls and docks.

Cade stopped in front of the parking lot entrance and let a primed 1966 Falcon Convertible pull in. He admired the progress. The sleek body with its dull finish and white patches was ready for painting. He wondered what color he'd use. Black. Black would work. Cade nodded his approval and the driver nodded back.

The parking lot turned from tar to gravel. The rumble of a cigarette boat caught his attention. He decided to head for it and catch the breeze off the peninsula.

A woman with long, wavy black hair seemed to be doing a little dance at the park. He squinted, honing in on her antics. She held a bottle of pills. She seemed upset. *Desperate?* He kept his eyes on her and the pills.

Her hand went up to her mouth.

Cade's stomach dropped. A snapshot of his sister, fifteen years ago, in the kitchen of her dank, filthy apartment flashed through his head. The pills she'd tossed defiantly into her mouth when he asked her to stop, and she replied to him how it was none of his goddamn business what she did.

Not again.

Cade reacted. He yelled to grab the woman's attention, but his voice disappeared with the wind. His heart slammed against the inside of his chest as he dug his feet into the gravel and pumped his legs forward.

Bam!

He tackled her and she hit the ground with him on top.

The sweet yet pungent scent of smeared grass reached Cade's nose.

The cigarette boat no longer idled in the bay, the gulls stopped squawking, and the seal that barked in the distance turned quiet.

First sound back was a clinking of metal on metal, then metal on wood as the masts from the boats in the marina rocked with the wind. Next came his own quick, short breaths while she lay still beneath him.

Her face, buried in the grass, showed no sign of movement. Slight panic squeezed his stomach. He grabbed her shoulders and turned her around, afraid he knocked her out. He waited.

The woman opened her eyes to the blue sky. He raised his head to see what she focused on. A few gulls circled above, nothing unusual. She snapped out of her daze and tried to get up. He refused to move.

She snarled. "Get the fuck off me!"

His rock-hard eyes stared at her. "Ain't gonna happen," he said in a voice as rough as course sandpaper.

She fumed. Dirt and grass fell into her mouth. She managed to slip her hand out from under his leg to wipe it away. Her other hand came up, the one with the pills, and he grabbed her wrist.

Like a feral cat, she batted wildly to keep him from pinning her down. They played a wild version of patty-cake. He clasped her wrists firmly with one hand and used his other to open her fingers. He focused on the pills. She snapped her hand downward. Cade lost his grip.

She used the bottle as a weapon and slammed the bottom edge into his chest; more pills fell out. Cade tightened his muscles and took the brunt of it. She tried again but this time he swatted her hand away. The vial flew upward and the remaining white dots spilled out. They danced above her and then bounced against the grass.

Cade kept his thighs firm and left her no room to escape. She turned her head to search for someone to help. He didn't care. She stammered with anger, "You got the pills. You got what you want. Now let me go."

Cade leaned forward and pinned her arms down with his hands. He loved her eyes, pure flecks of chocolate without hints of blue or yellow. She parted her lips, and he had the urge to lean in and kiss her, even as she shot a daggered glare.

She sized him up and then matched his stare like a fighter challenging an opponent. Her cheeks reddened as the anger rose. The woman brought her leg up and tried to buck him off. He stayed like a rock. She hit him again and managed to knock him halfway off.

"Chill out," he warned.

"Why should I?"

"I saved your life."

"Saved me?" She wrinkled her nose and then shook her head. "You attacked me!"

He hesitated for a second to think back if he made a mistake. He shook his head. "You're the one with the pills. And I'm not going to let you take them."

"*What?*" She seemed dumbfounded.

She rocked her hips and inched her way from underneath him. Her jeans rolled downward to reveal a flat stomach and the start of black panties. Her abs, tight and smooth, aroused him. The curve to her waist, the soft skin, and the cute belly button intoxicated him more than he wanted. The feel of her under his legs didn't help matters. He eased up and rose to his knees.

Free, she edged across the ground for some distance and hitched her jeans back up. She brushed away the grass and dirt from her face. She rubbed her wrists, still red from his attack.

"Taking pills ain't the way to go," he said and kept his stance in case she decided to run.

"And who said I was?" she shot back. Her black tresses fell across her shoulders in a wild and seductive way.

He liked it.

She explained, "I was throwing them at the gull."

The woman suddenly looked up at the sky, around at the peninsula, and then the marina. She pressed her hands against her forehead as if to relieve a headache.

Cade had to laugh and wondered if he heard her correctly. "A gull?"

She shook her head, not so much in frustration but as if she were lost or sad. When she turned to him again, the fire returned. She said, "I wasn't going to take the pills, you ass."

"Yeah, right." He snorted. The desperate look on her face told a different story. "They were going in your mouth."

"I sneezed." She eyed a couple of the white tablets near her feet and picked them up to discard them properly. She found another buried in the grass.

Without a second thought, Cade slapped the pills from her hand. The remaining tablets scattered.

He should have done the same thing to his sister years ago, taken away her pills and put her in rehab. Back then, he was always the bad guy. Too many times he'd let it go and allowed his mother to defend her daughter's habit.

"Great move," the woman said and gave him a hard stare as she sat up. "Now you can pick 'em up."

"I plan on it." Cade kneeled forward to rake his fingers across the grass. She continued to rub her hand. He knew his slap must have stung, but it was her fault. Cade found four of the pills and crushed them with his palms. He rubbed his hands together, and the wind blew the powder away.

She rose to her knees and distanced herself from him. He didn't like the sign, the way her eyes saddened. Was she plotting her next attempt?

He stood and asked, "Why the effort? What's got you so down?"

***

Gitana's first reaction was to tell him to mind his own business. But all that aside, she considered what he must have assumed. He found a lone woman close to tears with a handful of pills. She might have thought the same.

"I'm not down. I'm angry. I just lost my check."

The man presented a tough front. He cocked an eyebrow. His smooth-shaven head told her that he was confident in his own skin. *Maybe a cop?*

"I'm Cade," he said and offered her an outstretched hand.

She hesitated, but he seemed to offer her a truce. Gitana accepted and slipped her hand into his. She didn't expect the sudden tug or his strength as she flew upward and into his arm. Cade held tight to keep them both from toppling over.

"You all right?" He wouldn't let her go.

His sharp blue eyes warmed, and they caught her off guard. Was it the way he cared for her or his tough appearance that sent a tingle through her insides? Maybe both. She couldn't pull away.

Stop it! She had to get the thought out of her head. Gitana squirmed until he let go. The last time she had let a man be that close was her ex, John. He had come home from work and wanted to ravish her in the foyer. The next morning he asked for the divorce. No more was she going to let a man hurt her.

"What's your name?" he asked.

"Gitana," she said and brushed her hands against her thighs.

"Gitana," he repeated. "Gypsy in Spanish. The name fits."

"Pray tell?" She was curious. Her family had given her the nickname as a child. She loved to dance around the house with castanets in hand and to see the long, flowing chiffon scarves sway around her waist as she moved. She used her nickname, Gitana, again after her split from John. She hated how he pronounced Annabella, her given name, as if it were two words. Using Gitana gave her a new start.

"A little lost, yet spirited," Cade said.

She rolled her head, somewhat in agreement. Gitana liked his response more than the slam she had expected. Stepping back, her knee buckled. Cade's hands went out but she recovered quickly, not daring to touch him again.

"You hurt?"

"I'll b-be all right," she stuttered.

He kept his arm out, ready to save her if needed. She rubbed her arms and kept her eyes down. She was not supposed to have feelings, even slight, for another man so soon.

Needing a distraction, she spotted the empty vial and cap in the grass. Gitana swept them up and headed for the waste bin. Her back cracked, her side ached. She wanted to go home. Layne, her neighbor, should be home by now, and he could open her door. She could hide for the rest of the day in her boat and start over in the morning.

"Suicide isn't meant to be an end, you know," he said and trailed after her like a puppy when she walked away.

"True. But as I said before, I wasn't taking my life. Nor do I plan to." She cut across the grass to the sidewalk. He kept up. She wanted to walk alone, so she stopped to give him the message. Gitana faced him. "I don't owe you an explanation if that's what you're looking for; however, if you agree to go away, I'll explain."

He put his hands on his hips, copying her. He squinted from the sun shining in his eyes. "I'm not looking for one. You had the pills in your hand. End of story."

"My ex dropped by to give me the last payment from our settlement. Included was a bottle of Diazepam."

Cade cocked his head, a little more interested.

Bitterness ran from her mouth. "A little side stab on his part. He's a doctor. Anyway, yes, the pills were in my hand. I hoped the bird would take one and drop my check. I sneezed before I could toss them at him."

He turned to face her again. "Why would he give you pills?"

Gitana tightened her lips. Why was he so interested in the Diazepam? Did he want to hear how she went wild after finding out her husband had a mistress?

She had pounded her fists into John's chest when he told her the woman was pregnant. He knew that would hurt her. She tried for years to conceive. He obviously cheated on her until he got what he wanted.

Gitana swallowed hard to remove the lump in her throat. "Let me just say we're now free and clear from each other's lives."

His hard street face weighed in her believability factor. "Something like a sick joke? A last present?"

She flicked her eyebrows, then snickered but offered nothing else.

"I'm sorry." He seemed to mean it by the way his eyes softened again.

Up ahead, a white piece of paper flapped between two rocks. Gitana made a beeline to look. A hint of blue ink made her heart skip. She bent down, hoping she'd recovered the check.

"Ha!" She pulled gently on a corner, careful not to rip it. Rumpled and shredded at one end, she was sure the bank would still cash it. She held the prized possession to her chest. Thank God, she did not have to call the lawyer for a replacement.

Cade stood with his hands on his hips and watched her. She smiled and showed her proof.

"Next time, go for the check. Not the pills," he said.

"Okay, hero," she said and tucked the payment into her back jean pocket.

He smiled a little crooked turn of his mouth with full lips. It seemed to say their paths would cross again. He headed for the parking lot.

"Later, Gitana."

"Highly doubtful, Cade." She waved to dismiss him.

Lesson #2
Fear triggers reaction.

Living on a houseboat had advantages. The gentle rock of the boat on the water, the salty breeze in the air, and the closeness to nature worked together. Layne Jaroul enjoyed the dark before sunrise on the deck of his custom-made wooden boat. He settled into his canvas chair, popped a Corona, and relaxed. He needed the downtime after work, playing blues with the band.

Tonight, as had many nights in the last few months, kicked him hard in the ass. He strained his arms to get his drums to thunder the floor. He gave the band and audience what they required. He set the beat, made their blood pump, their legs move. Jake, the band's singer, and the others longed for a contract, recordings, fame—they wanted sex, drugs, money.

Layne had a different plan. His goal of becoming a full-time physical trainer distanced him from those things. Pumped muscles and sculpted bodies gave him the reward, the high, he needed. People loved the results of his work, and their appreciation meant more than a good night playing music.

As he focused on the moon's reflection on the dark, oily bay, he heard the sliding glass door of his neighbor's boat open, then close. He grabbed a Corona from the cooler and wiped the wet, icy bottle against his black cotton shorts. The sound of flip-flops shuffling to the back of the boat reached him. He heard the splash of water over the top of the makeshift raft tied between their boats as Gitana jumped from her houseboat to his. He twisted the cap off the bottle. The beer released with energy, and the hiss called to his friend.

"Mind if I join you?" Her voice poured over him like maple syrup. She appeared from the shadows and limped toward him.

"A little sore?" he asked with some amusement as she rubbed her thighs.

"A little." Gitana took the beer from him and plopped into the folding chair next to him. She laughed. "And this time my pain isn't caused by you and your workouts."

Layne chuckled. Earlier she'd grabbed her spare key from his boat and told him about her ex's visit, the gull, her check, the pills, and the idiot who tackled her. He teased, "Too bad it wasn't me. I can give you more pain if you want."

She made a face and then put her lips to the bottle. The woman knew how to enjoy a cold brew. She wiped her mouth when she finished.

Layne took a swig of his Corona and remembered the day they met, the day she moved into the houseboat. One by one, she'd hauled each box down the dock. She wore sandals with delicate pink straps and heels that were ready to break from all the weight she carried. Her white silk tank top and red capris sagged from the heat and her sweat.

At first, she avoided him. He'd offered his assistance, but she was too stubborn—like she wanted to prove to the world she could do it without a man. Watching her move in next door without help became torturous, and finally he had to interfere. He'd set an ice-cold beer on the post—like dangling a carrot in front of a mule. She took the bait and drank half without stopping. He unloaded the last of the boxes from the U-Haul van and carried them to the boat as she finished the remainder of her beer. Then she helped herself to a second bottle. Since then they'd developed an easy friendship.

"Only you, Gitana." He laughed as he thought about her crazy story with the gull and her stubbornness. "At least you got your check."

"Yes, a definite hallelujah moment." Her head went down, and he felt a change in her mood. She focused on her toes instead of him.

"So how come you be up this late?"

She shrugged. "A creepy monster slithered into my dreams."

Layne knew better. "You need to stop thinking about your ex."

He removed the black, skull-print bandana from his

head and let the night air cool him off. He rubbed the fuzz on his scalp and wondered if he should grow his hair long again. Not yet. He still liked being smooth and would shave in the morning.

Gitana shivered, so he grabbed his lined windbreaker from the bench next to him, then leaned over and wrapped it around her shoulders. He hated the tremble in her lip and the hurt in her eyes. That said what her words did not.

Gitana clutched the jacket together with one hand and took another drink of her beer. She studied the other boats tied to the dock. Some had lights glowing in a soft hue from the deck. Others were dark.

Her voice faltered. "Do you think the guilt keeps him up at night? Does *she* like sleeping across the king-size bed we shared for over seven years?" She tapped the bottom of the bottle against her thigh. "He replaced me as if I never existed."

"Does it matter anymore?"

"I should have fought harder." She stopped to think about the divorce and then restated her argument. "I could have made life more difficult for him and been a bitch about it. Why not, since he accused me of being one?"

"But you're not like that, are you?"

She let out a heavy breath. "At times I can be. I was this afternoon."

Layne gave her time to reflect, get all the bad stuff out of her system. He listened to their boats rub against the dock, the creak of wood. He kept quiet until she was ready to join him again after being deep in thought.

"Funny, I'm the one who became the outcast. I'm no longer important without my 'distinguished' husband. Our friends became his friends, not mine. Not one invitation to a cocktail party or even a charity event."

"Screw 'em," Layne said. He let out a belch that steamed garlic and pepperoni. Gitana waved her hand to clear the smell. He loved pasta and bread before a long set, and now came the after effects.

"Yeah, screw 'em," she said with an edge in her voice.

Layne straightened his wide, muscular back. He brought his arms up and flexed his Hulk-like muscles. "Should I beat him up for you?"

"Yes, go right ahead." She laughed. When he leaned closer to her, she rubbed the stubble on his chin with affection.

"And what do I always tell you?"

She deepened her voice and mimicked him. "Things happen for a reason."

"You got it." He smiled, lifted his beer for a toast, tapping his bottle against hers. "Here's to finding you a good man."

She snickered. "Yeah, like the suicide hound dog tackling me to the ground today? No thank you. Not in my crystal ball for a while."

"You never know what life has planned for you," he sang.

Gitana was gorgeous. Men noticed her dark eyes, long hair, and curves. But she always looked away and never gave that direct glance back. She wouldn't allow anyone near her, except for him. She knew he was safe—more like a brother.

Layne coughed and took another swig of beer. He was a lot like her. They each retreated into their own little misery. Maybe it was time for a change.

"Come listen to the band this Saturday. We're playing at the Bay Moon."

Gitana raised her eyes and thought for a second. "I can't. I work until seven."

"Band don't start until ten."

"I work all day at the winery. I'll be tired."

"Too bad," Layne said and refused to let her come up with another excuse. "I need you there. I'm tired of the women hanging on me."

"You want me to be your star-crazed fan?"

He smiled. "Now you're talking. And, you can fix that attitude of yours. Loosen up."

Gitana rolled her eyes but didn't say no this time. He knew he had her.

***

Gitana stood for a moment inside the haze-filled bar. Her vision adjusted to the dim lights. The walls were dingy and yellow from years of smoke, and the air lingered like stale breath after a heavy night of partying and drinking. The place was now smoke-free, but the yellow-stained tiles still dripped tar and nicotine and stayed true to the cigarette-loving people who'd occupied it before.

Gitana ignored the stares from the men as she walked back to the stage. She chastised herself for what she wore; her tight jeans, low-cut blouse, and black vest invited stares to her chest. Even a few of the woman eyed her as if assessing their competition. No competition here. Leather, big bellies, ratted hair, and thick black eyeliner characterized the men and women in the bar, and she preferred neither.

Layne played with his headset snug against the bandana that covered his head. He mimicked Johnny Cash—all in black. Two women competed for his attention but he brushed them off. He was happy to leave them when he saw her.

"Gitana." He dropped from the stage to hug her.

"No date tonight?" She referred to the two women.

Layne shrugged off the idea. "Not my type."

"What is your type?" Gitana had to think. Only once since meeting him, a year ago now, had she seen him on a date. Or, at least she thought he had been on one. The woman had been a cling-on to his arm, while he seemed stiff and uncomfortable.

"No one here, that's for sure." Layne scanned the room.

"Yes, thank you by the way. You could've picked a better bar instead of inviting me to this one."

"Next gig is in Oakland. Besides, you needed a night out now. Not next week."

"Gitana!" the bass guitarist grabbed her shoulders.

She jumped like a gun had gone off, then quickly recovered. "Hey, Jules."

"Layne said you were coming. Grab a seat."

Jules, a perfect clone for Keith Richards, balanced an unlit cigarette between his lips. He pointed to a chair for her to sit. The others already had jackets draped over them.

The band's space included three worn tables pushed together near the corner of the dance floor. Bottles of beer, ale, peanuts, and two baskets of half-eaten fries marked their territory.

"It's good to have ya here. We've missed our number one fan," Jules said and motioned for the server to bring her a Corona—he must have remembered her preferred brand.

From up on stage, Jake, the Ted Nugent singer, blew her a kiss with one hand and turned on his microphone with the other.

"Check. Check. Gitana," he said into the mesh ball. "Check. Hello, Gitana. Check. Check."

She smiled and waved.

"No wandering," Layne warned and pointed his drumsticks at her. He jumped on stage.

Their first set for the night started with an aggressive version of George Thorogood's *Bad to the Bone*. Freddie, the guitarist, teetered at the edge of the wood platform and worked his leopard-print Fender. He played with enough piss and vinegar to get the crowd going. A few older bar-goers moved closer, pounded their fists into the air, and bobbed their heads to the beat.

She sat back with her beer and watched Layne hit the drums effortlessly. He rocked, like the rest, but his eyes lacked the thrill. How many times in the last year had he said that he was going to quit the band?

A large man on the dance floor performed an exaggerated version of Freddie's solo with his air guitar. He held his hands a little too far above his head and stumbled back. He grabbed the chair next to Gitana and both stumbled. Afraid he might take her out, she scooted her seat backward.

"I'm okay," he slurred. His overgrown mullet hung across his face. His fingers, thick and deep-scarred, gripped the chair for balance. He tried to focus on her, but the booze didn't help. He smiled like an out-of-place porn star with a bad moustache. "Hey, sexy. You wanna dance?"

"No thanks." She laughed with some amusement. The guy had no idea how ridiculous he looked.

"I got the moves." He swirled his hips in Elvis fashion and wagged his tongue.

Gitana shook her head and hoped he didn't think he really had a chance with her—or any other woman for that matter.

The drunk went back to the floor to show her more of his moves. He humped the air with his legs bent, mouth open, and eyes closed. Not his best look. When he bumped into a woman who wore knee-high boots, short shorts, and a sparkling halter, he turned his attention to her.

How depressing. Gitana wondered if she'd ever find a decent man. She had thought John was ideal. He consoled her when she couldn't get pregnant. He cried as much as she had. What happened? Did he stop acting? When did he decide she wasn't worth it?

Gitana finished her beer and ordered another.

A hand jerked the back of her chair. Studded boots, leather pants, and spiked bracelet greeted her. She raised her gaze to the tough biker.

Asshole.

He tapped his drink against her arm. "Buy you a drink."

"No, I'm good." She stared at the sharp tip of his boot when he took a step to the side of her chair. He kept his hand on her chair back. Gitana shifted. She didn't want him in her personal space.

"Let me buy you a beer," he repeated.

"I already ordered one." She matched his growl.

Old whiskey, smoke, and sweat permeated his skin and clothes. He coughed. "Play pool?"

"No," she said and made eye contact. His beady eyes were hard and cold. A scar ran from his lip to the edge of his jaw. Not one to mess with. She turned back to the band.

"You some high-mighty bitch?" He kicked the chair. "Too good for a real man?"

"Leave her alone, Eddie." The waitress returned with her beer. With leathered face and hefty boobs, she was a better match for the biker. "Go back to the bar."

"Thanks," Gitana said after he left with a couple of grunts in protest.

"Just don't let him see you leave. He may follow."

News she loved to hear.

"Why in the hell did you have me come here?" she asked Layne when the first set was over.

He grabbed the towel draped across the back of his chair and wiped his neck. "What?" He had no clue.

"Do you really think I'd want to hang out with people like *this*?" She waved her hand up to the rest of the bar.

"There are some decent people in here," Layne said with a touch of hurt in his voice as he defended the patrons.

"Maybe. But these guys aren't my type."

"What's your type?"

She remembered their earlier conversation. "Excuse me. Even you said you wouldn't like anyone from here."

"But I'm not the one hung up."

"What the hell does that mean?"

Layne stalled. He took a swig of his beer. He seemed to realize that he was getting himself into trouble, but he didn't know how to get out of it. He stammered. "You need to come down a few notches. Get rid of that air about you. Loosen up."

"I have an 'air'?" What was up with him? She didn't come here to get picked on.

"Think about it, Git. What's your type?"

She shrugged. "A doctor."

"And how did that work out for you?"

She turned away. Prick.

Layne left for the men's room. She finished her beer.

A rush of people filled the place. Men and women squeezed sideways to claim small chunks of the long bar to set their drinks on. The pool tables were full and the sticks waved through the air. Men with big bellies let their rolls hang over their pants, while they hiked up their asses for better aim at the cue balls.

Definitely not her crowd, but she didn't like the benefits and cocktail parties either. She couldn't knock the experience of coordinating the different events the hospitals put on because that helped her land the temporary job at the winery. Gitana liked her work but knew she had to find something more permanent. Better pay too.

Layne came back with another beer for her. "Stop frowning."

"Stop being a jerk."

"All right. Sorry." He sat next to her and gave her an apologetic pout. He looked like a puppy with sad, droopy eyes. "I thought coming here would make you realize there's more to life than snobs, Stepford wives, and money."

"I get it." Her neighbor wasn't always the best with words or with women. She knew him enough to know his intent. Now that she'd experienced the spectrum of too good and not so good, she could settle for something in between.

A bouncer opened one of the side doors to allow some air into the overstuffed room. A perfect exit so she wouldn't have to fight the crowd near the bar and entrance.

"I'm going to head home after this beer," she told Layne.

"Stay. At least until the next break. I'll walk you to your car."

"I'll be okay."

"It's dark and not a good neighborhood."

"Don't worry. I'll be fine," she said. "I'm a big girl."

"Exactly my point. Big boys like big beautiful girls who don't fit the norm." He grabbed his drumsticks from the table.

"I got my cell phone on me, and it's only a couple of blocks to my car."

The other band members climbed on stage. Layne had to go.

"You be safe," he warned and gave her a peck on the cheek. "Stay in the lighted areas and head home."

"Yes, sir." She saluted him.

The bar became louder as the music started, and the crowd became rowdier. Each beat made her head pound. She dug into her black leather purse for aspirin and found the small bottle for such occasions. Empty. Damn.

The heavy Aerosmith song didn't help matters even though she loved the song. Next came Layne's drum solo. Her ears vibrated. She loved how he put his soul into those sticks. People stopped talking and dancing to listen and cheer him on. She would be right there with them but not with her headache. Maybe she had aspirin in her car.

Gitana made it through the solo and two songs after. She rose from her chair, and Layne's eyes were on her. His expression said to be careful. She nodded, then sneaked out the side door.

Fresh air. The cool San Francisco breeze helped clear her head. She stood for a moment to figure out which way to go. The side door was the back door. With purse tucked under her arm, she chose to go right and walk around the block.

She passed a drunk slumped against a building. Above him, iron grid windows protected bridesmaid dresses on display. She wondered who would buy a dress in this area. When her heels clicked on the sidewalk, the guy rolled his head, and Gitana stepped around him, in fear he'd grab her ankle. As she passed, he continued to look at her with dazed eyes but was too out of it for anything else. She began to think she should have waited for Layne.

Gitana decided to cross the street and hugged her purse even tighter as she left the lighted sidewalk. A shuffling noise over the click of her heels caught her attention. Two men who had been leaning against a black truck stepped out to block her way. The hairs on the back of her neck stiffened as they waited for her.

"Well, what d'know," said the taller man as he stood away from the truck. He twirled a key fob around his finger and sized her up. "The mighty bitch, eh?"

Gitana recognized the voice, the biker named Eddie from the bar who wanted to buy her a beer. She forgot to check, like the waitress had said, to make sure he didn't follow. She looked around. Where the hell was his motorcycle? If she'd spotted the bike, it would have triggered her to watch out.

She sensed the sneer, the slight evil grin before he moved under the light to show his face. Gitana stepped backed but had no place to go. The Bay Moon was now a distance away. The biker walked toward her with slow, predatory steps. He had an unlit cigarette in his hand. He placed it in his leather jacket pocket.

"My, my, all alone," Eddie taunted, scanning the streets to see if she walked by herself. A toothpick dangled from his mouth. His scrawny, pony-tailed friend circled around to stand behind her. She didn't remember Ponytail from the bar. She moved to keep both in view. Eddie asked, "So where's the mighty boyfriend of yours? Too much of a pussy to protect you?"

Gitana's lip twitched and she willed it to stop. She took another step back as the biker, Eddie, and his buddy stepped closer. Ponytail lit a cigarette and took a long drag. She feared what he might do with it.

"Had to ignore me in the bar, didn't you? Now you got a second chance." He leered and dropped his toothpick to the ground.

Eddie closed the gap, leaving only a couple of inches between them. She smelled whiskey on his breath, and with his face right in front of her, she saw that the space separating his stained front teeth was wider than she thought. Even the scar that ran across his chin looked nastier than it did in the bar. Fighting didn't seem to be an issue with him.

A door opened on the other side of the street. A short, stocky man stumbled out of a stairwell with a brown paper bag in hand. Glancing up, he saw the two men who hovered over her and eyed the situation. Gitana stared at him with pleading eyes, but he turned in the opposite direction and kept his head down—obviously not wanting to play the hero.

"Mighty fine ass, wouldn't you say, Al?" Eddie asked his friend as his eyes continued to devour her.

"You bet." Ponytail flicked his cigarette away and then rubbed his hands together. The lanky man, a mere shadow of Eddie, grinned with anticipation.

She could take Ponytail but not both of them. But would it help?

"Leave me alone." Gitana's heart pounded like Layne's drums. She stepped back, but Eddie squeezed her upper arm and pinched her skin. She winced when his fingers dug in deeper.

"Why?" He pressed his groin against her hip. "The fun's just starting."

Disgusted at his closeness, Gitana rammed her arms into his chest to shove him away. Her purse fell off her shoulders to the street. Coins and lipstick rolled off to the side.

"Fuckin' bitch." Eddie grabbed her roughly again, catching her off guard when she moved to grab her belongings. He wanted to be in charge but too much alcohol prevented it. The biker motioned for Ponytail to grab her other arm and help him. They forced her to walk with them.

"Get your hands off me," Gitana said with a choked voice. Her body tensed. She dug her heels against the cement, but her shoes dragged without much resistance. She jerked her arm downward to loosen the grip from Ponytail. Eddie then swung her around into a bear hug and half dragged, half carried her into the alley.

"You like it rough, huh?" the biker spat. "Well, I do too."

"Yeah, big man having to prove himself," Gitana kicked her legs at him. The dark and quiet alley closed her off from the safety of the open street, and she fought harder to get away as panic set in.

As she raised her elbow to slam it in his face, Eddie grabbed her hair and the back of her jeans. He raised her up as if she were a doll and then threw her against the wall. Gitana heard the crack to her head. Her temple exploded with pain. She swayed and tried to brace herself so not to fall. Layne always lectured, "Confront the attacker. Don't go down. Look for an escape."

The other end of the alley opened to another street. A possible way out, if she could run. She noticed the trash can filled with garbage behind Eddie. It leaked food. Not going there, she thought, as the sweet and rancid odor in the alley made her gag.

"Don't do this," she warned. "I'm not worth it."

"Oh, I think you are." Eddie grabbed her arms and pinned her against the wall. He glanced toward Ponytail with a nod to his head. "Gimme your belt."

The lanky man wiped his nose with his leather jacket before doing as told. The slick running of the leather belt against jeans had every nerve in Gitana's body jumping. Ponytail held the belt up. He slapped the buckled end against the cement wall. She cringed as the wind hit her cheek. He wanted a reaction from her and got it. Both men laughed.

"Please, let me go," Gitana begged. This wasn't how she wanted her life to end. Nor did she want her ex to find her in the hospital all beat up. Or his colleagues. They'd smirk. She was infertile, unfit to be a doctor's wife. She got what she deserved.

Eddie's hand went for her jeans. He tugged at the waist and rammed his knee between her legs to spread her thighs apart.

"Fucking prick," Gitana sobbed. His knee lifted to press against her crotch. She turned into a crazed cat. She hissed and twisted her arms until one of her hands came free.

Gitana dug her nails into his face, scratching his cheek. Tiny dots of blood rose above the biker's scar. His nostrils flared. Her attack angered him more, and he covered her neck with his hands. His thumbs pressed into her throat.

Gitana fought to move his fingers. She couldn't talk. She used her eyes to plead with him to let her go.

"What's that you say?" He laughed as she tried gasping for air.

"She said let go." A clear, deep voice came from the dark.

Eddie released his grip and turned in time for a fist to slam into his face. He cried out from the solid hit. He stumbled backward and had to steady himself.

The newcomer stepped between her and the biker. His voice roared again. "What the fuck you doing? You think you're a man by hurting a woman? Where's your tough ass now?" The yell sounded familiar. She remembered it from once before. At the park.

He pushed his hands against the biker's chest to provoke him. Eddie fell backward. Ponytail came to help. He threw the trash can at the man. The newcomer batted it away with his arm, the sound deafening as the can hit the ground.

The smell of rotten food and sour milk spread through the alley. Gitana coughed and pressed her face into her shoulder. She needed to breathe but couldn't handle the stench. She tried to get up. Her legs, like dead weights, kept her in place.

Lesson #3
Accept help in time of need.

"You hurt?" Cade asked. With arms out, ready for any surprise, and legs spread to keep steady, he watched the two assholes hightail it out of the alley.

The confrontation seemed to be over but his blood still pumped. He let out a breath, releasing the adrenaline.

When she didn't answer, he looked at her balled figure leaning against the wall. After hearing her cry out, he knew who needed help. He lowered himself to his knees and reached to touch her. She winced and he jerked back. The asshole got to her. Cade's anger rose even more.

"I'm not gonna hurt you. I promise," he said with more compassion than the day at the park. "I'm here to help."

Gitana brushed the hair away from her face. She wiped her temple and blood smeared across her hand.

"Let me see." Cade reached for her again.

She flinched when his fingers brushed her chin in a light stroke. He turned her head. Her eyes stayed on him—

staring, questioning—as he examined her face. A bump the size of a golf ball had already formed. With it, a cut an inch long. He couldn't tell how deep or bad with the alley so dark.

Cade glanced toward the street. He should have pummeled the scumbag; made him feel the hurt and fear reflected in Gitana's eyes. The way she cowered, too weak and afraid to defend herself. His anger boiled again; the biker had both hands around her neck. She didn't have a chance without help.

He shook his head. The dark-haired gypsy who'd consumed his thoughts since the day they met was now hurt. He suppressed his anger toward the biker and concentrated on her.

Gitana's lip trembled. She tried to get up, but her legs were too weak. Cade grabbed for her and pulled her into his arms.

"It's okay. Relax." He hugged her with care. "You're safe. I won't let anyone hurt you."

A sob rushed from her throat. She pushed him away. Cade understood her reaction. He wouldn't want anyone touching him either, but they didn't have time for an argument. They needed to get somewhere safe.

"Gitana," he said so she'd know he recognized her. He tapped his hand against her back to make her pay attention. "You up for walking out of here? Whoever you got into the fight with may not be alone if he comes around again."

Gitana's head shot up so fast she would have hit his jaw if he hadn't gotten out of the way. She wiped her eyes and glanced beyond Cade to the street, as if expecting a gang of men to come after them with bats and steel rods. She nodded and stood.

Cade slipped off his leather jacket and wrapped it around her shoulders. He brushed his finger across both her cheeks to remove the mascara smudged under her eyes. They didn't need to alarm the passersby when they reached the busier street. Holding her, he walked her out of the alley. They reached the street and she stopped.

"That's his," Gitana whispered. She stepped backward. When he tried guessing which vehicle, she pointed to the truck.

The inside was dark. He watched for shadows and saw no movement in the seats or on the outside. He listened. The rush of traffic a few blocks down and the beat of an amplified bass stereo stayed in the distance.

He never imagined his walk to the Blue Moon for a stiff drink would provide the opportunity to see her again. He'd set foot in the place maybe a handful of times. Tonight, he needed a change from the client who had a nose pointed to the top of the Golden Gate Bridge. No matter how he tried to accommodate her, the woman always had something else to complain about. Now he thanked her. If she hadn't annoyed him, he wouldn't have been on his walk that let him help Gitana.

"Come on." Cade tapped her arm. They had to keep walking to find a place where he could check her out, see the damage done.

"Wait," Gitana found her purse. She scooped it up

along with the contents that had fallen out and then hobbled back to his side. He led her toward the bay where a cooler breeze lifted the heaviness from the air. After a few blocks, they turned and left the dark run-down streets for ones lit and bustling with people.

Gitana stopped when she saw the droplet of blood that she had left on his shirt. It blossomed like a red flower into the fabric. She pulled a tissue from her jean pocket and wiped her temple. "Sorry about the mess."

In the light, he turned to see the cut. It didn't look too deep, but the blood was plenty. "Let's get you to a doctor."

"No," she said. "I'm fine. Skip the doctor. In fact, I got it from here." She moved away from him. She mumbled, more to herself than to him. "I need to get home. We're too far. My car—"

Cade reached for her, but she turned. He grabbed air. He was okay with not getting to a doctor, but she was still stunned from the attack. He wanted to make sure she was stable and cleaned up before letting her go. He knew of a coffee shop tourists would ignore. The place was more for locals.

"Have coffee with me," he said and tried to lure her back to his side by motioning his arm.

Gitana pointed in the direction they'd come from. Confused, she squinted to read the sign above a closed shop. She said, "I don't remember this building."

She tried to orient herself and walked a step to the left, then one to the right. Cade glanced down the street. A couple got into their car. No cause for alarm yet. He looked back at Gitana as she stepped from the sidewalk. She bumped into one of the parked cars and stepped toward traffic.

"Ohhh no, no, no!" He jumped after her and pulled her back. "You can't go that way. You want trouble again?"

His words hit harder than he expected. Gitana broke free from his grip, and she doubled over. She gulped for air and started to cry.

People shot curious glances their way. He feared this fragile piece of china, now in his command, would soon shatter. No need for calls to 911.

A patrol car slowed as it came up the street. Cade shook his head at his luck. The officer's eyes focused on them. He rolled down his window to get a better look. Cade laughed and blocked the officer's view of Gitana. He rolled his eyes and pretended embarrassment. He pulled her in closer to his chest. She swayed and he tightened his grip to keep her upright. He mouthed, "A little too much."

The officer frowned, but was satisfied she wasn't in need of assistance. He nodded to Cade and then drove on.

"Walk," Cade ordered. She refused and moved away from him. "Stop being so bullheaded."

Gitana's head snapped up. A spark fired from her eyes. A reaction, although small, was what he wanted. He hooked his arm around her waist and pushed her along, determined to help her whether she wanted him to or not.

At the café, the whitewashed door slammed against the outer wall as he escorted Gitana inside. The aroma of coffee, cinnamon, and cream welcomed them in like a warm haven on a cold winter day. Too bad the circumstances weren't different. He grabbed a couple of napkins. His other hand strained to keep her upright. He knocked over a shaker filled with sugar. He made a complete mess.

The barista came over to help and her eyes grew round when she saw the blood in Gitana's hair. She took a step back. Cade felt no need to explain. Instead, he pushed Gitana along as he tried to locate a spot for them sit.

The long, narrow cafe reminded him of the old-time bars in Colorado. A tin roof and dark wood paneled walls seemed quaint and private. A gas fireplace in the back kept the place warm. Perfect.

He plopped her down on a wooden chair next to a round table. A couple rose and left the leather couch across from them. How kind they were to give them some privacy, he thought. He nodded his thanks.

Cade leaned over the half wall and yelled to the barista. "Hey!" When she looked his way, he held up two fingers. "Large, strong coffees."

He turned back, grabbed a chair for himself, and then placed it in front of Gitana. He sat so his legs zippered with her right leg. Cade wanted her close to him.

***

Gitana watched the three vertical lines between Cade's eyes deepen when he examined the cut on her temple. He leaned back and shouted again to the front. "And bring water too!"

The coffee shop, a safe place with people and walls to protect her—versus walls to hurt her—calmed her nerves. She remembered the hit to the cement wall and raised her hand to her forehead.

Cade stopped her. He pushed her hand down. He took a corner of a napkin and wiped away the blood from her cheek, then worked upwards. Gitana jerked her head back when he touched the tender spot near her temple. She wanted to cry but bit her lip instead.

He dabbed in a light, quick motion, but the impact on raw skin was too much for her. She gave him a daggered stare and commanded, "Stop!"

"Sorry," he said in a flat tone.

"Yeah, that was convincing," she said with a glower.

He paused with squinted eyes. "Good, you're coming back around."

"No, I'm in pain. Press lightly."

"Quit being a baby."

"Fuck you," she said when the tips of his mouth curled into a smile. Her eyes glared at him. "I see your smirk."

"Not a smirk," he said and continued to clean her cut. "I'm remembering the Gitana from the park."

"Well, this one tonight is more bruised." The reaction in the park was her being upset at the gull and then at him for tackling her. Now she felt violated. The biker and his friend added the layer of fear. She hated being vulnerable. As a child, her brothers protected her, especially after mama died. While she was married to John, he kept her preoccupied with his life and shielded her from the true world. Now she was alone.

Gitana felt the cold, even with the heat from the gas fireplace at her back. She pulled the front of Cade's jacket together, closer to her chest. She wanted to go home. "Are you done?

He pressed his fingers against the top of her head, behind her ears, and the back of her neck and watched her face for any sign of pain. His fingers caught where the dried blood matted the strands. She winced as he pulled too hard on her scalp.

"How bad is my head?"

The barista arrived with two mugs of coffee and a glass of water. After setting them on the table, she removed a handful of napkins from a pocket in her apron. She slid them toward Gitana. "You want me to call 911?"

"No," Cade said and soaked the corner of a clean napkin in the glass of water. He used it to wash around the cut on her temple. He lowered the napkin again into the water.

The barista kept her distance but waited for a sign from the woman who was hurt. It took a moment before Gitana realized what she wanted. She attempted a smile toward the girl to assure her how she wasn't in danger any longer.

Cade turned to the barista. He intimidated her with a Vin Diesel stare as if to say she was taking up their time and it was none of her business. Gitana felt bad for the girl. It wasn't her fault. "I'm okay. Really."

The barista scuttled away as if happy for the distance.

"She was only trying to help." Gitana cracked her bottom lip when she spoke and she winced. She tasted blood.

"And I'm trying to get you cleaned up." Cade wrapped a couple of ice cubes in a clean napkin. "Here, hold this to your head."

He cupped his hands alongside her face and checked to see if her jaw was broken. His hands were firm and warm, unlike the biker's rough, callused ones. He asked, "What were you doing in a rough neighborhood all alone?"

Gitana thought of Layne wanting to walk her to her car. "Being dumb on my part, I guess."

"I'd say." He touched the marks on her neck and she flinched. Cade exhaled. "Jesus Christ. You'll be hurting for a while."

She snorted, thinking about the tackle in the park.

"You're damn lucky."

He didn't need to tell her. "How'd you know I was there?"

"I saw the purse. I heard you cry out. In fact, I think you said 'fucking prick.' I didn't know it was you until seeing…" He stopped. His neck thickened and his teeth clenched together. Cade reached over. She jumped when she thought his hand was going for her chest. She had enough of quick moves for the night. Her heart pounded as she thought of the biker grabbing her throat.

"Jesus," he swore at his stupidity. "Sorry, just going for my jacket."

This time he moved slower. He opened the flap with

one hand and reached inside with the other. Gitana turned rigid but allowed him to get closer. The jacket became lighter as he pulled out a silver flask. As he did, the backside of his hand brushed against her breast. He didn't appear to notice what he had done, but Gitana shifted in her chair, uncomfortable with his move.

"Here's a little something to take the edge off," he said and unscrewed the cap. Clear liquid came out as he poured a shot into their coffees. He set the flask on the table.

"Drink," he ordered.

She had forgotten about the coffee. Gitana removed the soaked and shredded napkin from her cut. Half the melted ice tumbled into her lap. She scooped up the chunks, then dropped them into the cup of water.

Peppermint Schnapps. She inhaled the steam from her coffee and took a sip, mindful of her cracked lip.

"Here's to me being nearby," Cade raised his cup.

This save she was willing to give him credit for, but not the tackle. She raised her cup to salute him, then drank half the coffee. The Schnapps helped. A little more clear-headed, she asked, "Why were you out? Roaming the city like a caped crusader?"

A slight smile evolved from his lips. He shook his head. "Your caped crusader had a hard day. Actually, a rough week. I was getting some air."

"In a bad neighborhood?"

He remembered. "You didn't answer my question. Why were you there?"

"A friend's band was playing at the Blue Moon," she

divulged between sips. "The biker harassed me there. He wanted to buy me a drink." She took another sip. "I guess he didn't like my answer when I told him no."

"He dragged you outside the bar?"

"No, I left. I was walking to my car."

"What happened to your friend? Couldn't take a moment to make sure you got to your car?"

"Like I said, he was in the band. *Playing*. I left."

She finished the last drop of coffee, then set the cup down. With her stomach warmed, she felt better yet tired. Her bravery left for the night. Her head spun when she closed her eyes—not a good thing. She opened them again.

Cade placed his hand on the side of her leg and leaned in. "Let me take you home."

She shook her head. "Not your job."

"I didn't say it was."

Gitana went for the flask but stopped and looked for permission.

"All yours." He gestured for her to continue as he sat back to give her space.

The straight Schnapps burned her throat. She didn't care and tipped her head back for more. Her thoughts circled back to her life. The last few years had been consumed with trying to get pregnant. Devastated by the negative results, she'd push herself into coordinating the benefit events at the hospital, one right after the other. Her middle name was Pick Me I'll Do It. No wonder John left her.

Disgusted, she said, "I can't even go out and have fun

anymore. What kind of a sorry ass am I?"

"Not a sorry ass," he corrected, "just a foolish one." When she kept silent, he said, "It wasn't your fault tonight. You were the most vulnerable."

"Does it show that much?"

He motioned toward his jacket again. This time she did not flinch when he pulled out a matching flask from the other side.

"A little drinking problem?" Gitana cocked her eyebrow. And he thought she was bad with the pills?

"Like I said, I was out clearing my head."

"The suicide hound dog, troubled? My, my. What life issues are haunting you?"

"No, no, no." He shook his head. "Tonight's about you. Your wake-up call. Not mine."

Whatever, she thought.

He opened the new flask and set it in front of her. Gitana stared at his initials engraved in the side. Her vision blurred.

His voice softened. "You all right?"

She put her elbow on the table, then rested her head on her hand. She gave a stupid, noncommittal response. "I don't know."

"You don't know?" His expression turned to one she had seen many times before. John would give her the same steady-eyed stare when she didn't think things through.

"Life hasn't been easy for me. This is just another one of those incidents to remind me of how I shouldn't be. I'm great at planning a party," she raised her other hand in the air, then let it flop back down, "but when it comes to my life I haven't a clue."

"How much have you had to drink tonight?" He raised his eyebrow with concern.

"I'm not drunk if that's what you mean." Gitana shook her head. "Sorry, I don't mean to babble. It's just been rough."

"What do you mean rough?"

"I haven't had what most girls need or want."

Cade shook his head, not understanding. Why would he? He was a guy. The pain in her head intensified. Her stomach churned from the Schnapps.

"Can we leave now?" Gitana pleaded. He was not keeping her against her will, but she couldn't just get up and walk off. "I'd like to get home before my friend does. He'll worry."

"That should've happened already."

"He didn't know."

"You live with him?"

Gitana shook her head. "He's my neighbor."

"Where do you live? I'll take you home." Cade gathered up the trash and stacked the cups with one hand.

"I'm all right."

"No, you're not. If you were, you'd think about the asshole who attacked you. He's still roaming the streets."

Gitana put her hand up to her throat. Her heart skipped a beat as she imagined the biker waiting for her again.

"You said you drove, right?"

She nodded. Her hand still covered her throat.

"We'll take your car."

We? My car? Yeah, right. "No, I can manage."

"I've saved your ass twice," he said.

"Once. You saved me once," Gitana corrected. "You were the idiot who thought I was committing suicide. Not me."

"All right. Once."

She rolled her eyes and rose from her chair. "Whoa." The room spun and she fell back down. Everything hurt.

Cade capped the flasks and tucked them inside his back pockets. He helped her up and let her stand for a minute until she had her balance. Gitana leaned into him. She loved the smell of his cologne, clean and fresh. His arm went around her. Safe. Warm.

"Come on, let's go," he said.

They walked to the front. As he stopped to throw a twenty on the counter for the coffees, she went outside with hope the fresh air would help clear her head.

The street was empty. The night was cold and lonely. Gitana stopped and waited for Cade, hesitant to walk alone.

Lesson #4
Take chances.

At seven in the morning, Layne lost his patience with waiting for Gitana to get up. All night he had paced. Back and forth across his boat, the deck, then to her boat. He watched the clock tick away the seconds. Let her get some sleep. Let her be. Another fifteen minutes...ten more.

He pounded on the sliding glass door to her boat. The business card, stuck in his door when he came home from work, left no hint to what happened yet everything to his imagination.

"Gitana!"

When his knock went unanswered, he used the spare key she left with him. The sliding door rattled as he entered.

The place was dark. With all the blinds closed, the sunlight streaked through. The sink in the galley had bloodstains, and a white washcloth, now pink, lay on the counter. His stomach churned and a hard lump rose to his throat.

"Gitana?" he said more softly, afraid of how he would find her. He went to her bedroom. The tiny room was a mess. Clothes were tossed on the floor, and her bed sheets half ripped from the mattress. Her pillow was missing. No Gitana.

"In here, Layne." Her voice was deep and hoarse.

He left the bedroom and found her huddled on the chair in the living room. How had he missed her?

In three steps, he hovered in front her. "What the hell happened?"

"I was attacked by the biker from the bar."

"What?"

He leaned sideways to study the side of her face. He moved away her matted hair, some sticking to skin, to see an ugly looking cut. She flinched. He turned on the light next to the chair and she flinched again. She raised her hand to shield her eyes and blinked hard to adjust to the brightness.

Layne ignored her frown. He needed to see what was going on. The bleeding had stopped, but the wound was still raw and swollen. "You need stitches."

She shook her head. "I'm okay."

Guilt soaked into every pore of his body. Layne cursed to himself for letting her leave the bar alone. "I'm so sorry, Gitana. This is my fault."

"No, it's not."

"I should have protected you," he said and choked on his words. "That asshole would never have touched you if I had walked you to your car."

Gitana's frown deepened. Her eyes went to him and she looked confused. She asked, "How...how did you find out?"

"I got this." He flipped up the business card. "Wedged in my door."

"What's it say?" She tried to focus on the print as he held the card in front of her.

Layne helped. "Gallery One, San Francisco. Gallery Two, New York. Cade DeVerine." The dark steel lettering popped against the white background. A logo, an orange glass-and-metal sculpture, adorned the left side of the card. He flipped the card over so she could see the handwritten note. From memory, he read, "Gitana was hurt last night. Make sure she's okay. Cade."

Layne sat on the edge of the couch and hit his fist against the palm of his other hand. His mouth twisted with anger. "The man's dead."

"Cade? He's the one who saved me."

"No, the biker," Layne said.

"It's over," Gitana said. "Let it go."

"How can I?" Since he'd found the card, he'd considered all scenarios of her getting hurt, over and over in his head. Layne regretted telling her to "get out" and have some fun. He knew the Bay Moon was not the place for his friend. But still, he'd insisted. He rubbed his face, angry at his stupidity. He reached to rub some dried blood from the side of her jaw.

"Ouch!" She batted his hand away.

"Sorry. So, did he follow you out of the bar?"

As she turned, he saw the marks on her neck. Red blotches, fingerprints pressing in. The asshole choked her. Layne rubbed his shaved head, distressed. "Jesus Christ."

"Well, he was waiting for me when I left," Gitana continued and then corrected, "Not Jesus. I mean the biker who wanted to buy me a drink. The waitress warned me to watch for him. I forgot."

"Fucking idiot," Layne cursed.

"I know." She lowered her eyes in shame. "I should've waited."

"Not you." He put his hands on top of his head and growled in frustration. "Me. I'm the fucking idiot."

Layne, now shaken, stood up and looked out the window toward the bay. He wanted to find the guy. Take him out. He spun back around. "We'll get him. This shouldn't have happened. I'll take care of it."

"No, you won't. I'm not blaming you."

"I am."

"Stop being so stubborn," she said. Her words turned sharp. "It's done with. Over." Her eyes turned downward.

Layne sensed something else troubled her. He helped to pull her up when she struggled to get up from the chair. "What's going on, Gitana?"

She hobbled toward the galley as she held her back. "I used to live in a six-thousand-square-foot house with a pool and gardens. I shopped, organized events, met with friends...or at least I thought they were friends...and had no idea I'd lose it all in less than a day. After John kicked me out, I stayed in my own little fog." She picked up the coffee pot and stared inside the empty container as if seeing her life inside it. "And then last night, the fog lifted. I couldn't accept what I was forced into. I kept hoping I'd wake up in my king-size bed with the sound of the ocean coming through the open window. Now I realize it's over." She turned on the faucet and filled the container with water. "The biker and getting attacked was my slap to reality."

"A new dawning," Layne said as he thought back to a month ago when he watched Gitana sit at her table in the galley with papers strewn about. For six nights, he thought she had buried herself in work. She always talked about the number of events at the winery she had to coordinate, and he was pissed she wasn't taking care of herself. He went over to yell at her, until he spotted his name on the paperwork. She had given up her spare time to develop a business plan for him to open his own gym. That was his reality hit. Dreams can happen. He refocused on her. "So what are you going to do?"

"I need to reconfigure my plan." Gitana patted him on the back. "And you gotta go."

"You nuts? I'm not going anywhere."

"I'll be fine. Besides, I don't have to work until tomorrow, and you have a class to run today."

Layne glanced at the clock on the wall. He had a half hour tops, before the class started. It took fifteen minutes to get there, but no matter. He already called one of the guys to take over for him. "I'm staying."

He sat at the table to show he wasn't going anywhere.

He also knew she would argue, so he needed to change the subject. Layne studied the business card in front of him. "So who is this guy, the one who saved you?"

"He's the one from the park. The one who thought I was taking the pills." She grabbed two mugs out of the cupboard and set them on the counter. She snorted. "He actually saved me this time."

"Ahh," Layne remembered. "I thought I recognized the name."

Gitana took the card from him and read the print below his name. "Sculptor. Gallery owner." Her eyebrows shot up in surprise. "I figured him to be a mechanic, or a carpenter. She wrinkled her nose and gave the card back to him. "Aren't gallery owners usually gay?"

Layne coughed and his cheeks reddened. "Now there's labeling at work."

"This guy is definitely not gay."

"Ah-ha, is that a tone of interest I hear in your voice?"

Gitana stopped filling the mug with coffee. "I'm just saying...he..."

Did she have a slight curl to her lips? Layne helped her when she was at a loss for words. "You liked him."

"No," she said. "He just had a great smell."

"Something you need." He rose from his chair. "Let's get you cleaned up. You need a hot shower."

"No, you need to get the hell out of here."

"Not a chance." He pointed a finger at her. She may have him wrapped around her fingers, but Layne knew how to be stubborn as well and keep his ground. Gitana needed him, and this was not a time to leave a friend. "We stick together, Gitana. You and me."

She smiled. "You know, I thought about you, when the biker cornered me in the alley."

Layne's heart dropped with guilt. He kicked himself again for not being there to help.

"Oh no." She flailed her hands after realizing what she had said. "I mean, I remembered what you taught me, how to defend myself. Unfortunately, I should have paid more attention."

"We'll get you toughened up." Layne had a mission now. He would teach her how to protect herself.

"I don't know," she said, and her voice faded for a second. "I don't think anyone could have been prepared for what I went through."

She lowered her head and wouldn't look at him. She was going to the dark place in her mind again. One he'd seen many times before when she thought of her ex or not being able to have kids. He had to get her smile back. "You should go see Cade."

Her brown eyes lit up for a second. She did have an interest.

Layne had to keep going. "You owe him a thank you."

"I did thank him." She took the card he held up for her.

"Twice, Gitana. He's been there twice for you."

"What is that supposed to mean?"

"Go pay him a visit."

***

Three days later, Gitana stood on the other side of the street from Gallery One. She held Cade's jacket close to her chest as she looked up at the crisp, white building nestled between two larger marble buildings. Brushed steel plaques hung on each side of the doors with the name *Gallery One* and *Cade* written in signature form—elegant yet industrial.

She had figured his place would be a weathered 60's style nook with a large window display of oil canvases propped against black velvet blocks. Instead, one of the tall windows had a wide steel sculpture woven with multi-colored glass in the middle of the display, while the other side had impressionistic paintings with gold carved frames on easels.

Artist and gallery owner. She was intrigued. His jacket was the perfect excuse to see him again. Gitana took a deep breath to calm her nerves before crossing the street. She grabbed the solid handle and pushed to open the tall glass doors before losing her nerve. Like a bird flying toward the reflection in the window, she slammed into the glass when the door refused to budge. Gitana jarred her shoulder. Stunned, she stood for a moment before pushing again, this time on the other side. Still no luck.

Pull, dummy. Pull. Gitana pulled and the door opened.

"Welcome to Cade's. May I assist you?" A petite, polished male stood behind the thick, steel counter. His dark features drew her in. He smiled, showing perfect white teeth that contrasted against his trimmed beard and moustache. His bedroom eyes were deep brown, which she assumed were for men only.

"Is Cade around?" she asked, her gaze drawn by the curved stairs that spiraled to a loft. Was that where Cade worked? She then spotted the crystal chandelier above them, very intricate with the beaded ropes and droplets. He had eclectic taste, industrial metal with elegance. She couldn't wait to see the rest of the gallery.

"He's not in today," the man said, bringing her back to why she was there. He sized her up, and then his eyes rested on the jacket she carried. He hesitated as if wondering whether she were a friend, a client, or a jilted lover.

Let him guess. All morning Gitana had paced the boat as she tried to build up the courage to go to the gallery. Twice she talked herself out of it. Layne was adamant, and in the end he won out. She should at least return the jacket. So be it.

She said, "He loaned this to me the other night."

His eyes grew as he recognized the jacket. "Mr. DeVerine had to fly to New York this morning."

"New York?"

"His other gallery."

Ah, yes. Duh. Both were on his business card. "How long will he be gone?"

"He returns next week."

"Think I'll look around...if it's all right?

He nodded.

Like a kid in a candy store, Gitana turned her attention to the gallery. The front featured an artist by the name of

Edward Yaell. He painted full portraits, mainly children on the shore. She walked through to the next section. Her greeter turned into her shadow. The gallery was long and wide. The midsection had portable, angled walls slanting like gills to display the different works of art. Large and small paintings lined both sides of the hall.

"Nice set up." She nodded her approval. Gitana liked how the walls let her view the paintings without having to crane her neck or swing a panel to see them fully.

She stopped at one painting and took in the different thicknesses of silver paint, the textured canvas, and thin pieces of steel. Interesting. The white plaque near the framed art read: Josie Waters. Gitana thought the artist did watercolors, but this was an acrylic. She winced at the price tag of five thousand dollars. Not in her budget.

"Does Cade show his own work?" Her abrupt question made the man jump. She pressed her lips together to keep from grinning.

He was quick to recover. "Cade's pieces are in the front windows and in the back of the gallery."

Gitana's heels clicked on the polished white floor as she walked toward the back. His echoed behind.

She shot quick glances to the right and to the left. The paintings became brighter and bolder with magnificent hues jumping from each canvas. When the angled walls ended, she walked through a short arched tunnel to another room.

The domed ceiling and white Grecian columns against the marbled walls were like works of art themselves. Her mouth dropped in awe. She loved how the long curved windows filtered in natural light to enhance each piece of art. In the center, on a black circular platform, were different-sized sculptures formed from steel, bronze, and copper. Each had blown glass set within and around the metal pieces. A small plaque, a white tile on brushed steel, marked Cade as the artist.

"Beautiful," she said more to herself than to the man. She walked around the platform to get the full depth of his pieces. Metal fused with glass. Some were three-dimensional while others were flat. The glass pieces were opaque, spotted, clear, and swirled; a talent not everyone could master. She tried blowing glass once during college, but her vase lacked form and had turned out to be a curved blob.

A clock chimed three o'clock. She had to leave for work before rush hour started in the city. Gitana spun around. She knew Mr. Gay still waited behind her. She asked, "Will you be seeing Cade?"

"I'm his assistant." He held out his hand. "Rex Victor."

"Gitana Sothers." She liked his firm handshake.

Rex brought his focus back to the jacket.

She held it out with some reluctance. She hoped to be the one to give it to Cade, an excuse to see him again. "Would you give this to him?"

He took the jacket and folded it across one arm. He smiled as if wondering again how she knew his boss.

"Thanks," she said.

"My goodness!" He saw the cut on her forehead.

"Not a big deal." She tried concealing the wound by

slicking her hair down over it. Customers at the winery didn't need to see the ugly mark.

With her business finished at the gallery, Gitana walked out of the domed room. When she reached the hall, she stopped and turned back. Giving Rex a large smile, she added, "Tell him I washed most of the blood off."

Rex's eyebrows rose. She smiled. Let him think.

"Stop in again, Wild Child."

She glanced back and saluted. She liked the guy.

"I will," she promised and left the gallery in an upbeat mood.

She drove across the Bay Bridge to get to the winery and stopped for gas near Sonoma. With her tank at the quarter mark, filling up before work sounded better than afterwards when her main goal would be to get home and sleep.

She parked behind a laundry truck. Someone had written "wash me" in the layer of dirt coating the back panels. The words had been there for a while. Clean clothes and a dirty vehicle. She wrote a mental note never to use the company.

As she pumped the gas into her Honda, her thoughts turned to Cade as she'd first met him at the park. What would she have done if he had kissed her then? He wanted to, and that had pissed her off. Would she have hit him in the face? Would she have relented? He did have full, kissable lips.

"Hello, Annabella."

At first, Gitana didn't register the voice, still deep in

thought about the man who tackled her.

"Don't be rude," he chastised her.

She stared into her ex's face and then at the baby blue Mercedes parked on the opposite side of her pump.

"John," she said. He knew how to kill the mood.

Tick, tick, tick, a tick. She focused on the pump. Six gallons left and she would be on her way. *Damn it! Why did he have to here at this very moment.* Her heart ticked faster than the numbers adding up her cost. Gitana's hand started to shake as she squeezed the handle on the pump.

"What brings you here?" Her ex smiled as if they were old friends. Of course, she was no longer a threat. The divorce was final and he'd gotten what he wanted.

"Same reason as you," she said. He wore a blue pinstriped suit and silk shirt. He was so perfect— professional yet easy-going—as usual. It made her sick.

He chuckled. "No, I meant this side of town."

"I'm on my way to work."

"How's your *career* going for you?" he asked and held the nozzle away from himself with his hand. God forbid if he got a little gas on his expensive suit.

"I enjoy what I do," she said. Parts of her struggled with answering. She hated having to defend herself, but his grin irked her.

Gitana jumped when her pump clicked off. She lifted the nozzle from her car and put it back in the holder.

He squinted his eyes at her and tilted his head sideways. "What happened to your temple?" He wiped his hands on a white handkerchief.

She turned away and smoothed her bangs over the cut to re-cover the side of her forehead. "I fell on the deck of my boat."

He changed the subject, more into himself. "I just had lunch with George Hersan. You know, the investor."

Why did he think she wanted to have a conversation with him or care who he was with? She ripped her receipt from the slot when it rolled out. That part of her life was over. The Hersans—Mr. and Mrs. Poodle with their curly white hair—ignored her after she invited them to her last charity event. An event she cared about and hosted despite the fact her husband called it quits on their marriage three days beforehand.

Gitana walked around her car and opened the driver's door. She owed him no good-bye.

"Wait!" He stepped over the median and avoided the stone-pillared garbage can. "You remember Larry Hawthorne?"

"Of course," she replied and waited for him to continue. How could she forget his college roommate? John dissed him, but she had kept in touch. She sent them a Christmas card each year. Come to think about it, she didn't receive one from him last year.

"He died two days ago. He had a massive heart attack."

"What?" Gitana had one leg in the car and a hand on the open door. She froze, stunned at the news.

"He was golfing."

"Wow, how sad."

"Yeah," John agreed as he jingled keys in his hand.

"When's the funeral?" Gitana asked. She should have called when she hadn't heard from him. But he was John's friend.

"Friday."

"You going?" The friend lived in Connecticut with his wife and two kids.

John nodded. "I'm leaving Thursday."

"Give his family my sympathies," she said.

"Why should I?"

Gitana fell back, not sure if she heard correctly. The bastard had the nerve to refuse to pass on her condolence?

"No." He wrinkled his face at her misunderstanding. "Aren't you going?"

Gitana blushed, embarrassed by her too-quick reaction. She said, "No, I can't. I have to work. Not to mention, I just found out."

He started to say something else but changed his mind. His pump clicked off.

Time to leave, she thought and got in her car. She closed the door. John rapped his finger on her window, and she pressed the button to open it a few inches.

"I'll tell them you said you're sorry."

Gitana eyed him for meaning. He liked playing with words. Yes, she was sorry for the loss. Yes, she was sorry for her failed marriage. Knowing him, he'd be telling them both.

"You take care of yourself, Annabella." He laughed. "You are so gullible. Just wait."

"What the hell is that supposed to mean?"

He walked away with a smirk and no response.

The anger and bitterness at seeing her ex kept her fuming on the way to work. Another reminder of how she needed to move on. Now his comment made her think.

What the hell did he have up his sleeve?

Lesson #5
Learn how to drive.

A week had passed since Gitana ventured into Cade's gallery. She leaned against the bar at the winery and listened to the drone of a professor discussing the bitterness of grapes. She suppressed a yawn, having learned early how to hide them without gaping her mouth and showing her back teeth. The boring lectures and hospital events she had to attend throughout her marriage had given her plenty of practice.

The large clock at the side of the bar chimed ten. Two more hours and she could go home, once the event was over. She turned her thoughts to Cade. Gitana knew he was away on business, but a call would have been nice.

"Reisling, please." A guest with a gourdlike nose set his glass on the bar and slid it toward her.

She grabbed the white pinot grigio. They didn't make Reisling at the winery. He left the bar without thanking her or caring what she poured for him.

Alone again, Gitana gazed out across the floor at the people milling about like bees building their hive. Most of the men wore white polo shirts and blue casual pants. If not the blue and white, they dressed in tweed jackets, differentiating the geeks from the professors. The women wore black or gray, no bright or light colors within the bunch.

Digimagnum, Inc., based out of the San Jose area, invited different universities to entice them with their new products. Two hundred employees and guests—geeks and more geeks—mingled together.

She liked weddings better, with their beautiful gowns and dressed-up guests and how the hall glowed with candles and fabric draped across the arched walls. Pete, the owner, took pride in his winery. Customers always looked up toward the coved timber ceiling as they walked through the arched doors welcoming them in. Next, they ooh'd and aah'd at the deep mahogany high-back chairs and round tables for a cozy sit while tasting his wines. The day she walked in for her interview, she was in awe. Like she had with Cade's gallery, she wanted to be a part of the beauty.

This time, Gitana did not suppress a yawn when she checked the wine stock on the shelf. They had enough bottles to last the evening without opening additional cases. A professor in tweed brought three water glasses up to the bar and set them down. He splashed the contents across the shiny Stone Legend Hall logo she had just cleaned. She removed the glasses and wiped up the mess with a towel.

"Another success," Pete said as he surfaced from the

back office. The bear-like man set a pile of napkins in the wooden holder next to the wine list. He released a lion-sized yawn and rubbed his round belly as he looked at the guests still mingling the hall. She did not feel so bad about her yawn. His was gigantic in size compared to hers.

"Yes, another success," she agreed. Her toes pinched together inside the red shiny pumps. They wanted out of the 3-inch heels.

"Everybody likes a good wine." He yawned again. He had not mastered the skill of suppression.

"Why don't you head home? I'll close up," Gitana offered.

He spent all day at the winery, and his face sagged with exhaustion. Over twelve hours made anyone's bones hurt, even those of a tough old Lithuanian. He needed to retire and enjoy life. His granddaughter would be taking over the business once she came back from her studies overseas. Again reminding Gitana she had maybe a year before her replacement arrived, which would leave her without a job. She had taken the temporary job to pay bills, thinking she'd continue looking for a better, more permanent, job. Unfortunately for her, she loved working there. Planning the events was a piece of cake compared to the charitable parties she hosted.

"You did enough." Pete groaned while bending over to pick up a napkin from the floor. He used the bar to brace himself.

"You did more." She had the place covered. The crowd was thinning. She waved her hands to shoo him out. "Go.

Get."

"You're a tough broad to kick me out of my own place," he half teased and shook his finger at her.

Gitana laughed. "And you're an old man needing his sleep."

"Ahh!" He flicked his hand up as if brushing her off. "I can race you blindfolded across my vineyard and win hands down."

"I bet you can," she agreed without a doubt.

Pete had a special place in her heart. He reminded Gitana of her own papa with strong opinions and a good work ethic. Born and raised on the land, he loved what he did.

"I can stay," he said like a father watching out for his daughter. "You shouldn't be here alone."

On her first day back after the biker's attack, he took notice when she tried hiding the cut on her forehead. "I have a trained eye, you know," he had said to her. "I saw many fights growing up, and it looks like you'd been in one." He kept at her, pumping questions, until she divulged what happened.

"I'm good now," Gitana assured him.

After five more minutes of pressuring him to leave, he relented on the condition she parked her car closer to the back entrance. He didn't want her walking across the dark parking lot after she locked up for the night. Even if no crime had ever been committed at the winery, he made sure she felt safe. Gitana was more than happy to oblige before he left. She learned her lesson.

Slowly, the guests at the event began to trickle down. The castle turned quiet just after midnight. The click of her heels on the wood floor echoed in the large room as she walked to the arched doors and bolted them shut. She dimmed the lights and the hall grew dark.

Many times, she stayed well into the night to pick up remnants of a party or finish paperwork in the office. She liked quiet, but tonight the winery carried too much silence as she went to the grand room to clean up alone.

The hairs on the back of her neck stiffened when the ice cubes in a cup from one of the tables shifted. She hated how the attack in the alley affected her, never having been afraid of her own shadow before.

Something moved in a flash across the room. Gitana froze. Her eyes widened and she caught the reflection of her face in one of the mirrors hanging from a pillar. She laughed. The flash had been her walking.

Gitana went to the mirror and leaned forward. She pulled her hair away and touched her temple with a fingertip. Still a little tender, but at least the mark turned from an ugly blue to a soft yellow. She moved closer, avoiding the wine glasses on the table, to wipe away a smudge of mascara from under her eye.

The arched doors rattled as someone tried opening the door. She jumped. Quick reflexes kept a glass half filled with wine from toppling over. Her first thought was Pete. He always forgot something. The doors rattled again, and then a fist pounded against the heavy wood. Not Pete. He would use the back door, not the grand entrance.

Gitana's face froze. The biker. He found her. A lump hit her throat.

No. Don't go there.

She grabbed an empty bottle of wine from the table and held it tight in her hand. She was determined not to let the asshole rule her life. Pete's house was about a half a mile up the road. Her phone was in the office.

Another three hard raps. This time they echoed throughout the hall.

Why tonight? Her heart pounded. The whites on her knuckles glowed against the bottle when she raised her arm up. Standing near the crack where the doors met, she asked, "Who is it?"

"Gitana?"

She recognized her name called beyond the thick arches. The voice sounded familiar. One side of her wanted to ignore this person, while the other had to know who was trying to bust down the doors.

"Who is it?" She lowered her voice to make the person think she was a tough male.

"It's Cade."

She released the latch on the lock. Metal against metal screeched louder than expected. She winced as the door moaned when she opened it just a crack. So much for being quiet.

"Nice try with the voice." He grinned, amused by her tactic, when she saw it was him.

Gitana tried slamming the door shut after his snide remark, but he had placed his foot in the opening. He didn't try to enter but waited instead until she gave him permission. She took two short breaths to calm her nerves and then opened the door wider.

"How are you, Gitana?" He seemed so casual as he slid inside before she changed her mind.

"How'd you find me?"

"I stopped by your boat. Layne gave me the tip."

"He told you where I work?" Gitana frowned. Her friend should know better.

"Only fair I find you since you came to my place."

Lame excuse, she thought.

He looked up at the ceiling as he walked to the center of the hall. "Wow."

"That's pretty much what I thought when walking into your gallery," she responded, then closed and locked the door behind him.

"Sorry I missed you." He continued to check out the place.

"Your assistant said you were in New York." She followed behind him and picked up the empty bottles scattered about by poking her fingers into the openings and becoming Edward Scissorhands.

Cade went to the middle of the open room with his hands on his hips. He wore a blue shirt with jeans. Crisp was the first word to enter her mind.

"One of my pieces sold," he explained. He smoothed his hand over one of the carved chairs. He seemed to be into the detail like a true artist. He picked up a half-filled bottle of wine and read the label. The blue speckled design distinguished the blueberry flavor mixed with the common red. He set the bottle back down and continued to roam. She watched from the corner of her eye as he noted the long, narrow windows. He stopped in front of a painting with a princess overlooking a moonlit valley. Her blonde hair and velvet blue dress flowed behind her as if she defied the wind. Cade zoomed in to study the brush strokes.

"So why are you here this late at night?" Gitana asked, but in realty she wanted to know what he thought of the painting. His expression offered no thoughts to whether he liked the piece or not. Just a blank stare while he scratched his chin. She went back to her task and dropped the bottles from her fingers into the recycle bin. She grabbed a smaller trash container and started picking up the rest of the debris from the tables.

"I was hoping you'd grab a bite to eat with me."

"At midnight?"

"I'm starved," he said and rubbed his hand on his hard stomach. "My plane landed three hours ago. I haven't eaten since this morning."

She curled her toes inside her shoes. They pounded against the leather in protest. Her back ached. She wanted to crash. Go home. Slip into her nightshirt and curl into her soft down blanket.

"Sure," she said instead. "Give me a few minutes here to close up."

While Gitana cleared the tables, Cade went from painting to painting. Most were acrylics: a vineyard in the sunset, a castle in the valley, a knight amusing a beautiful woman in a courtyard. He closed in on one of the two oils, a river scene with the moon dancing across the water. He seemed mesmerized.

"Let me help." Cade rushed over when she struggled with the garbage bag. "Outside?"

"Black bin," she said. "Go out the back. There's a piece of wood to prop the door open."

She went behind the bar to inventory the full bottles left from the night. When he returned, she had them lined up in rows.

"Good stuff?" He picked up a sealed bottle of Merlot and read the label. His broad shoulders were straight and perfect. All muscle. Even his shaved head was lean and fit. His chiseled jaw, full lips, and large nose did not advertise a heartthrob, but he did style magnetism. He seemed intimidating yet safe.

She remembered to respond to his question when he tilted the bottle up for her to see the label. "Yes, one of my favorites."

"Perfect." He smiled and tucked the wine under his arm.

Gitana smirked but remained silent. She inventoried three bottles of Merlot instead of four.

"So you came all this way to grab a bite with me?" She flicked off the upper bar lights. She left one on to stave off total darkness.

"And to see how you're doing." He followed her to the back room. "You weren't in the best of shape when I left you the last time."

"True, but I am getting better." She lifted her bangs to expose the cut. "Almost gone."

After retrieving her purse, Gitana set the alarm and they headed outside. A peaceful quiet lulled the night, and a light mist blanketed the grounds, hiding the rows of grapevines lining the valley. Frogs croaked their tune. Above, an airplane passed and the stars twinkled against black. It was a perfect evening to sit on the porch or on her boat with a glass of wine.

Gitana studied Cade. She envisioned them together, sharing a kiss. Heat rose to her cheeks when she realized what she had done.

"I could get used to this," Cade said. He nodded as if reading her mind.

Gitana flushed even more, and she turned to the cars, her old Honda Prelude next to his new Dodge Charger. He bypassed hers, opened the passenger door to his silver bullet, and waited for her to get in. She slid into the seat and ran her hand down the black leather. She had wanted to test-drive one since they came out on the market.

"Oh yeah," she meowed, liking the power already. "This has a HEMI, right?"

"You bet." He smiled.

"Nice." Gitana missed the '68 red Mustang she owned in college. John preferred his Mercedes. She still kicked herself for letting her ex trade the car in for a C500 after they married.

The Charger roared to life and the engine overpowered the night. Cade gripped the silver skull shifter and placed his beast in reverse. Gitana wondered if she could buy one in black for Layne. He would like the skull for his Falcon convertible.

The dual exhaust rumbled as they crept down the driveway. Once on the main road he hit the gas. The car flew into motion. Gitana gripped the door handle, ready for the ride. He glanced her way and smiled. "Glad you like it."

The car hugged the road as they weaved around a couple of bends. Gitana took her hand off the door handle and then pointed her finger to the intersection. "Turn right up here. There's a diner up a ways, with great food."

Cade took the turn. His gaze darted from the road to her, then to the road again.

"What?" she asked after he repeated the motion too many times. She fixed her hair. She checked her teeth with her tongue.

"I've been thinking about what you told me," he said. He slowed as they neared a sharp curve.

"What do you mean?"

"You and your divorce."

Gitana shifted in her seat. "Since when did my divorce become your problem?"

"It's not." He hit the gas again and shifted.

"So why were you thinking about my personal life?" She should have dropped it, changed the subject. A lecture was not what she wanted. A nice night out sounded better. She turned her head and watched the trees pass by to hide her disappointment.

"Because you're bitter. Stuck."

"Who says I'm stuck?"

He shot her a "you know what I mean" look.

Gitana rolled her eyes. So he witnessed her antics in the park. She had a good excuse. Her seven-year investment wiped out by a twenty-four year old hurricane.

She sank into the seat and nibbled on her fingertip.

"It's like driving a car," he said and focused on the road.

Why did I agree to dinner? Why is he preaching? She sighed, and the window covered with fog.

Gitana wanted to avoid the subject, but he didn't take the hint. He said, "You were the passenger in your marriage. You took it all in, enjoyed the ride, and let him drive. Don't let him be the driver anymore."

"Just like that?"

"Just like that," he replied.

"Fine. Pull over," Gitana ordered. Enough of his shit. "I'm driving."

Cade slowed to a stop at the side of the road. She unbuckled her seatbelt and got out. If he wanted her to drive, then so be it.

She stepped around the Charger. The heat from the exhaust hit her legs. She placed her hand on the trunk and felt the vibration of the car running. From the rearview mirror, he stayed attentive. A deep line creased Cade's forehead as he waited. She came around to his side, and he opened the door.

"Out," she said.

He turned the engine off.

A truck sped toward them. Gitana leaned closer to the Charger and waited for the headlights to pass. She waved, impatient at the driver when he slowed. Bright lights on a dark road were blinding.

"Out." She turned back to Cade.

His black polished shoes hit the pavement. He stood with his chest out to play the tough guy. Gitana ignored his intimidation and pushed him aside. She slipped into the warm seat behind the wheel, and a wicked smile crossed her face when she turned the key and revved on the gas. If he wanted a ride, he had better hurry.

He got the hint. He spun around the front and fell into the passenger side. She pressed down on the pedal before he buckled in. The tires sprayed gravel into the air like two tails.

Gitana caught how he held his breath. His hand gripped his knee, but he kept his cool.

"Now, what were you saying?" She dared him to lecture her on not taking the driver's seat.

"Nothing." He shook his head and hid a smile. "Not a thing."

Gitana forgot how fun it was to drive a stick. She fell in love all over again as she maneuvered the curves and hills like a kid in a go-cart. However, her skills at shifting were rusty, and she jerked the car more than once. Cade winced each time. She apologized, and he had to get over it.

Gitana pulled into the diner and parked so the Charger was visible from the inside. One light glowed in the front of the parking lot and she took advantage of it.

If she had been with John, he never would have considered stopping at a dingy place for a bite to eat. How many places with good food had she missed because of him? She now preferred the small quaint restaurants to the spendy, high-class ones. After a hard night at work, the diner became an odd yet comfortable place to hang out. While everyone else fell into a fitful sleep, a few lost souls took on the dark to enjoy the peacefulness of being somewhat alone.

Gitana got out of the car and met him at the sidewalk. She held his keys up and then dropped them in the palm of his hand.

"Hungry?" she asked with a smile.

***

Cade liked the comfort of the diner. Soft classic rock whispered from the speakers to keep the place from total silence. One booth in the corner held a couple presumably out on a date. Four big guys took over one of the center tables. They leaned back in their chairs after they finished eating. One had the bill and appeared to be calculating the tip in his head. Another stared at Gitana and ogled. Cade glared at him, and the guy quickly turned his head.

A middle-aged waitress with speckled gray and black hair saw them come in and grabbed a pot of coffee and two mugs. She sat them at a booth, in line with the Charger.

"Thanks, Kathy," Gitana said and slid into one of the red vinyl seats. The waitress poured the coffee into their mugs.

"Good to see you back," she said in a deep, smoker's voice.

Cade watched Gitana smile as she nestled in. He wondered if he would get the same expression from her after making love and pictured them tangled in white sheets with her leaning toward him, a black curl tickling his chest.

His jeans tightened. He was just as bad as the guy looking her over when they entered.

He leaned to sit, and his knee bumped hers under the table. The one touch intensified his senses and sent fire to his belly. He caught her short gasp. She jerked her leg away from his. They had a connection. He felt it the day he tackled her and now confirmed it all over again.

"So, why do you need to save me?" she asked and sipped her coffee.

"Not save. Just help."

"Am I some poor pitiful person?" Her back straightened.

Cade had to redeem himself. "I'm not saying you need help. I'm saying you need to move on."

"What's your version?" She set her cup on the table, and the coffee inside splashed upward.

He decided he wasn't the only one trying to help her by the attitude he was getting. Cade raised his eyebrow and gave her a silent "calm down" stare. She softened her hard bitchiness after taking a deep breath. She did not apologize, which made him believe he was still on shaky ground. His goal wasn't to alienate her or lecture her. He wanted to spend time with her. "I was like you. I hated the world."

She was about to interrupt. He shook his finger to stop her. "Your deal is a divorce. For me, I left my family. I disowned them."

The waitress headed for their table. When Cade looked up, she stopped. He realized what she wanted and motioned her over. He grabbed two of the laminated papers from the steel holder at the edge of the table and handed one to Gitana.

"The hamburgers are good here," she told him and glanced at the menu before Kathy arrived. She then ordered. "I'll have mine with cheese this time. A coke and fries too."

Cade held two fingers up. Kathy nodded without writing down the order and left. Gitana turned her full attention to him and leaned forward with her elbows resting on the blue Formica and her hands against her chin.

He tried to hide his grin. She was acting like a shit and knew it. She waited for him to continue. His cocked smile broke through, showing he was amused yet serious enough to become Aesop. He continued his story. "I grew up in New York. Brooklyn."

"Where's the accent?" she asked.

"Gone. Different life."

"So you had a rough childhood?"

"Not my childhood," he corrected. "I had a normal life growing up. My mom stayed home and raised us. My dad took us places on weekends. At fifteen, it all changed. My mom changed."

Cade had to do something with his hands. He liked to keep his past behind him. No one needed to know his business. He wanted to tell her though. She had something about her that mirrored himself. Was it loneliness? The need for love?

He grabbed a white sugar packet from the holder and started playing with it. He crunched the sugar against the paper and continued his story. "She began arguing with my dad. He worked long hours, and she would get on his case about not being home. When my sister became pregnant at sixteen, all hell broke loose. The fighting continued from the minute my dad got home until he left for work the next morning. Meanwhile, my brother joined a gang. Everything escalated out of control."

"How about you?"

"I worked. I went to school. I worked."

"No trouble?" She made a face to show skepticism.

"Not where I got caught," he chose his words with care. "I was seventeen when my dad died in a car crash. His fault. My mom turned to me. Suddenly I was supposed to be the man of the house. Take care of everyone. She wore me ragged."

The sugar packet broke open, and the white crystals danced across the Formica. He was about to brush the mess to the floor but caught the hard stare in her eyes. He changed his mind. The sugar went into a pile at the end of the table near the salt and pepper. So much for the packet.

"Why did your mom change?" she asked.

"She got hooked on pain medication and booze." He

rubbed his hands together to remove the sugar stuck to the side of his palm. "I decided if I stayed, I would end up like them. I would hate my life and get nowhere fast. One night I went for a drive and kept right on going."

He stretched his arm out to symbolize his car on the road. Off to nowhere. "The guilt stayed for months. I couldn't sleep. One part of me said to go back. They needed me. The other said 'don't be a fool' and I listened to the latter."

Gitana frowned. She picked at her fingernails, deep in thought. Cade allowed the silence between them, giving her space. He shifted positions. He rested his arm against the back of the booth with his elbow hanging over the edge.

Where in the hell was the food? His stomach growled.

He tried not to think about the months he stayed awake at night, guilty for having left. He caved and contacted his mom and then listened to her cuss him out. Called him a loser. A pathetic asshole who didn't know how to take care of anyone or anything. Not even himself. He was going to rot in hell.

Cade let out a laugh to hide the hurt.

Gitana leaned closer, as if drawn to the emotion behind his eyes. He looked away. He made a decision to bury his past a long time ago. He stuck to his choice. "I never went back. I made the decision. How about you? You have family?"

She nodded but lowered her gaze. "I grew up with two sisters, two brothers, lots of drama, love, and protection. Papa worked over fifty hours a week, but he was always home to tuck us in when we were little. A month after my sixteenth birthday, Mama died in a car accident. Papa shut down. He was distant for many years, until I became engaged to John.

"For some reason, Papa liked John. Papa bragged about him to co-workers, neighbors, friends, and even strangers. Having a *doctor* join the family was big. He begged us to come over whenever we could spare the time."

She looked everywhere but at him. Cade realized how hard this hit her. At least his troubles escalated until he couldn't take it anymore. He *wanted* to leave. For her, it seemed she had no choice.

"After we split, my papa withdrew again. The divorce hit him hard, as if it were my fault. He wanted me to forgive my husband because men, he hinted, make big mistakes but they learn. Only it wasn't about me taking him back. With a pregnant girlfriend, forgiveness was out of the question. She won hands down with the baby."

"He got her pregnant?" Cade was surprised. He remembered what she said about not being able to have kids. "Ouch."

They both turned when a young couple walked into the diner. They entered arm in arm with whispers and giggles between them. Gitana's expression changed. The lines on her forehead dented in.

Cade sat forward and grabbed her hands. Her arms jerked back on instinct, but he kept a firm grip. "You have to let go, Gitana. Even when it hurts like hell, you have to move on. I did."

Gitana nodded her understanding. She let him hold her hands for a moment longer before withdrawing. This time he released, not wanting to push his luck.

She asked, "Did you ever return?"

"I saw my sister, maybe three times." He looked toward the couple who sat in the booth near the jukebox. He stretched his back, once again uncomfortable how the conversation switched to his family, but he let it ride. "She has four kids now, and each one has a different dad. She's on her third husband, chain smokes, and works at a dry cleaner. My brother is in jail for armed robbery. He won't be getting out for a while."

"How about your mom?"

"Last I heard she was working at a bar. Literally. She likes moving around. I think she's in Texas."

Kathy, the waitress, came out with their Cokes. She placed the red plastic glasses on the table, then dropped the papered straws between them. "Your food will be here in a minute."

"Thanks," Cade and Gitana said in unison. The waitress smiled at the cuteness before heading over to the other couple.

Gitana pushed her coffee aside and turned to the Coke. After taking a sip, she asked, "Do you think if you'd stayed, you'd have made a difference? At least with your sister and brother?"

Cade wanted a beer. No, something harder. Like Scotch. "I believe if I stayed, I'd end up in jail. They made their path. I made mine."

"Didn't you feel guilty leaving?"

"I was in hell with all the guilt. I sent money back home. I wanted them to get away, start fresh. They were too deep in trouble at the time to make a break. Nor did they want to. They wanted my money. I had to make a decision. I stopped being the enabler. Like a divorce, my ties with them ended."

"Ah," Gitana exclaimed. "So what you're saying, if I stayed with John, I would slowly rot. I would always have the fear of him leaving or hiding a mistress." Her cheeks sunk in as she headed into a dark place. "What about the hurt? The betrayal? Unlike you, I didn't have a choice. He made it for me."

"Yes, but you can decide what comes next. Don't let him drive."

She curled her lips into a slight smile. "Back to the driving, I see." Gitana raised her eyes again. "And when you ran, where'd you go? Here to San Francisco?"

More questions. *How did this turn to me again?*

He put his hands on the table and stared at the scars on his fingers, the short cuts made when he bent the metal without gloves. He wore one of the first rings he made, a simple braided silver band.

Cade sighed, not wanting to spill his life on her but liking their connection. "For a while I moved to Montana. I figured the wide-open space would do me good and it did. After a time, I missed the sounds of a city. I left for Colorado. I worked on a ranch where one of the handlers, a local, had a small shop in town. He sold beautiful pieces of glass, ones he hand-blew. His work floored me. This guy was the meanest, ugliest man in town—not the artist type. For some odd reason, he saw a talent in me I didn't know I had. He taught me his trade."

"And the galleries?"

"I was blessed with a new start and wanted to help other local artists sell their work."

"And where do I fall in?"

He frowned, not understanding.

"The damaged puppy needing to be saved?"

He squeezed her hands. "You're definitely not a puppy."

"I am damaged."

He wrinkled his forehead. "Because you were married?" He snorted. "That's an everyday occurrence."

She became agitated. "I can't have kids—keep the generations going."

"Guys are out there who don't want families."

"Are you one of them?"

"I left my family. You think I'm cut out to be a daddy?"

Gitana sat back, creating distance. His words startled her. He wasn't sure if he'd said them too curtly or if she didn't like the fact that he didn't want kids. The word family had importance to her. She turned too quiet.

He asked, "Are you okay?"

"Yeah," she said and tightened her lips. "I'm just hungry."

Lesson #6
Bring your talents forward.

On and off, Layne looked toward Gitana's boat. He was dying to find out how her night with Cade went. He sat in his usual spot on deck with a cup of coffee in one hand and the *San Francisco Chronicle* in the other. The morning sun brightened the sky and kept the fog away from the bay. Normally he stayed inside cleaning. But having the blue sky and wanting Gitana to come out of her boat, he stayed visible.

He glanced from paper to boat, boat to bay, bay to boat, boat to paper. He tried reading the news, but the sentences blurred together.

He thought back to when Cade showed up after sunset. Layne knew who he was when he knocked on her door. The man seemed disappointed when he noticed the closed windows and dark interior.

Layne liked the man's solidness. His arms and chest radiated muscle, but not the steroids-type where the bulk did not fit the body. Instead, he had a healthy stance, one earned by physical work and not gym-bred. Most of the men and women he trained never gained that status. Besides, he liked the shaved head. Cade's was shiny and perfect-shaped.

Layne rubbed the fuzz on his own head and wondered if he should try the shine again. Scrape the hair down to skin instead of leaving a shadow. He didn't think he had the right head shape, but Gitana thought he did. As a trainer and a drummer, he liked a little bit of hair to give him a rough sexiness that his clients seemed to go for.

He saw movement and jumped out of his chair as Gitana, with tousled hair and her robe tied, popped out of her boat to check the weather. Layne folded his paper and set it aside. He walked to the edge of his deck and asked, "How'd last night go?"

Gitana ignored him. She raised her head to the sun to enjoy a moment of warmth and blue sky. She took another sip of coffee before turning to him and shaking her finger. "I'm thinking I have a bone to pick with you."

"Why?" He feigned innocence. He leaned his elbows against the silver polished side rail.

"Telling him where I work?"

"He's a good guy. He saved you twice."

She rolled her eyes. "Once."

Layne grinned. "You got home pretty late."

"Not too late." She yawned.

"Almost four. Four o'clock in the morning." He pointed to his watch. "Did you have fun?"

"I guess," she said.

Layne went back to his chair and grabbed his coffee cup. Empty. He made instant. She had a percolator. He jumped onto the raft and over to her houseboat.

"You guess you had fun?" He gave her a peck on the forehead. "How can you say you guess? The guy's handsome. He's a watcher. Watchers are good."

"A watcher?" Gitana wrinkled her nose at the description.

"He'd protect you," Layne explained and slipped inside the galley. He poured himself a cup of hot coffee.

She waited until he came back out and then said, "He's not necessarily looking for a relationship."

Layne shook his head once. "You're wrong. He wanted to see you."

"No, I don't think so."

He took a sip of coffee. He tasted the Columbian blend with the salty air of the bay. His patience was just about shot with her. "For chrissake, Gitana. The man came here the minute he got off the plane from New York to find you. When you weren't home, he drove to another state, looking for you. He's interested, darling."

"I work near Sonoma, not another state," she corrected. A smile curved on her lips, and she hid her mouth behind the coffee cup.

Layne's eyes narrowed. The twinkle in her eye ratted her out. "You little…"

Gitana let out a laugh. She nudged him. "You get so riled. I couldn't keep a straight face any longer, Butthead."

Layne mimicked her laugh, but he was relieved to be right. He knew she and Cade would get along. He sensed their chemistry by the way Cade said her name and the way she suppressed her liking for him. "So tell me about your date."

"Well…" She rolled up against the steel rail and leaned forward to look at the water lap between the boat and the pier. "He gave me a lesson on driving. He told me a little about himself, his background." She turned her head to him. "He doesn't want a family."

Leave it to Gitana to figure it out right away. "I suppose you flat out asked him?"

"No, we were talking about families."

"You didn't let it ruin the night, I hope."

She glared at him, pulling her robe tighter around her chest.

"I know how you work." He lowered his eyebrows in disappointment. He had hopes for her.

She went inside to grab more coffee.

"Gitana…" he growled.

"I didn't ruin it," she snapped. "Yes, we had a little setback, I admit, but I let go. I eased up."

"Is he gonna call you?"

Her eyes focused on her coffee cup. She shrugged.

"Did you give him your number?"

She made a face at his ridiculous question. "I didn't have to. You gave it to him."

Layne smiled. She may not admit they had their first date, but they did. She put up a good front, not wanting to think her life could change.

"What's your plan for the day?" He flipped his leg over the side of her boat.

"Sleep and sun," she said and gazed up at the late morning sky. Not a cloud wisped overhead. A perfect day graced Sausalito.

"Enjoy your lazy ass." Layne hopped back across the raft.

"No showing off," she warned in a playful way. She knew he would be working with his buff client, the FBI agent in the making. The woman had defined curves and more muscles than most of the men at the gym.

Layne liked the agent because he was in charge of keeping her fit. His other clients still needed to lose weight and define muscle. He pointed his finger at Gitana. "You need to get your sorry ass in for a good workout."

"One day," she agreed, "but not today."

***

After a late night and little sleep, Gitana deserved to be lazy. She dressed in a purple bikini, her best for limited coverage, and climbed the ladder to the roof of her houseboat. She laid her towel out. It still smelled of sand and salt from the last time she had been at the beach. She thought of driving to the ocean but the comforts of home had privileges.

Already lathered with a light sunscreen, she stretched out, stomach down, on the bright peach terrycloth. She found the plastic claw clip in her bag after removing her book, IPod, and sunglasses. To keep from getting the zebra-look as she tanned, she clipped her hair in a bun. She then undid the strap to her top to eliminate the tan line. Settled, she closed her eyes.

A few gulls squawked overhead. The birds flapped their wings and hovered, looking for food from the tourists gathered in the park and along the shore. Her thoughts went to Cade, and she wondered if he enjoyed the night and if he was thinking of her.

A seal barked in the distance and echoed across the bay. Someone's radio played from a few boats down—she assumed from the neighbor who was always on her deck with a lit cigarette in her hand.

Back to Cade. Gitana thought of his gravelly voice and the way his eyes squinted, showing little creases when he laughed. He had a tough appearance, yet his personality had a softer side that didn't seem to come out as often. Was she the same? Hard and jaded?

Layne kept telling her to lighten up. Cade's crystal blue eyes shined at her...

The lapping of water against the boats, the clang of metal, and the traffic in the distance lulled her to sleep.

"Hello?"

Gitana jerked her head up. She reoriented, wondering how long she had been out.

"Gitana?"

"Up here," she yelled and wiped away the drool from her mouth. The sun was still high in the sky.

Sitting up, she covered her breasts as the bikini top shifted. She peeked over the side of the roof while clasping it back together. Boat and water. Wrong way. She rolled over. Skin touched hot metal.

"Shit!"

"Did I come at a bad time?"

Cade stood on the dock. He shielded his eyes with his hand and looked upward.

"It's open," she said and pointed to the sliding glass door. She wrapped the towel around her waist and gathered her belongings. He stepped aboard and the boat rocked. She grabbed the low rail for balance.

Still not awake, she tumbled down the steel ladder to the wheelhouse, her legs not ready to work. The small room she used for a studio was a mess. Stacks of different-sized canvases were on the floor and propped wherever they could find a home. A large wicker basket tipped over, spilling tubes of oils and acrylics across the counter. The wheel, in the middle of the mess, hid underneath rags and hand towels. And tucked in the corner, an easel held her latest painting of a naked woman on top of a stallion.

Cade walked up the spiral staircase as Gitana gathered up the rags. She stuffed them in a drawer, a fruitless effort to make her studio a little neater. He slowed as his head popped above the opening.

"Sorry for the mess." She apologized and dropped another rag into an old coffee can.

He drank it in. And of course, he would, being an artist and gallery owner.

"You paint?" He honed in on her current work in progress.

"Keeps my mind off things."

Of all paintings for him to fixate on, he had to go for the naked woman. The wheelhouse became hot, stuffy. She leaned over and opened one of the windows as he stepped into the room. He stood next to the easel and scrutinized the detail of her work in progress.

As he shifted over, his knee hit another canvas propped against the stool. It fell forward. Gitana grabbed the painting and moved it to a stack with ten others stored nearby.

"Sorry," she said with some embarrassment at the tight quarters even though he didn't seem to care.

"You paint a lot?" He touched the palette next to the easel. Ochre smeared on his finger. He rubbed the color away with his thumb.

"When I can. I find it costs less than a therapist."

He nodded as if knowing what she meant. His attention went to the canvases on the floor. He crouched on his knees to flip through each one and stopped at a castle. He bit his lip, deep in thought. Reaching the end of the stack, he reversed order and found the painting of a knight holding a sword to a man kneeling before him.

His eyes lit up. "You painted the ones at the winery."

"I did," she said and smoothed her hands across her hips.

Mesmerized, he stared at another painting of a young man and woman sneaking a private conversation in a barn.

He tapped his finger against his lips. "You're good."

"Watch..." Gitana started to say, but it was too late. He stepped on the steel shackle bolted to the floor. His hand went to the counter to keep his balance. Dark umber and crimson streaked his palm as he hit her palette of oils. She'd painted the day before without cleaning the leftovers from the board.

"A little hazardous up here," she apologized again. She pulled his hand toward her waist and used the clean edge of an old white rag to wipe off the paint.

Cade's eyes found her breasts tucked into the bikini top.

Gitana glanced down to make sure she was still presentable and not too exposed.

"No problem," he said, a little delayed. He took over the rag and in a casual move wiped his hands like a mechanic after changing the oil in a car. "You never told me you painted."

"It never came up."

Her paintings were for herself. She brushed the white canvas with intricate strokes until they came to life. In a dark mood, a good splotch of midnight blue against black strokes did wonders for shadowing a face or for threatening a clear sky with an incoming storm.

"You have any more?" Tiny beads of sweat formed on his forehead. He used the back of his hand to wipe it away. He still seemed surprised at her mess.

"You mean finished work?" She opened another window, hoping for a cross breeze. "I do, but not here. No space. I store them at my papa's, where the air is less humid and salty."

"How many you got?"

She stopped to think. "A roomful?" She never counted them.

He pointed to the canvas on the easel and said, "You know, you could do a show with your paintings. You ever try selling them?"

"I did eons ago to help pay for some of my college tuition. Of course, I sold them out of my car from the parking lot, not in a gallery."

"A few of these would fetch more than enough for tuition," Cade said under his breath while leafing through another stack of paintings. He held up a canvas with a child playing in a sandbox. "You could sell these. Easily."

He was kind. She said, "Thanks but I think I'm in the category of a starving artist."

He laughed. "All starve. Some do make it." He stopped at the last one in the stack, a portrait of an old man sitting on a bench in a park. "Your father?"

"No, a guy at the Sacramento courthouse. I sketched him as I waited for my turn with the divorce judge. I then put him on canvas."

"Interesting face." Cade, deep in thought, kept looking at the way she cut in the shadows with the blue paint. After a moment he said, "Can I borrow this one?"

"You may have it."

He jerked his head up and frowned. "Oh no. Do not give away your paintings. Not when you can sell them."

Whatever, she thought. Being a gallery owner, he had to be careful.

"Would you like a beer or wine?" Gitana asked, ready to head down. She was thirsty from her nap, the hot sun, and now the cramped quarters.

"Thanks for the offer, but I can't stay."

She had to get out of the oven-like room. She made a move toward the staircase and hoped he would take the hint. He stood in place.

She turned sideways to pass, careful not to touch him or smear him with suntan lotion. She slid by, but his warm hand pressed against her waist and stopped her.

Gitana's skin danced with pleasure. She swayed, a little light-headed. He smelled of sexiness. The lure to pull him in was overwhelming. When she looked up, his eyes glazed with the same desire. She flicked her tongue across her bottom lip.

The gesture was enough of an invite for him to lean down for a soft kiss. And then another. His tongue fluttered with hers. She tasted pure male, and her knees weakened.

The stubble on his face roughed her skin when he came in for a stronger kiss. Gitana stepped back, but he kept her from pulling away. His other hand rested against her upper back. He went in for a deeper kiss, and she had no control.

All sounds fell silent. When he released his mouth, Gitana breathed in. She savored his pleasurable touch. She returned to the present.

He cleared his throat. "I want you to come to my

studio, the garage where I work. Would you like to?"

She wanted him to lay her flat on the floor and take her instead. She knew it was wrong. How could she have such feelings when she wasn't over her divorce yet? Gitana nodded, afraid she'd reveal her feelings if she spoke.

"Tomorrow night?"

She nodded again.

The swish of the sliding glass door opening below made Gitana jumped. Soon Layne called her name. Her fridge opened, and the rattle of bottles came next.

Cade stepped back. The spell broke between them.

Gitana turned to compose herself. She fixed her bikini top and imagined the smirk on her neighbor's face. She motioned to Cade that she was heading down.

Cade cleared his throat as if working on his own return to earth. She could tell their kiss had gotten to him as well.

She clutched the rail for support, her knees still weak from their connection as she took the narrow steps.

"Hey…" Layne started to say but stopped when he saw Cade behind her. He shot her an "I-told-you-so" look.

"What's up?" Cade stuck his hand out.

Gitana watched the two greet each other as if they were old pals. Their thick arms wrapped in a light, brotherly-like embrace.

"Tomorrow?" Cade turned back to her for a confirmation. He held her old man painting with care.

"Huh?" She still felt dazed.

"I'll pick you up at seven?"

"Seven," she agreed.

Lesson #7
Try new things.

Cade was prompt.

Wearing a white T-shirt and jeans, he walked with confidence down the long dock to her boat. Shoulders straight, head back, he waited for a young woman to whiz by on her rollerblades. He did not turn around to admire the short shorts and Barbie legs, but she turned, obviously hoping he would. Gitana liked his focus.

She shook the nervousness out of her hands. *I'm not ready for a relationship.* She repeated the words under her breath. As he passed Layne's boat, her breasts tingled with excitement. She wanted to feel his kisses on her again. Run her hands down his naked back.

No! Stop it.

Gitana straightened her dress, a favorite with sheer white and pink floral chiffon over black silk. The belt cinched her waist and the low-cut front showed enough cleavage to stir any man's interest. The A-line skirt stopped above the knees to reveal sculpted legs but no thighs—fun, summery, and sexy. Ten times she'd pondered whether the dress was too much. But she looked so good in it. What if they went out afterward? She would be ready.

When he reached the dock extension she shared with another neighbor, Gitana grabbed her purse and did one last check in the mirror. She opened the door before he could knock.

He pulled down his Ray-Bans to take in the view. "You look great."

A smile curved her lips with silent pleasure. After a small kiss, he took her hand and they walked to the parking lot. Every nerve opened like a circuit and all points connected into one charge. Gitana strained to stay calm and collected.

The ride from her place to San Francisco flew by. They chatted about paintings and the art world. She was glad he left Dr. Phil at home; yet another lecture may have helped distract her urge to touch his arm, his leg. She liked the way his jeans tightened when his thigh came up after shifting. She should have taken care of herself last night. Get rid of some tension.

Cade parked on the street in front of an old renovated garage. He warned, "My studio isn't anything special, nothing like the gallery. I don't have to worry about the mess here."

"Understandable," she said, thinking about the wheelhouse where she painted.

"And private. Very few are allowed in."

"So why's the opportunity for me?"

His smile came out. "I'm showing you my other side. You opened your life and work to me, so now I get to do the same."

She laughed. *Open my life to him?* She used him as a dropping ground when he kept bugging her about it. "I bitched and moaned. You didn't get the friendly version. I used you."

"You can use me anytime." His eyes dropped to her cleavage.

Gitana's cheeks burned, so unlike a thirty-year-old. She wanted to be herself, let loose, yet her other side kept the warning bells tolling. Hot and cold clashed together. Her pulse raced, mixing excitement with nerves.

His studio, a rustic, quaint stone building had two larger green garage doors for cars to enter and one smaller door for customers. No signage on the place claimed what the inside treasured. His name, painted in small letters above the entrance, offered the slightest hint.

The air turned warm and humid as they entered, which Gitana imagined was from the furnaces glowing yellowish-orange on the far wall. The work area took up most of the space. Wood-slab workbenches and cabinets shelving tools, sheets of metal, and glass panels replaced the car stalls. His office with a small bathroom, kitchenette, and a desk occupied the other part of the building. A large, high-legged table divided the two areas.

Gitana walked over to a yellow line painted on the floor. "What's this for?"

"Danger zone. I bring kids in during the holidays to make ornaments for their parents. They can't cross the stripe until it's their turn."

"Smart." She was more impressed that he volunteered his time than with the safety issue.

A multicolored glass piece caught her eye from one of the shelves. Feeling naughty, she crossed the line to the danger side for a better look at his work. She picked up the bright orange tangle of glass and admired the detail. Faint red swirls danced like fire from the base, then darkened into blue tips, the ends fanning out like flames. Fascinating, she thought, how the colors blended without halting lines.

The room brightened when Cade opened one of the furnace doors. Gitana turned to watch. He stuck a rod into the orange glow, twirled it around, and then checked the end. As he played, she returned the glass piece to the shelf and went to the table to wait.

The place had warmth and an old-style comfort. A faint dusty smell of old oil clung to the air when she walked further in. She wrinkled her nose. This was a man's hideout; all closed in like a cave. Even she would hang out there just to get away from the bustle of everyday life.

Cade returned to the kitchenette. He grabbed a bottle of wine from the fridge and two glasses. He held the bottle out with label up, wanting her to see it.

She laughed. The Merlot he snatched from the winery.

"I knew this would come in handy." He smiled and uncorked the top.

Still thinking about the tangle of glass, Gitana motioned

toward the other pieces on the shelf. "How long does one of your sculptures take to complete?"

"Depends on the size. For most, two or three months. Sometimes longer if the galleries keep me busy."

"Do you create the glass first? Or metal?"

"Usually glass first." He poured the wine and offered her a glass.

Gitana held the glass to the light. The tulip-shaped base spread out at the top like the petals on the flower. Tiny clear bubbles raced upward from the pale green bottom, changing to yellow at the top of the rim. Simple yet complicated at the same time.

"I made these for you." He raised his and pointed to it.

"The glasses?"

Cade nodded.

Gitana liked them. She brought her glass to his and clicked in a toast. "Thank you. Here's to cool glasses."

"Here's to beauty," he added.

Her cheeks heated again as he stared with more than a platonic interest. He moved closer, ready to take her in for a kiss when a loud whoosh from the furnace grabbed his attention.

Cade set his wine on the table and walked over to the danger zone. He lifted the rod and a glob of glass stuck to the end like honey on a stick. After setting the rod down again, he checked the temperature. "You ready to make something?"

"Me?" Gitana stood straighter.

He took the wine glass from her hand and set it on the

table by his. He led her over to the back corner of the building.

"First, let's cut some metal."

"I should've wore jeans," Gitana said when he picked up a rectangular copper sheet and placed it on the worktable.

"You won't get dirty. Besides, I love the dress."

Gitana did too, except the fabric was a bitch to clean and iron. She could not afford the expense of a drycleaner. She should have known better than to dress up for a date in a garage.

"Here, put on these gloves. I have an apron if you'd like."

She slipped them on and wiggled her fingers around, the grit on the inside going underneath her nails. She refused the apron, taking her chances. He handed her the cutters.

"Where are your gloves?" she asked, remembering the scars on his hands.

"You'll be doing the cutting." He held the sheet against the table so the metal stayed in place. "I already marked the lines. All you have to do is cut."

Gitana turned her head. She looked for his markings. The copper shined brightly with the lights reflecting off the sheet. She leaned over for a closer look. Her backside aligned with his front. His jeans pressed against her. She closed her eyes to feel his touch flow through. *Keep steady.*

"R-right here," Cade stuttered. He pointed out the three lines.

She refocused. The sheet was long and tricky to cut. The edges were sharp and raw. She made him move his hands, afraid she would slip and jab the scissors into his skin.

With his continual coaxing, Gitana snipped three narrow strips—less than an eighth of an inch—along the length of the sheet. Her cuts were not perfect, more like a drunk attempting a straight line.

Cade took the strips and twisted the three pieces together with a sharp, angled tool. He continued to turn the metal until the end became a new-formed rope. He passed the tool to her while holding the copper. She mimicked his moves and started twisting.

Over halfway done, Gitana dropped her arms and leaned back. She confessed, "This is tough!"

He was still behind her. His hand came up and rested on the side of her waist.

"You're doing great. A little more."

"A little more?" she protested. She had a few inches left. With the tiny twists, it was no small feat. "I deserve at least some wine."

Taking the hint, Cade went to retrieve their glasses. She continued to form the rope. Returning, he took over to finish the end, then dangled it in front of the light.

"Nicely done," he said and made slight adjustments so the metal sealed together. "Take a look."

Gitana removed her gloves and took the rope from him. The lines were perfect, smooth—no raw edges or spaces.

Cade slipped in behind her and lowered his head. Gitana closed her eyes as he feathered her hair away from her shoulder and traced his hand against the curve of her neck.

It had been way too long since a man touched her.

"You smell *sooo* good," he said, inhaling her scent. His lips kissed the side of her neck. His arms circled her waist. He pressed against her backside, and she leaned in to enjoy the moment. Cade cupped her breast. Gitana's nipple hardened and she closed her eyes to enjoy the touch of his fingers massaging her.

The wine glass slipped in her hands. She turned and placed both the glass and the twisted copper on the stool next to the worktable.

"Come here, you." He moaned and brought his lips to hers. His tongue was playful and teasing.

Gitana wanted him—wanted sex. But taking it further would mean more than just friendship. If they continued, she sensed something deeper would result, a bond not easily broken.

They found the edge of the worktable. Pinned, she let him plant soft kisses across her shoulder. She moaned. Every nerve opened to his feathered touch when her head went back.

Gitana gasped. The flick of his tongue left a cool tingle between her breasts. She leaned on her elbows and hit the tool that twisted the copper. Cade pushed it out of the way, along with the remaining metal sheet. Both crashed to the floor, and neither of them cared when he grabbed her legs and lifted her onto the table. He continued with his searing kisses, his breath warm and heavy.

Gitana ran her hands across the top of his smooth head. At first she was afraid. Don't give in by touching him—to the feelings that would follow. She trailed her fingers down the back of his neck. How could she resist his hard body?

Cade was more wild and exciting than what she experienced before. The tough side of him played with her curiosity. His hands flamed the desire in her body. She pushed away the guilt wanting her to stop. She ignored the warnings.

Both of Cade's hands slipped under her skirt, and he spread her legs apart. Gitana gasped again. She wanted him yet knew this would seal them together. He stopped and waited for permission. Their short breaths filled the space between them. He was ready.

What am I doing? Gitana responded with a kiss. Her tongue to his. Permission.

Cade's large hands smoothed over her hips. He clipped her thong into his fingers. She lifted up, allowing him to pull the satin away. Her skirt shifted upward, revealing bare thighs.

She pulled off his shirt and took in the broad chest and sable nipples. Unable to resist, Gitana scratched her nails into his skin. She dragged them down to his solid abs and then found his belt. She fumbled to unclasp the hook. He helped. In one swoop, his pants and briefs were at his ankles.

He was a work of art, pure male—rough and muscular without any polish or softness. She bit her lip, ready for him. He guided himself in without using his hands.

They held each other. The desire intensified as he rocked. The rhythm of their bodies kept pace with their breathing. His blue eyes, like water cresting, deepened as they concentrated on her.

No distractions. No shame. Gitana lifted her hips. She welcomed the sensation. Her hands cradled his head as he buried his face into her neck seconds before coming. He let out a cry of pleasure as he released himself in one long stroke.

"Holy Jesus," he gasped between kisses to her breasts. His chest heaved up and down.

Gitana could not move, did not want to. She soaked in their closeness until his mind came back around.

Giving her a squeeze, he pulled away. With a playful smile, he said, "Now for your delight…"

He ran his hands down her sides, then fell to his knees. Gitana moaned with anticipation. She wanted to come a thousand times over when his soft tongue found her pleasure spots. Still in her heels, she pressed them into his back. She cried out as she came. Months of pent-up desire released in one long convulsion.

As they basked from their high, Gitana stared at the wood-framed ceiling. She became part of the table, too weak to move. Cade came back up to kiss her belly. He wrapped his arm around her waist and lifted her. When her feet reached the floor, he caressed her cheek and waited until she got her balance before letting her go. He pulled away a strand of hair. "You good with this?"

She liked how he knew her place, her emotions. Lustful desire overtook any thoughts to what was proper.

"I'm good," Gitana said and meant it.

As she fixed her dress and recovered her panties, he refilled their wine. She met him at the table near the kitchenette. They toasted. The glasses clicked, but they remained silent. Cade drank half his Merlot, then grinned. He set his glass on the table and wanted her to do the same. He said, "We're not done yet."

Gitana raised her eyebrow.

He hooked his fingers around her hand and pulled her across the yellow line again. "First metal. Now glass."

"If that was metal," she said, "I'm looking forward to glass."

Cade laughed as if he found no words to describe what he wanted to say, even though he tried. He squeezed her into a hug instead.

He had her stand near the workbench, the one he used for his glass-blowing. He went to the furnace and opened the hatch. Intense heat, like their lovemaking, glowed toward them. She waited as he kept turning the rod until a blob of glass stuck to the end. Over his shoulder he explained, "This furnace contains the molten glass. We're at about 2,200 degrees here."

"I bet," she said, referring more to the tryst than the furnace.

He took the rod out and sprayed the handle of the pipe

with water to cool it down. Cade motioned for her to join him at a table. He sprinkled out colored glass shards on the metal top from an old coffee can. Together they rolled the blob of glass across the shards and coated it, like dipping an ice cream cone in sprinkles.

"Now we're going to melt in the colored glass." They walked over to another furnace. "This is called the glory hole."

Gitana raised her eye at the name but kept silent. They twirled the rod until the glass blended.

"Where'd the color go?" she asked after he took over again. Once the orb left the glory hole, it turned yellow again.

"You'll see the color once it cools," he said.

Fascinated with his work, Gitana liked how he handled the rod, his bare chest glistening from the heat. She wanted to concentrate on what he was doing, but the vision of skin took over. She took a snapshot in her head, wanting to capture it on canvas.

After putting the orb into a metal form on the floor, he placed a tube on the end of the rod. He took the orb out of the form, then handed her the side with the mouthpiece.

He pointed to the end of the rod. "Blow into this end."

"Me?"

"You have to use some lung power, but not too forceful. Take a good breath. Blow long."

"What if the glass comes up into my mouth?" She pictured her mouth glowing orange like the furnace.

"It won't happen," he promised.

The rod was heavier than she expected. Cade held the other end. He made sure the glass did not hit the floor. Gitana inhaled. He gave a nod, and she wrapped her lips around the mouthpiece. She exhaled; her face turned red as the air left her lungs. The orb started to grow.

"Keep going," he said, keeping his eyes on her and the other end of the rod.

She blew again.

"Steady…" he warned.

A swirl of faded green and purple expanded into a round bubble. He held out his hand and she stopped.

"Nice!" He seemed impressed.

He took the rod back from her and removed the glass ball from the end with a diamond shear. He then grabbed another rod, walked over to the furnace, and grabbed more of the molten glass. He dabbed a small piece onto the ball, closing the hole with a Dairy Queen curl to form a hook.

"We'll have to let the glass cool. Once ready, I'll loop the metal rope you made through the hook so you can hang it above a window."

"How cool is that!" Gitana clapped her hands together. She made an ornament, not a blob.

"Good job for your first time."

"I totally agree." She gave him a wicked smile. The thought of his lips on her skin sent another round of pleasure through her body.

Cade didn't catch on at first. But soon the chuckle came and he grabbed her waist.

"What would you like to do while we wait?" He pulled

her in.

"How long will it take to cool?"

"I don't think it will." He placed his hand on her ass.

Gitana caught her breath. How could she refuse?

The first time was raw and unyielding. Now she wanted control and pushed him away. Her terms. She removed her dress one shoulder at a time before letting the fabric fall to the floor. His eyes stayed right where she wanted them.

Lesson #8
Look out for surprises.

The glow of the evening stayed with Cade as thoughts of Gitana branded his insides for the next few days. He dreamed of her with a half smile and those sexy brown eyes tilting downward. He loved how she teased him to come forward but didn't allow him to touch. She had the power to hold him. He would have done anything to keep her for the night. Make love a dozen times over. But he behaved.

Cade's head spun. The first time they made love, he came out of lust, need. The second time, he enjoyed the visual and physical to make sure it wasn't forgotten. Her shyness disappeared. She knew what she wanted, knew what he wanted.

Hard again, he shifted his pants to uncurl the steel rod now between his legs. One more night and he'd see her. She said yes to going to a birthday party with him. He'd introduce her to his circle of his friends and acquaintances. Until then, he called her every night. He wanted her to remember their chemistry, how well they fit. He loved hearing her laugh on the phone. At times her beauty opened, and she let down the wall sheltering her insides. Other times, her self-doubt crept back in. He wanted to erase the bad, keep her spirits lifted. She was too talented to have dark clouds holding her back. One way he could help was to see her thrive as an artist.

The clock on his desk chimed twelve and brought Cade back to the present. He worked all week at the gallery, burying himself in the financials of the business. He caught up with his paperwork. He wanted to make sure he had time for Gitana.

For the party, he picked her up at eight o'clock sharp. She greeted him in tight black pants, a black bra, and a buttoned white shirt. She kept her hair down. He loved how it bounced when she walked to meet him in the parking lot. The setting sun put her in the spotlight and enhanced the fine curves. He smiled a helpless grin. His lips parted. If he weren't wearing his sunglasses, she would have seen his eyes dance like the water in the bay.

Cade dressed in dark gray pants and a black shirt. Sharp yet casual and the right choice by her smile. Always a plus.

"You look amazing," he said and pulled her in for a kiss. He swept his gaze downward to catch the swell of her breasts against the sexy, tight bra. He knew their roundness, the taste of each nipple as he wetted them with his tongue.

"Thanks." She flashed him a brilliant smile.

"I made something for you," he said after they climbed into his car. He pulled out a box of small glass beads attached to studs for her nose. He played it safe and made four with different hues in hopes to match her outfit.

"How cool!" She used her finger to separate the studs and found the black with a dark, silvery-blue swirl. "These had to be hard to make."

"Not too bad," Cade lied. It took one full day. He had to find the studs and then make the glass stone. Some came out too big, some broke.

Gitana changed out the stud in her nose as they headed into San Francisco. Cade strained to watch the road instead of her. Between shifting gears, he placed his hand on her thigh and liked the firmness. They created small talk. He told her of his day catching up on paperwork. She gave him bits about the event she hosted at the winery, the late morning "tea" with a group of older ladies and the second shifting into a wild bachelorette party's first stop. He continued to listen as the buildings grew taller inside the financial district. He enjoyed the purr in her voice and the little laugh before she said something funny.

When they pulled up to the Marriott, a uniformed man stepped out to open Gitana's door even before the car came to a stop. Cade got out on his side and tossed the keys to another valet eager to park the Charger. He pointed a finger to intimidate him. No pulling any shit with his Charger.

Gitana flowed out of the passenger seat, and he was quick to catch up to her. He put his arm possessively around her waist. Heads turned as they walked through the doors.

"Now what's his name again? The birthday boy?" she asked.

"Billy Friedman." Cade nodded to the attendant when he opened the wide gold-plated door for them to pass through. "I sold his first painting five years ago. He lives here, close to the tower."

"What's his style?" Her heels clicked on the tile floor to the elevators.

"Fish."

"Fish?" she repeated as if not having a clue what he meant. "So he uses a rod and reel to splash paint onto the canvas?"

Cade laughed. "He paints different types of fish using flecks of gold for the scales. He sometimes uses silver. I'll show you a painting. Pretty clever, actually. The gold looks like the sun is reflecting off the fish."

They entered the elevator along with another couple. Cade pushed the button to the top floor, then turned to face her. He pulled her in and intoxicated himself with her scent. He had the urge to kiss her shiny lips but refrained since they shared the small space with strangers. He kept his hands on her hips and just stared. She giggled with shyness and glanced toward the other people.

Cade waited. The elevator stopped at the 18th floor. The doors opened and the couple got out. When they were alone, his mouth covered her lips in a lustful kiss. Gitana gripped the elevator's rail with both hands, her head tilted back against the corner walls. Her tongue reached in to play with his.

The elevator stopped way too soon. He didn't hear the bell, but she did. She tried pushing him away. He resisted, but then her tightness slapped his mind back into gear. He cursed himself for being thoughtless. Not too long ago a man had attacked her. Those thoughts must haunt her.

"I apologize sincerely," he rasped. He took her hand and planted light kisses across the palm. "I haven't been able to stop thinking of you."

She stayed quiet. She didn't back away or seem frightened, just unsure of her own feelings. He'd work on it.

As they got out of the elevator, Gitana wiped the edges of her mouth to make sure her lip-gloss was in place. Cade adjusted his pants, then fixed his collar. Musk perfume drifted through the corridor as they walked to the double doors at the end of the hall. He rapped twice against the wood panel. He turned to face her.

"This evening," he said, "if you feel uncomfortable let me know. We can leave at any time."

She gave him a nod as the door flew open. The noise from inside the suite blew out like a gust of wind. A short pudgy man wearing a purple coat and red beret greeted them with a giddy smile.

"Welcome! Welcome! Come on in!" His thick black glasses poked out from his face like Truman Capote's. He sucked on an unlit cigar, rolling it between two fat fingers.

"Randy." Cade shook the man's hand.

The host gave Gitana the once over. He smiled his like. He let out a high-pitched laugh and said to Cade, "It's about time you jingle-jangled your balls in here. Where the hell have you been?"

"Keeping life straight," Cade responded and put his arm around Gitana's waist. "Randy, this is Gitana. Gitana, Randy. He's a jeweler with lots of money."

"Loads, baby. Loads," the man corrected and took her hand in a kiss. "So sweets to meets you."

He led them into the living area. A colorful palette of flamboyant outfits splashed the room. A transvestite in a white-sequined, red-feathered pantsuit mingled with a Diane Keaton look-alike. A woman wearing a hot pink mini and white knee-high boots conversed with a man in a yellow pinstriped suit. Two other men in shimmering blue shirts stood mesmerized by another woman with white hair. They devoured the words coming out of her mouth. Their silver-spiked heads bobbed up and down in unison as she rattled on.

Cade watched Gitana. She seemed amused with the vivid scarves, hats, and accessories adorning the people who came to greet them. The introductions flowed from those curious to meet the new person hanging with him.

Scanning the crowd, he spotted his assistant.

Rex's eyes lit when he saw Gitana. In black slim pants and a white shirt, he used a sharp eye to scrutinize her outfit and ignored Cade.

"You win," he said, referring to their similar attire. He took her hand and kissed it. "So we meet again, Wild Child."

"Devil Man," she said, heavily pronouncing her new

name for him.

Cade had no time to protest when Rex pulled her away from him. Gitana glanced back, amused.

She was fine.

***

Being an artist, Gitana needed to know more artists, so she had gone shopping the day before the birthday party. She wanted the right outfit for a good first impression. Seeing Rex's reaction, she was happy with her choice.

Her income did not allow for a huge clothing budget, but the clearance racks offered something cute and simple at a decent price. She was happy to find the right outfit.

She glanced back as Cade turned to talk to Randy again. Gitana smiled inwardly and lingered on the moment she seduced him at his garage. How the dress fell from her shoulders after she untied the front lace. He became mesmerized the second her fingers curled around the string and started to pull. She loved using her womanly power on him. She took full advantage and teased him until he turned to mush.

"You got something on your mind..." Rex wanted her attention. His bedroom eyes twinkled with mischief.

Gitana smiled from ear to ear. She returned her focus, not indulging him with her thoughts.

He pulled her toward the back of the room where mounds of food decorated the tables. Rex grabbed two plates and handed one to her. He picked at the sushi and settled on one with a pink center.

Gitana wanted to wait before eating. She shot a look toward Cade again. He was talking to a woman with straight red hair and large, green-rimmed, tinted glasses.

"This is fabulous." Rex nudged her and pointed to the deep-fried clams.

The devil man kept her in place, near his side. She feared he would start piling what he wanted on her plate so decided to fill hers with fruit, raw vegetables, and skewered filet medallions. She spread everything out to pretend she had more than she did.

"Cade showed me your painting of the old man. Fantastic." He dragged her to the bar. "We need to do a show."

He stopped to say hi to a woman in a purple jumpsuit and matching peacock hat. She had bright red lipstick and smeared the color on his cheek when she kissed him.

Stunned, Gitana stood for a moment to absorb his words while he did his thing. When he came back to her, she asked, "What do you mean, a show?"

"Sell your art. We have a spot for you. Six months from today." Different types of drinks lined the bar. He handed her a strawberry margarita, then took one for himself. She wanted a beer but didn't argue. She wanted to know what he was talking about.

"A spot?" She followed him to a tall side table. They set their plates and drinks down.

"You're sellable, darling." He clicked his tongue with some slight irritation. "You'd make money. Fruitatious money. Not just lamp-post leg money."

A well-dressed man interrupted their conversation. He placed an arm around Rex, showing ownership. "Who's your friend, sexy?"

"Binny, this is Gitana."

"My pleasure!" He twirled his words with a feminine swirl. He wore lipstick, a pink shade with a darker lip liner.

"Gitana, this is Binny." Rex pushed his friend's arm away.

"I'm his bitch." The man smacked his lips.

Gitana's eyes inflated like two balloons. She brought them back in before the shock wore off.

"You wish." Rex rolled his eyes.

She held out her hand and tried not to laugh. If she were gay, she doubted bitch would have been her choice of words. His handshake was soft, his skin smooth, with nails polished and pink.

"I hear you're Cade's new woman." He fluttered his fake eyelashes as he talked.

"He means you as an artist," Rex explained and gave Binny a heated stare.

"Nice pics by the way," his friend smiled.

This time Gitana looked to Rex, confused.

"Bin and I went to the winery…" he stalled, trying to remember the name.

"Stone Legend." Binny helped him out.

"What?" Gitana choked. She turned speechless.

Lucky for her, Rex felt the need to explain. "Cade raved about your artistic talents and wanted me to go see for myself after showing us the old man painting."

She scanned the room, finding Cade still deep in conversation with the red-haired woman. When he did glance her way, he tried leaving the woman, but she wouldn't let him go.

A waiter passed by with a tray. Gitana grabbed a green drink and took a gulp. A Mojito. Yuck. She wanted a margarita—something with tequila. She had half of it gone when Cade walked over to them.

"He told you, didn't he," Cade said more than asked. He turned to Rex and posed like Yul Brynner with folded arms and raised eyebrows.

"Don't you glare at me," Rex scolded. "She's fine with it. See?"

Gitana finished her drink. The mint made her stomach turn. She ignored it.

"Come on," Cade said and took her hand, "before he corrupts you even more."

"He went to the winery," Gitana said, a little peeved.

"I know. I asked him to. He has a keen eye. Better than mine." He guided her to a corner, then spun her around. He put his hands on her shoulders. "Rex likes your work. He's excited about your style."

"My paintings?" They were quick dabs of oil to give the winery a regal theme and make the place more romantic.

"Yes, your paintings. You have an eye for creating beauty on canvas."

Gitana grabbed a dark pinkish drink from a passing waiter. She took a few gulps. Strawberry margarita. Yes. She slowed down. If she consumed too much alcohol too fast, Cade would have to carry her out.

Their private time was over. He was being the popular one at the party. She did not lack attention as his friends filled the space, eager to talk to the one who caught Cade's interest. Gitana had to drop the painting issue. Instead, she enjoyed discussing art and discovering how those she mingled with knew Cade or what brought them to the party. When hosting her ex's charitable events, she had to be pleasant, smile, bring out conversations in those who would rather sit in a corner and drink by themselves. But tonight she relaxed. She had fun with the bouquet of people who attended the party. She did not have to pull words from their mouths, offer fake smiles, or remind them to be generous with their money.

More guests crowded into the suite, and she still had not met the birthday boy. The drinks were making her woozy, or maybe it was the overstuffed, heated room. She needed a break and slipped out to the deck with a glass of champagne in hand. The cool air was welcome. She closed the door behind her to keep the voices inside muffled and distant.

Gitana leaned against the rail, looked out at the lights, and listened to the sounds of the city. The traffic volume rose from below. Cars drove by, a motorcycle rumbled down the block, and a horn honked impatiently in the distance. Past the buildings, the Bay Bridge arched toward land with a few boats specking the dark patch of water in the bay.

"Nice cool night, isn't it?"

Gitana jumped. She thought she had the balcony to herself.

The woman chuckled at her reaction before stepping out of the shadows. The female with red hair, the one clinging to Cade, took off her large, tinted glasses and revealed green eyes. She was striking. Her porcelain face shined like a China doll's.

"I'm Madeleine. Maddy for short."

"Gitana." They shook hands. Her shake was not even a squeeze to the hand. More like a brush stroke with air. Handshakes with little energy didn't impress her. Gitana discreetly rubbed her hand across her hip. She needed to feel something solid against her palm.

"He's adorable, isn't he?" Maddy took a cigarette from her purse. The woman reminded Gitana of a model with her lithe arms and legs. After exhaling a line of smoke, she continued. "You have quite the eyes on him."

She had to be talking about Cade. Gitana's guard went up as she watched Maddy continue to inhale her cigarette with the same amount of drama reeking from a black and white movie scene. Her cheeks swelled when she blew a circle of smoke into the air.

Gitana bid her silence. She wondered why the woman seemed agitated. Was it with life or with her?

Maddy looked up at the night. "He's so hard to get over, but they all do eventually. He's my little pea. And he means well."

She sighed and took another puff. Gitana debated on

excusing herself. She was not sure where Maddy was going with the conversation. She assumed but asked, "You've known him long?"

Maddy ignored her question. "Love is so confusing isn't it? So complicated." She saw the stud in her nose and by the surprise look on her face, she must have realized Cade made it. She glanced down at the street, then at Gitana again. "Are you his next...his next starlet?"

The woman fished. Did she want gossip? What she meant to him? Gitana was not about to divulge their private life.

"Cade raves about your paintings," Maddy commented.

"Always nice to hear." Gitana took the compliment.

Maddy raised her eyebrow as if downplaying their conversation. Gitana had the sudden impression the woman was competing with her. Maybe Maddy was his favored artist? She tried thinking back to the names on the little white plaques in the gallery. She would have remembered Madeleine or Maddy. "Are you an artist?"

The woman laughed and took a longer hit from her cigarette. She dropped the butt to the floor and snubbed it with her red buckled spike. "No darling, I'm not one of his artists." After another amused look she said, "More like his wife."

Gitana's breath sucked in as the words punched her in the stomach. She refused to show the hurtful blow.

"Ciao," Maddy sang with a cat smile and slipped back inside.

Lesson #9
Remember to breathe.

Gitana backed into the rail. How easy for her to flip over and fall to her death. She covered her mouth with her shaking hand. She choked back a cry.

Married?

Did he ever hint at having a wife? She shook her head. Cade never mentioned being married. He had no reason to keep Maddy from her. He could have said something at the park or the café after her attack or even at the winery. He had many opportunities to bring the subject up.

She thought of his loft. A man's place. A work area. He didn't take her to his house. Was it a sign he was hiding something?

A wife. Maddy. He'd stuck with Maddy, not her, since arriving at the party. The two of them together, close. She saw the intimacy, how he knew her. Gitana felt the vibe between them when they talked.

Fuck.

Gitana's throat swelled with hurt and anger. How stupid of her to think they had a chance. Her first glimmer of hope at spending time with a man, and she let her wall down. *For what?*

She turned to face the suite. Beyond the glass, Maddy stood again, of course, with Cade. Her hand was on his shoulder and his arm rested on the small of her back. They laughed at something she said. Was she telling him how she sprang the news to her? Their little joke they played for kicks?

Gitana spun around and leaned over the rail to watch the cars below as she tried controlling the knots in her stomach. A taxi. A limo. A truck. All heading somewhere. She raised her eyes toward the windows and balconies on the building towering over the next street.

Layne was wrong. Cade was not a watcher or a keeper. Tears threatened to burst from the pores in her body. She had to go.

Do not ruin the birthday party.

Breathe. Stop shaking.

Gitana closed her eyes to gain her composure. She erased emotion from her face. The door was not too far away. Just get past the crowd and disappear.

Better to know now than later. One great night filled with passion and nothing else. Another deep breath. Gitana opened the door to the noise inside. She crossed the line from the balcony to the suite. The density in the air from all the bodies and tongues wagging back and forth choked her.

The doorway out became her focus.

"Gitana!" Binny waved her over.

She ignored him. "Don't stop," she mumbled to herself. "Keep moving."

Nothing mattered. His friends were not her friends. She doubted if she would see them again.

Binny was on her faster than she could walk. He grabbed her hand—the annoying little prick—and dragged her over to Rex.

"Wild Child, there you are!" His expression lit up. He stood near the couch drinking a margarita. He had no idea how the emotions inside her rumbled like an unpredictable storm. Her mask covered the clouds twisting through her. "Your paintings. We need to decide which ones to put in the show."

More words came from his mouth, but Gitana barely picked up half of what he said. She waited for an escape.

"You want to bring them by?" He repeated a little louder.

She shook her head. "Call me. When you're ready."

"Precious, you don't look so good." Binny frowned like a worried mother. "You need a pill or something?"

Gitana coughed. "I just need some air."

Tears poked from behind her mask and burned her cheeks like barbed wire branding her skin. Each leg dragged like cement across the carpet. She faced forward, afraid of seeing everyone laugh at her. Afraid of seeing Maddy, in victory, watch her leave. She opened the door enough to slip out as if she had never entered.

Gitana sprinted to the elevator and pushed the down

button. She tapped her hand rapidly on her thigh and pushed the button again.

"Come on, come on!" she said under her breath. Why was it taking forever?

She jumped when the elevator dinged, then walked into a man coming out as it opened. Gitana averted a scene by twisting around to avoid a collision. She punched the button for the lobby.

Alone, she leaned back and rested her head against the wall. Tenth floor, the elevator stopped. A group of four entered, and she cowered in the back corner. Everyone stood facing the door. No one talked.

Typical elevator rules, feet forward and awkward silence. She too lived by rules. She stayed away from other people's spouses and refused to mess with a guy who had a girlfriend. She went to school, earned a degree. She got married, honored her husband.

Did the rules change? Was she so naïve—so out of date? Was it acceptable to steal husbands now?

The elevator stopped with a little bounce. The doors hesitated but finally opened, and they all piled out to the bustling lobby.

A bellhop rattled words to a co-worker as they struggled with a piece of luggage. They tried stacking a small tote on an already overloaded cart. Gitana tripped on one of the bags still on the floor. He apologized and moved it out of her way.

She headed for the revolving doors, her chance to disappear into the night. But she felt light. Too light.

Shit. Cade drove. She had to call Layne. He would come pick her up.

"Fuck," Gitana swore a little too loud.

She crushed her hand into her forehead. *Idiot!*

Her purse was in the suite. She left the clutch by the table where she ate with Rex. Her shoulders slumped. She did not want to go back to the party.

Gitana's head hurt and began to pound. A man's laugh cackled from the bar, and then the voices in the lobby grew louder. A group of women came to meet more women. A family strolled passed, and the little girl skipped while holding her mom's hand. She asked when they could go swimming.

Gitana stood in the middle of the hotel bustle. She needed to move before someone knocked her over. *Think.* She rubbed her temples. The front desk would let her make a call.

She spun around and ran into a broad-chested wall. When she looked up, Cade's blue eyes stared back at her. She turned—not wanting to talk to him.

"Gitana, what's wrong?" He moved so he was in front of her again. He held her silver bag. "I told you we'd go whenever you wanted."

A clue she should have caught. Her teeth clenched. Her face heated. She grabbed her clutch from him and stormed toward the entrance door.

"Wait!" he called from behind. "What happened? What'd I do?"

Air steamed from her nose like a bull ready to charge.

He had the gall to catch up and stand in front of her like an innocent bastard. She tried passing him, but he stepped to block her.

"Unbelievable," Gitana said. Her voice shook. She slapped the clutch against his chest. "You think I'm a fool?"

Cade opened his hands, upset and clueless.

"You have the nerve to take me to a party with your *wife*?"

People stared and whispered when she hit a high note.

Cade's mouth shut tight.

Gitana stood her ground. His eyes turned away. He did not deny it. Her heart shattered with each stabbing moment of silence.

"I should have known." She became way too calm. Defeated, she said, "Too good to be true, huh?"

He raised his hands and rubbed his head. Now he seemed angry. "What did she say to you?"

"Maddy? Does it matter?"

"What did she say?" He pronounced each word. His face turned red.

Caught. She wanted no explanation or excuse. She went around him and headed for the door.

A skinny teenage bellhop stepped from the curb and raised his hand when she ran out. He asked, "Taxi?"

"Please."

One whistle and a hand signal. The taxi came forward.

Cade flung through the revolving door.

"No!" he shouted.

Too late. She dived into the cab.

People watched. Cade stood with clenched fists. He kicked the curb.

Gitana faced forward, not daring to glance out the back window. The driver sensed the urgency and sped off into the night.

***

The breeze helped cool the anger boiling inside Cade when he flew through San Francisco. He made a stop at his loft to find his file. In less than five minutes, he was back on the road. Gitana's words struck like a hammer to his heart. Maddy had pulled the stunt before to make his dates believe they were still connected. Her kick was seeing their reaction, and the game had cost him plenty. No more.

Gitana had been through enough with her divorce, her ex treating her like shit. What a slap to the face, ousted by her ex's girlfriend and now his ex.

Cade made his way down the dock with papers in hand. She had to know he would never do this to her.

The traffic on the street was only background noise. A boat on the other side of the pier lit up the night. Voices and music carried across the blackish bay. Layne's houseboat cast no light or movement. He thought Gitana said something about his band playing in San Jose for the next two nights. No lights were on in her place either, but she was inside. He knew. The faded-red boat tipped when he stepped aboard.

She stood at the galley with her face to the window, her back to the outside. She had one arm wrapped around her stomach, while the other held a glass of wine. He rapped on the door.

"Go away," she said over her shoulder.

"Maddy's not my wife," he half yelled through the glass pane. He rattled the stack of papers in his hand, hoping to catch her attention.

She took a sip of wine and ignored him.

"Gitana," he groveled. "Don't do this. Give me a chance to explain."

She twisted her head toward him.

"Here, I have proof." He continued to press the papers against the glass door. "I promise I'll go away. But first, hear my side."

She caved to his relief. Gitana unlocked the door and swung it open, then went back to her spot by the sink. Cade entered and closed the door behind him before she changed her mind. He searched for a switch and flipped it on. The outside light turned on. Good enough for her to see the papers he set down on the counter. He positioned them so she could read the first page. The legal heading. His name. Maddy's name.

"We're divorced."

"You never even told me you had a wife. Not once did it come up in our conversations," she said.

"I was married for one month," he said, calm and slow. He tapped the papers with the tips of his fingers, and pleaded with her in silence to look at the proof. He continued. "I met Maddy when I moved here. I was twenty-two and she eighteen. We sat next to each other on a bus heading for San Francisco. We were both starting over. We made a vow to watch out for each other."

He moved closer. She hid behind her arms. She had been crying. Mascara smudged under her eyes. She wiped her cheek with her palm.

Cade continued and hoped she'd see his side. "Broke, we decided to live together to share expenses. People assumed we were married. It helped us get an apartment, find jobs." He leaned against the counter, edging a foot closer. "We had separate lives, she went her way, and I did the same. One night we went out. We got drunk and had the brilliant idea to elope." He tightened his jaw. "At the time, it seemed like a good plan since everyone thought we already were married. We drove to Vegas.

"Not long after, we knew we'd made a mistake. We had no connection, like two people should be when they are in love. We used each other. Luckily, her uncle was a lawyer. We got a quick and easy divorce. No assets."

Gitana set her glass down and faced the sink. Her voice cracked when she asked, "Why didn't you tell me? Not once in our conversations did you mention her."

"We didn't have a marriage."

"You didn't bring it up. *At all.*"

"I'm sorry. I didn't think…" He stopped to pick the right words but shook his head instead. He let out a long, audible breath and said, "I don't talk too much about it. In my heart, I was never married."

"At the party, why did she call herself your wife?"

Cade cursed Maddy under his breath. She could catch a mouse, make it bleed, and then discard the body. His girlfriends were toys for her to play with. He stepped closer. "Why she said this to you? Maybe you're a threat to her. I don't know."

His arm came out to rest on the counter beside her. Gitana straightened her back and became stiff. He slid one hand to her waist to test the water.

"Don't be upset," he pleaded, then buried his face into her neck. He inhaled her perfume as if making sure to savor what he may have lost.

"I've done this route, being a second fiddle," Gitana said with a strained voice.

"Maddy is a player. She tested you."

"And you?" Gitana turned around to face him. Her brown eyes wanted the truth.

"I don't play games." He wisped a piece of hair away from her cheek. Her stiffness melted.

"This wasn't supposed to happen," she whispered.

"What do you mean?" Cade trailed his finger across her shoulder and found the buttons to her shirt. He waited. She didn't protest. He unlocked each one, then pulled back the white fabric. The black silk straps to her bra went with it. The light coming in from the windows revealed round nipples against the white fabric of her shirt.

"I'm…I'm just not ready for this." She pushed him back, not hard but enough to show defiance.

"What do you mean by 'this'?" He cupped her breast

and she stifled a moan. He kept his hands on her to soothe away the rest of her anger.

"I mean a relationship."

Cade stopped thinking of the curve to her hips, her breasts. He brought his hand back up to her chin and raised it until she looked him in the eyes. "Too late."

Her fresh scent saturated his senses. When her hands came up to rest on his chest, Cade pulled her in. Their mouths met. Soft and sweet.

Gitana's hands went around him and her nails went into his back as if telling him she felt the same. Too late was right. Her touch drove him wild. He'd never felt this way with any woman.

Between kisses Cade said, "I want you, Gitana. No one else."

She placed her head on his chest. Her soft black hair tickled his skin. He couldn't wait any longer and knew she felt the same as their fingers danced when he unbuckled her belt and unzipped her pants. She tore at the buttons on his shirt. He slipped his hands around her hips and lifted her onto the counter. Gitana helped him slide her pants down. They fought with his shirt, the sleeves caught on his wrists. He pulled until the first button popped off. The second managed to come undone.

Gitana slid to the edge of the counter and wrapped her legs around him after he flung his pants across the floor. He lifted her onto him. They rocked together. His thighs hit the cupboards, and his knee slammed into one of the handles. He winced but refused to stop.

She motioned for the bedroom. He was too into the moment to heed her, until she pushed him away and jumped down. Cade caught his breath; his brain still throbbed between his legs. He wanted her back, but she grabbed his hand and pulled him toward her bedroom. He dwarfed the full-sized bed in the alcove as he spread out, ready for her. Gitana straddled on top of him and tightened herself around him until he shuddered in uncontrolled gasps. She took the last drop out of him; his body drained of all energy. Cade closed his eyes. He swam with pleasure from their lovemaking. He held her. He wanted her to stay with him and know she had his heart.

Lesson #10
Look before you leap.

With its large windows and a square façade, the three-story brick building Cade and Gitana entered seemed more like a factory than his home. Like his studio, the outside of the place hid the true life inside.

In the morning, after she made him breakfast, he invited her to his loft. He wanted to prove he had nothing to hide, no wife or girlfriend hanging at his place. She accepted his invite.

Instead of taking the industrial-sized elevator, they climbed the wide, solid steel stairs to the third floor. Gitana held on to the rail for balance. Her boots clanged with each step. Double doors made of thick wood and black iron greeted them from a wide platform when they reached the top.

"You own the whole floor?" Gitana asked. She noted one entrance besides the caged elevator.

"I own the building," Cade said and pressed buttons on

a keypad next to the door. The lock clicked one of the doors open. "My place is the third."

"What's on the others?"

"Storage on the first. A renter on the second." Cade waited for her to enter. Music played from inside.

"Wild Child!" Rex greeted her with a bright smile. He sat on one of the white leather couches in the great room. A stack of papers rested in his lap. He set the pile aside before standing to greet them.

Swaying his hips, Rex sauntered over and gave her a hug with two big, fat air kisses to each cheek. He then grabbed her arm and pulled her inside.

Like the building, the loft was industrial, yet warm. Rustic brick walls and earthen-stained cement flooring covered the spacious room housing the kitchen and the living area. A large granite island separated the two, and Rex offered her one of the leather stools to sit on. The granite had a charcoal mix with white crystal veins, and she smoothed her hand across the top of the cool stone. Rex went to grab his stack of papers from the living area.

"I'll be right back," Cade said and squeezed her hand as if wanting one last touch before parting. She gave him a smile and watched as he hiked the staircase to the lofted second floor.

Glancing about, Gitana took in the full stainless steel kitchen, made for a chef, and the dining room, tucked into the corner for cozy meals. The dining room was out of place with an ornate gas fireplace, an antique table, crystal chandelier, and red walls compared to the rest of the place.

Yet, she loved the design.

"I decorated the room," Rex said as he passed by. He crossed the kitchen and went down the hall to an office where a huge desk and bookcases lined the back wall. Partially open doors in the other two rooms down the same hall hinted at a gym and a bathroom.

Instead of sitting, Gitana went over to the large slanted windows in the living area and gazed out. Gray clouds rolled in from the bay, and tiny drops of rain began to patter on the glass panes. Even with the dreary weather, the view was amazing with tapered houses coloring the hillside. She could perch there for hours, soaking in the scene.

Rex reappeared. He carried his appointment book with him. He tapped his pen to one of the pages and announced, "We are all set."

She had no clue what he meant. She figured he was talking to Cade, but the devil man kept staring at her.

"Set for what?" she asked.

"You, Wild Child, are set for a show." He waited for her response.

Gitana was befuddled. What show were they seeing? A play? A movie?

Rex shifted, flaring his hip to one side in disappointment. He then rolled his eyes as if annoyed he had to spell it out. "Gallery One on Saturday, the sixteenth of November. Right before the holidays. We're going to show your work."

"My work?" It then hit. Gitana remembered their discussion at the party. She thought he was joking or providing idle conversation, which she often heard from the doctors' wives. They would say, "Oh yes, let's get together for lunch. I've been meaning to call you."

Rex wrinkled his face in frustration, and he rolled his eyes. He then perked up and widened his grin as if forcing himself to stay positive and patient with her ignorance. She saw amazingly bright teeth against his olive skin.

"You want to show my paintings?" she repeated. "Like in three months?"

"Three months and one week. Exact."

"You're kidding me, right?" The skepticism bled through again. Why would an established gallery want her work? Her paintings were therapy. She portrayed her mood into art, as a hobby, not a profession.

Gitana rejoined him at the kitchen island.

He went into work mode. "We need to select your paintings. I hope you have more than just the ones at Stone Legend and your boat."

She cringed. Pete would cry if she took his treasured pieces from his castle. She confessed, "I can't sell the ones at the winery."

"Why not? They're yours. Right?"

"Well, yes, but I just can't rip 'em off the wall and tell Pete I'm taking them back. He loves those paintings."

"We need them." Rex was adamant. "We can't do a show without something to sell."

"Arguing already?" Cade returned in a change of clothes, jeans and a light blue, cotton, button-down shirt.

"I can't take my paintings from Pete." Gitana stared at

Cade, keeping her ground.

"Why not? They're yours," Cade said and walked over to the wine cooler in the hall. He grabbed a bottle.

"I…but…" Gitana stuttered. She remembered the emotion in Pete's eyes when he saw the paintings for the first time. His tears rolled with joy. She painted those scenes for the castle, not for a gallery. "I can't take those away from him."

Rex stared at Cade. He put full responsibility on him.

His boss was opening the wine. He took the hint. "This is your one chance, Gitana. You got other paintings to match the depth of those at the winery?"

"I have some good ones," she said to defend her work. "I keep them at my papa's so they won't get ruined on the boat."

Rex looked puzzled. He took out three long-stemmed glasses from the cupboard.

"She lives on a boat," Cade explained. He turned to her and asked, "Can we go through them? Bring back the ones worthy of a show?"

"They are worthy." Gitana was insulted. "Some better."

"Words I like to hear." Cade smiled.

"If not," Rex said, straightforward, "we need the paintings at the winery."

Cade raised his hand to keep him still, not wanting an argument. "When?"

"To get the paintings?" She needed clarification. He nodded, poured the wine, and joined her. He handed her one of the glasses. She said, "I'm heading to my papa's place, not this Friday but next Friday, for dinner. Layne is coming with me. I can easily bring two more guests."

"Friday, Friday, Friday," Rex repeated after opening his black book again. He frowned with lips out. He leaned toward Cade and used his pen to point to the date. He shook his head. "We have a meeting at seven. Barry's studio."

"Reschedule," Cade said.

"But he's…"

"Reschedule."

Cade lifted his glass to Gitana. She raised hers. He toasted, "To you, Gitana."

More meaning came from his eyes than from the spoken words. The crystal blue pools sparkled as if he replayed their makeup sex.

"Wait for me." Rex scurried to join them in clicking glasses.

As she drank her wine, their discussion sunk in. A show? Why not? Rex and Cade were not the only ones who commented on her paintings. Numerous customers at the winery asked if her work was for sale.

"Wow," was all she could say. Blown away, her mind raced in all directions. If she did have a show, the extra income would help. Sausalito was not a cheap place to live. Anywhere in the Bay area, rent was out of control. She'd toyed with moving to Sonoma or Napa Valley, but her job was temporary. Soon, she had to search for work in the city, closer to home. Hopefully she could find something tied to the art world.

Gitana remembered her favorite paintings, the Muir woods set. Those would be perfect for the show. The deep greens and rusty browns burst off the canvas as the sun shined through the trees. Cade would like them.

"Welcome back." Rex said in his devilish way when she noticed he had been watching her. He had waited for her reconnection to earth.

"I have a set of oils I think you'll like," she said and emphasized, "Devil Man."

"I can't wait." He smiled and gave her a real kiss on the cheek. He picked up his coat from the far bar stool and put it on. "I'll mark the date for next Friday. What time?"

She had to remember what she told Layne. "How 'bout two?"

"Two it is." He quickly wrote in his book and then placed it in his briefcase. "Bye-bye, Wild Child." He waved to Cade. "Later, boss."

He wiggled his ass and gave one last wave before disappearing out the door.

Gitana turned to Cade. "Where'd you pick him up?"

"He came with the gallery. He was too cute to fire when I bought it. And, I will say, he's the best investment I made by keeping him on."

"He seems to like his job."

"He knows his job."

She gave him a squeeze. "I should get going too."

"Stay."

"I've taken enough of your time. Besides, I'm getting a business luncheon together for the winery. I should be working."

"Ummmm…" He nuzzled in and nibbled on her ear with his lips. "It's too rainy to go outside."

The overcast skies called for a lazy, curl-up-and-watch-movies type of day. Gitana tightened her lips, determined to keep ground. Work. If the day was going to be crappy, what better time to sink into paperwork and make some phone calls.

"I didn't get to show you the rest of my place," he said. He hovered over her and pressed his hips to hers.

Ahhh, the temptation he provided. Cade had a point. Maybe if she stayed just long enough for a tour…

He carted her up the stairs to his bedroom. The spacious king-size bed graced the room, and a huge oval skylight centered the ceiling like the one at the gallery. His taste called for a lot of white with splashes of color here and there. Even the bathroom was like a hotel with plush white towels and a robe hanging from a hook.

"Impressive," she said.

"Try the bed." He sat and pulled her with him. "I think you'll like it."

Layers of white clouds took her in. He kissed the top of her lip and flipped his leg over to straddle her stomach.

***

Gitana stretched like a cat and loved how her legs felt against the cool, crisp sheets. Sunlight streamed in from the dome above, and she realized that she had stayed the night.

So much for working.

Cade was cocooned somewhere in the white fluff, and she went in to find him. King-sized beds were roomy enough for hiding. She tugged at the comforter until she found his nakedness between the sheets. His tan skin contrasted with the white, providing a perfect calendar shot. She traced the scar on his leg and continued upward. He shivered in delight.

"Can you believe how long we've been in bed?"

"Can't we stay?" he asked with his eyes still closed. He stretched his leg across her thigh as if to keep her in place. "What time is it?"

Gitana leaned over him to see the clock on his side of the bed. The silk sheets fell from her shoulder, and she loved the feel, cold yet smooth against her skin. In her little cubby on the boat, she would have fought the heavy flannel blanket and then rammed her foot into the wood frame as she struggled to get free. "Nine-fifteen."

"Ten more minutes," he said and yawned again.

"You do that." Gitana slipped out of bed and headed for the bathroom. "Mind if I take a shower?"

He grunted and she took his response as a yes. She walked into the stone shower room and turned on one of the showerheads. She enjoyed the beads of heat streaming her backside. A ledge lining the walls held man stuff—a blade, shaving cream, mirror, shower gel, but no shampoo or conditioner. Great. She was going to smell like a guy.

She let the spray pelt her face and fell into a trance. She hated how comfortable she felt, in his home, his bed.

The shock of cold hands iced her hips. Gitana screamed. She grabbed the ledge to steady herself.

"Jesus!" Cade's foot slid on the wet floor. They shuffled a dance as she tried to hold him up, but slipped herself. She laughed at how comical they looked.

"I came to give you some hair stuff." He laughed too and picked up the small bottles he dropped in their scuffle. He handed them to her.

She read the labels. "You got these from the Hilton?"

"I knew they'd come in handy," he said with a grin.

Gitana finished showering with his help. She wanted to ask how many others used the hotel shampoo but refrained. None of her business.

Getting out first, Cade grabbed a fluffy towel from the counter and wrapped it around her. Gitana tucked a corner in near her breasts to make a cover-up. He handed her a second towel for her hair. He seemed to know what to do and this time her curiosity unlatched.

"Do you do this often?" she asked in a husky come-hither voice.

"I'd do it over and over for you, especially seeing you out of the shower...so sexy." He growled with lust.

Not what she meant. Was he avoiding the hint of giving her some assurance? He said he had few dates, which she had a hard time believing. He was a woman magnet.

Since their fight about Maddy, she noticed a change in him, as if he wanted to prove his trustworthiness. Cade's tough exterior melted into a playful lion. A side she liked. But she liked his edgy side too, a slight roughness earned respect when people spoke to him. The rough side also held some anger. She dared his anger to come out. "And how many others have you catered to?"

He hesitated. His eyes widened briefly. "I've had my share."

She smiled and shook her finger at him. "I don't want any more surprises."

"No snakes biting me either," he shot back and snapped his towel at her.

Gitana yipped and jumped to the side before his weapon hit. Their eyes connected. His gleamed with mischief and she teased, pointing her ass toward him.

Cade came after her again, this time in war. Ready, she whipped her towel off and spun it up to strike him with the end.

They dried off playing *Crouching Tiger, Hidden Dragon*. In slow motion, they did somersaults across the bed, then rose with invisible swords in hand. Even in fun, laughing until their stomachs hurt, she became aroused seeing a naked man bare all with no shame. But then, he had nothing to be ashamed of—his hard muscles were sculpted and easy on the eyes.

A cough from downstairs stopped them in midstream. Cade stretched out from the double doors and looked to find Rex at the kitchen island. Waiting.

Giggling, Gitana found her clothes and pieced them together. Cade threw on jeans and a black tee. He went downstairs. She stayed in the bedroom to finish getting ready.

She listened as they talked over the noise of pans clanging and eggs cracking. The two men reviewed the schedule for the day as they made breakfast. Rex kept rambling on. She counted at least four meetings they had to make. Finding her cell phone, she called Layne to pick her up before she joined them. Cade did not need the delay of taking her home, and she knew her friend would be in the city giving a private training session.

"Good morning…" Rex hesitated for a second when she descended from the stairs. "Not sure if I should call you Yu Shu Lien or Wild Child today."

"Hey, Devil Man." Gitana suppressed a grin.

"Quick breakfast and we'll head off?" Cade wanted her approval.

"I overheard your schedule. Layne will be my carriage home."

"I can take you home." He seemed offended.

"Don't worry." She welcomed the cup of steaming coffee from Rex. "Just feed me something and I'll be happy."

"So who was the tiger?" The devil man snickered.

Cade threw a piece of toast at him.

Gitana kept out of the way while the two went about their business. She devoured the poached eggs, toast, and bacon they set before her. When the doorbell rang, she stuck the last piece of bacon in her mouth. She announced, "Layne's here."

Cade went to welcome him in.

Rex gasped and hid behind her. He mouthed, "He's

Layne?"

She chuckled seeing the devil man drool. His gayness seeped out. She waited for the trumpet call as Rex presented himself and bowed before her neighbor.

"Layne, this is Rex, Cade's assistant," she introduced the two. "Rex, this is my neighbor."

"Nice to meet you." Rex played it cool yet gave him more than a friendly glance. If not mistaken, she thought he undressed him piece by piece.

Layne provided a smile with some curious interest. He knew how the devil man hung.

"Firm hands. Good grip. You work out, right?" Rex asked.

"I'm a trainer." Layne looked him in the eyes.

"Ouuee!" Rex no longer held it in. He flirted. "Do you give private lessons?"

Cade and Gitana glanced at each other, amused by his assistant's boldness. Layne did not seem to mind.

"I do," he responded.

Lesson #11
You can't please everyone.

For the first time in a long time, a rush of excitement ran through Layne. He learned to follow his instincts years ago. Being a drummer in a band, he knew when to kick up the beat for the crowd, and being a trainer, how to push harder or ease up with his workouts. In the truck, heading to the Merino's house for food and paintings, his instinct fell on Rex.

Something triggered inside Layne's gut when meeting him at Cade's. He wanted to know more about him, spend time with him. Now was his chance, yet he knew to stay reserved.

Soft rock hummed from the speakers as they weaved around the hills. Layne sat in the back of Cade's Escalade with Gitana curled in his arm.

Rex swung his head around to look at Gitana. "Thanks for letting me sit in front, Wild Child. I tried twice last year to sit in the backseat. That didn't go so well. Luckily I brought bags both times, just in case."

"Did you use them?" she asked.

"First time I didn't. Second time I did." He plugged his nose and made a face. "The client wasn't too happy with me."

Gitana laughed. Layne smiled. His thoughts roamed from Rex to her. She was nervous about their evening. She had told him earlier how her family might react with Cade. Her ex held pedestal status with her papa; Layne learned the first time he visited. Being a neighbor, not a boyfriend, he posed no threat. Cade might since the man's eyes lit up just being in the same room with her. Maybe not love...yet...but soon.

Gitana sat up and peeked around Rex. He stayed half twisted in his front seat for the entire two-hour ride as he chatted.

"Turn right, up here," Gitana said when a narrow dirt road appeared.

Cade took the road slowly. A cloud of brown dust trailed behind as he drove around a sharp bend and into a valley. Trees shadowed the road.

"Where in the criminy hill are you taking us, Gitana?" Rex asked as he peeked over Cade to look out his window. The road seemed to disappear. "You'll protect us, right, Layne?"

Gitana flicked her eyebrows at Layne. He ignored the look, not sure how to react. In a way, Rex's attention flattered him. Like at the gym, he stayed casual and innocent. His eyes wandered discreetly. He knew the gays from the straights. They hid, not wanting to offend or find a fist to the face if they stared too long.

Layne offered a small nod. Another tug of war played inside him. For a few years now, he knew something wasn't right. At the gym, he would run his hands down a woman's thigh. He'd never get stiff when his face was next to their hips, smelling their scent. He never imagined ripping off their clothes or riding them. But with the other clients, the men, he found himself comparing bodies and deciding which one he preferred.

"Oh, thank God!" Rex exclaimed when they turned again to a meadow.

Ahead was the ranch-style log house perched on a hill. As they drove up, two dogs rose from their spot in the driveway and watched. Shep, a mutt with short legs and gray hair, began to bark. The other, a collie named Rico, sniffed the air, then joined in.

"Do they bite?" Rex seemed a little nervous as the dogs continued their protective stance.

"My family's worse," Gitana said with a tease. She jumped out of the truck. Shep and Rico were on her. The dogs wagged their tails, pawed their feet at her thighs, and yapped for attention. She greeted both and scratched behind their ears, like she always did when Layne tagged along. While Rico enjoyed his scratch, Shep pounced on Layne.

"Hey, you!" He got the dog to all fours again.

He laughed as Rico sniffed at Rex's crotch. Gitana pulled the dog off. Cade came around to join them, and

Rico bounced over to greet him with the same type of sniff.

"I never knew they had gay dogs," Rex said and went with the flow.

"Go on!" Gitana yelled and waved her hand to shoo them back. Neither dog wanted to leave. She warned, "You behave or I'll put you in the kennel."

They ignored her as they continued to get attention from Cade and Rex. She stepped away to let them have their time.

Layne leaned against the truck, glad it was white, not black. The day was a scorcher, and he wore a white shirt and khaki shorts to keep cool. Inland always sizzled with heat when the bay's temp turned cold from the ocean. He already felt the sweat on the back of his neck, even with his bandana wrapped around his head.

"Annabella!" Gitana's sister Maria came from the house. She was all smiles with big white teeth and black hair braided to her waist.

Cade and Rex eyed each other, confused. Layne explained while she went to hug her sister. "Annabella is her given name."

Maria tucked a kitchen towel in her back pocket as Gitana introduced her to the new additions. Layne had to smile. Her sister acted like a mother. She gave both men the once over, and he wondered if she had done the same with him. He never noticed. Maria turned to give him a big hug. "Welcome back, stranger."

"I haven't seen you in the cities," he said and kissed her cheek.

"I'm thinking I should come visit you more often," she said low enough for his ears only. She continued to ogle the two other males.

Layne chuckled. Cade in his Vin Diesel stance and Rex with his warm, earthy glow were quite the pair.

Mr. Merinos came from around the house. He wore his usual cowboy hat, plaid shirt, and jeans. He dressed like a rancher, but by profession had been a farm mechanic.

"Hey, Papa." Gitana hooked her arm around his and guided him to their guests.

Her papa greeted the men with a handshake but nothing more. They were her friends. For Layne, he managed to grunt his name.

The chaos continued as more introductions took place. The others were on the patio in the back: Maria's husband Marco, her sister Jane, and her brothers Charlie and Tony. Jane's husband was missing, off visiting his family in L.A., which was fine by Layne. He didn't like the guy. And then the two nieces and three nephews appeared. They giggled and ran between the adults with their helium balloons batting against them.

"What's the occasion?" Layne asked when one pounded him with a balloon.

"Charlie thought it'd be fun for the kids. Gave them each a balloon," Maria said, rolling her eyes.

"Clever idea," he said with a smile. Charlie and Gitana liked riling the little ones. Last time, they brought plastic lawnmowers that made noise like an engine when pushed. The faster they ran, the louder the engines.

Tony, the youngest at twenty-three, carried a steel bucket filled with ice and beer. He set it on the picnic table and said, "Hey, Layne, how's it going? How's the car?"

A great start to get the men rolling. Gitana had hoped Layne would ease Cade and Rex into the mix. She was concerned about each brother's reaction to having a gay man at the house. Charlie was old school without much exposure to life beyond farming. He lived ten miles east of the family ranch and used part of the land to let his cattle roam free. Tony should be okay, but she wasn't sure.

When Gitana disappeared into the kitchen with her sisters, Layne updated Tony and the rest on his '66 Falcon restoration.

Rex chimed in. "I had my Barracuda restored a year ago. Guy did a great job and I'm lovin' the drive."

"You have a Barracuda?" Layne asked. Rex was full of surprises.

"A first generation?" Charlie asked.

"Formula 'S' package." Rex beamed.

"What color?" Tony drooled.

"Red. Cherry red."

Gitana came back with two pitchers of margaritas. Her sisters carried chips, salsa, and peanuts. She gave Layne a look to ask how it was going. He winked. All was good.

Rex went on to tell the story of how he raced his car against some punk in a Mustang. His Barracuda flew like a rocket down Highway 1 and right into the hands of a cop.

"The cop wanted a close-up of my car. Gave me a warning." Rex laughed. He loved the attention.

Layne liked watching him. He had a smoothness and was easy on the eyes. Rex talked to fit the audience. At Cade's, he didn't shy away from letting out his feelings about his preference. At the ranch, he relaxed his aura, being business casual. He stood out against the family, due to his crisp white tunic and blue linen pants versus the jeans and T-shirts, but it gave him a different presence. He joined the conversation, portrayed confidence, and spoke the right words, comfortable in his skin. Layne, on the other hand, was like the quiet grasshopper Gitana always teased him about being. Maybe the difference was Rex made no pretense as to who he was.

The drinks flowed as they relaxed on the patio and enjoyed the late afternoon sun. Gitana sat near Cade with Shep the mutt sitting between them. Cade had his hand resting on her arm, a light yet possessive touch.

She was happy with him. Every time she talked about him, her eyes sparkled. Her face smiled. Layne knew the day Cade came to find her after his New York trip, the man would be good for her.

Gitana caught Layne watching them and made a face. He smiled back and stuck his tongue out at her. She was his family. She gave him reason to think and be himself.

She glanced over to her papa when he coughed. The old man sat in his rocker with beer in hand. His mouth turned down, and the sides of his face wrinkled in. He stared out at the day.

Gitana tried bringing him into the conversation, but he just grunted. When Cade spoke, the old man ignored him.

Layne saw the hurt and frustration in her eyes. He rubbed his fist and wanted to smack him for being an asshole.

"You all right?" Rex asked.

Layne shifted and shook his hand. "Yeah, just a little stiff."

"Anything I can do to help?"

Layne was curious with his new friend. Rex's gaze seemed to suggest more than a simple offer, but he wasn't sure. "Thanks, but no."

"I heard about her papa," Rex whispered. "Cade filled me in."

How much? Layne wondered. Gitana had many issues with her papa. The old man put her ex, John, above her brothers. A doctor above family. He still pouted about the divorce, making Gitana insecure.

"He is a little anal, isn't he?" Rex asked in a lowered voice after Gitana got up to help Maria with dinner. "I was talking to Tony. He's been staying with him but not for long. Mr. Merinos isn't too happy his youngest wants to be a chef and not a ranch hand."

"Or mechanic, or a farmer," Layne chimed in.

"There's nothing wrong with being different. Not a thing."

Layne thought of Gitana. "Except when your father's against you."

Rex crossed his legs and leaned toward him. "There are two types of family, the blood kind and the ones you make. My true family is one I surround myself with. How 'bout you?"

"I'm an odd duck. I'm different. Quiet," Layne said.

"Odd duck isn't the word for it," Rex corrected him.

***

Gitana watched Layne and Rex from the kitchen window as she grated fresh parmesan into the large bowl of salad. Rex leaned toward her friend and opened his mouth in a smile. He said something and Layne's eyes softened.

Women were always flirting with her handsome neighbor. But he never had the eye or the interest. What he lacked around females, he expressed toward the devil man.

"It's ready," Charlie hollered. He removed the steaks from the grill.

They ate dinner outside: steak, fried potatoes, salad, and plenty of drink. Tony used his special dry rub on the New York strips, the rave of the night as everyone dug in. Even papa commented on the good food. A big step, she considered, since he spoke fewer than ten words all night.

To her surprise, he followed the men to the garage after they ate. They went to uncover his old 1950 Cadillac, his pride and joy, now in need of some loving care. Gitana stayed back to clean the kitchen and blend another batch of margaritas.

"Are you sure you're ready for this?" Maria asked.

"What do you mean?" Gitana still had her mind on her papa.

"A relationship. I see how the two of you ogle each other." Maria smiled like their mother. A broad smile suggesting she was happy for her, yet cautious at the same time.

"I like Cade. A lot. But he doesn't want children."

"Is that all you think about, Annabella?" Maria turned her face into a frown. "Having kids isn't the only thing in the world."

Gitana bit her lip. Her sister, of all people, knew the heartache she went through.

"I'm sorry." Maria grabbed her in a hug. "I want you to be happy. Change course. Have some fun."

"I have," Gitana said as she let go of her sister. "I've had a lot of fun with Cade."

"And he's ripped." Maria gestured with her hands to emphasize how hot she thought he was. "Enjoy him."

Gitana nodded. She had to remove herself from the kitchen before Maria offered suggestions on how to keep him. She disappeared and found her brothers and Layne at the side of the house discussing workouts. Layne pumped his arms in the air, as if holding a large set of weights. Cade and Rex were missing. She went to the front in case they were near the truck. Not there. She returned to the backyard.

"You looking for the shiny head man?" Her oldest niece, the one with big curly hair, asked. She sat at the table kicking her legs back and forth.

Maria attempted to wipe the melted ice cream from her daughter's hands.

"You know where Cade is?"

She said with round, innocent eyes, "He's in the

bedroom with Jane."

Gitana's eyebrows went up. "Thanks, Chrissy."

A light glowed at the end of the hall. She found them in the boys' old room, a storage dump now. Cobwebs trailed from the ceiling to the floor, and dust covered the veneer dresser with all the knickknacks cluttering the top.

Jane was bent over with her ass in the air when Gitana arrived. Her sister dug out the canvases from the closet and handed them to Rex. She turned and saw her. "Hi, Sis!"

The little turd, Gitana thought.

Jane's cat smile said it all as she paraded in front of the men.

Rex, unaware of her antics, took the paintings she unearthed and separated them into piles around the room. The large canvases were on the floor, leaning against the bed, while the smaller ones lay on top of the white chenille bedspread.

"Jesus H. Christ, woman," the devil man cried his praise, "You have a gold mine here!"

Cade flipped through a stack of the larger canvases and removed two from the pile. His gold bracelet hooked on the corner of one painting, and he carefully freed the links. He held the canvas up to examine the detail of a faded red barn with cows in a field.

The light in the room came from the single socket in the ceiling, the cover long gone. Gitana wished they had better lighting to see the true colors without the glare, but the two did not seem to mind.

Cade handed Jane the rejects to put back in the closet.

He stepped over to the door and squeezed Gitana's waist. "My god, woman. When did you find time to paint these?"

"I had plenty of time during my divorce. Great therapy," she explained.

"You must've been fuckin' miserable," Rex mumbled. "Years of pain."

"Here's my middle finger," Gitana raised her hand.

Cade laughed.

"Annabella has always been an artist," Maria came to her sister's defense. "Even as a little girl, she would sketch and paint with such detail. She's good, no?"

"I wouldn't be here in the middle of nowhere if I thought different," Rex said and then was lost again in the paintings.

Gitana noticed the separate piles. She figured the ones by the door were those they wanted. She leafed through them with her finger by catching the top edge with her knee to hold them in place. None of her favorites made the pile.

She went to the hall closet and opened the door. The shelves held a variety of games they played as kids—Life, Monopoly, and Scrabble. She pushed back the thick worn coats from their childhood and crammed them together to get a better shot of the floor. Nothing was stacked against the wall. She shut the door. Where had she put the Muir woods collection? She went back to the bedroom.

"What happened to my other paintings?" Gitana asked Jane.

"You mean they're not all here?" Rex's mouth gaped.

"No," Gitana said and crouched to peek under the bed.

She dragged out a few more paintings, two with flowers and another of a creek. Both needed work. She shoved them back under the bed. "I brought some here a couple of months ago."

"Hey, remember this one?" Jane laughed. She held up a canvas of her daughter, dressed in a clown outfit. Simple strokes set off her daughter's eyes and big lashes. Gitana smiled, remembering the Halloween outfit. Her niece was too cute not to paint.

"Is this the starving artist's sale?" Layne popped his head in and clicked his tongue with disbelief. He stayed in the doorway with beer in hand.

Out of a hundred canvases, Cade and Rex decided on fifteen with ten maybes. They wanted thirty for the show.

"I've got them. I just have to find them," Gitana muttered. She ducked under Layne's arm and headed for the patio.

"Tony," she yelled to her brother. He was talking to papa. His head came up. She asked, "Did you move my paintings?"

"Which ones?" He rubbed his chin.

"Any."

"I found them," Jane hollered from the basement.

Rex shrieked, not as bad as seeing a mouse but close. Gitana, afraid of what she would find, raced down the stairs.

The devil man had his knuckle in his mouth as if to refrain from swearing in front of the children. Her nieces used the best paintings for a Barbie mansion. Each canvas held the other one up to make walls. The larger ones made up the roof. Her heart dropped. She hoped none had cuts or bends in the canvas. However she did have to give her nieces credit for their creativity.

The girls cried in protest when Maria dismantled the roof. Their shrieks of horror rang through everyone's ears until Layne masterminded the plan to replace her forest paintings with some of the rejects. They kept the Barbie house intact with the girls directing them on how to angle the walls when they didn't get it right.

Rex examined each one of the wooded scenes. He found no scratches or marks in the paintings. She now had twenty additional canvases for the show. More than enough.

The chosen paintings, plus a few extras, made it to the back of Cade's truck. They stacked into two crates with thin dividers holding them in place. After loading them up, Charlie convinced them to have one more drink before hitting the road. And no leaving without dessert.

Tony's rum cake with a sugary glaze drizzled on top was worth the delay. Everyone had seconds. Gitana took hers to eat by Papa where he sat alone.

"You're quiet tonight, Papa."

He grumbled. "Times aren't the same."

"With Mama gone?" she asked.

He grunted.

She flipped back in her chair. A slight annoyance ran through her. She knew he was thinking about her ex.

"John's not here anymore, Papa."

He took a swig of his beer with one hand and gripped the edge of the rocker with the other. She shook her head in sadness, never seeing him so stubborn about one thing. Why did her ex hold such a soft place in his heart?

Keeping her patience intact she said, "He has a wife, Papa. He married the day after we divorced, I believe."

She wanted to yell at him for taking her ex's side. It wasn't fair, but she curtailed by telling herself how Papa wasn't the same with Mama gone. He went through the motions of day-to-day living but had lost his fire.

Gitana patted him on the leg. "One day, Papa, you'll understand. You'll take my side instead of his."

The night was getting late. Her eyes stung. She went to Cade at the picnic table, slid her arms around him from behind, and whispered, "You ready to go?"

He nodded and grabbed her hand, giving it a little squeeze. "Long day, huh?"

She responded by drinking a glassful of margarita.

He finished his beer and set the bottle on the table. Everyone took the cue.

Another half hour went by before the last goodbyes waved against the night.

"Did you all have a good time?" she asked, then rested her head on Layne's shoulder. She noticed how Rex, again, seemed like a jealous little puppy who longed to be in her shoes.

"I had a wonderful time," he spoke first. "Your brother Charlie is just too much."

Layne snickered. He stared out the window. "I don't

think Charlie knew how to take you."

Gitana raised her head to Rex. "Did you behave?"

He laughed. "I asked if he liked riding stallions. He told me he liked Arabians. I don't think he got me."

"You're bad." She smiled and put her head down again. She pictured Charlie asking Tony or Marco if Rex had questioned them about horses. She would be hearing about it.

All in all, she agreed the night had been fun. Her men were accepted. Only Papa was quiet, but better quiet than raving about John, which would have been worse.

She caught Cade looking at her from the rearview mirror. He smiled and his eyes wrinkled at the corners. "Thanks for letting us tag along. You have a great family."

"My pleasure," Gitana said, then closed her eyes. She drifted off to the thought of the four of them spending Christmas together at the ranch with her family.

She woke when the truck came to a halt near the front of the loft. A blast of cold air rushed into the cab when Rex got out. Gitana opened her eyes, dazed. She tasted the salt from the ocean as the wind came across the city.

Gitana stumbled out with the rest of them and had to stretch her legs from the long ride. They decided to unload the paintings and bring them inside for the night. They spread them throughout the living area by leaning them against furniture and walls. She stood in the middle of the room and took note of the ones they picked. Gitana agreed with their selection. Her confidence lifted, happy she had an eye for show material.

She yawned and Cade reached over to give her a hug. She rested her head against his chest and apologized after another yawn. "Sorry. I don't know why I'm so tired."

"It's two in the morning, a good explanation why."

Gitana plopped on the couch. Rex was deep in conversation with Layne. They analyzed one of the paintings, too critique-ey for her. Rex had his hip flared toward Layne. Their heads were close together. It would be too rude to interrupt. Let them get their time in.

"You want something to drink?" Cade headed to the kitchen.

"I'll have a glass of water." Gitana covered another yawn.

"Wine." Rex overheard. "Red."

"Make it two," Layne agreed.

"Gitana," Rex called out and held up a painting. She forced her eyes open. "This one is amazing. The gold you put into the forest, like sun reflecting off the bark—I love the quirk."

"That'll fit nicely in a wood and metal frame," Cade said and handed her a glass of water. He headed back for the wine.

"Who do you think should frame them?" Rex asked Cade. "Delanio?"

"I'll do the forest scenes. Let Delanio work on the Renaissance pieces and the old man," he called from the kitchen.

Rex instructed Layne to place the forest paintings in a stack by the large window. He then moved the ones for

Delanio to the corner wall.

Cade changed his mind as he gave the boys their wine. "Wait. The white knight. Bring him to FrameSet. Use the silvery peach liner to compliment the armor."

Gitana listened to them debate framers. She had no money. Framing had a price.

"Ahh, Cade?"

He spun around.

In a meek voice she said, "I can't afford the frames."

"You'll make up the price when they sell," he assured her.

"No," she said. "I don't have the money to pay for the framing."

"Get a loan." Rex thought nothing about it. "Artists do it all the time."

Gitana sunk deeper into the couch and felt about the size of a mouse. She wanted to scurry into the walls so they would not see her embarrassment.

Rex turned to Cade. "No frames. No show."

Cade rubbed his hand down his mouth. He nodded his head as if discussing business with himself. He then said, "I'll pay for them."

Rex raised his eyebrows in surprise. "What?"

"No, I'll pay for them," Layne chimed in.

The devil man seemed relieved. Gitana knew he watched out for Cade and the business. She understood and respected him for it. But she could not have Layne pick up the cost. He had his stash sitting at home—the down payment on his gym.

Rex clapped his hand. "Settled. I'll have the contract printed, and we'll get rolling."

Gitana was about to protest, but Cade reacted first.

"No," he said. "I'll pay for them. Personally."

He sat on the couch next to her and squeezed her thigh. Gitana was too tired to think or argue, but her heart melted for the watcher in him.

"All righty then," Rex nodded. "We can discuss the pricing later."

Thank God, she thought.

Cade agreed. He cradled her in his arms and continued to discuss with Rex the supplies he would need. Even Layne got involved. He came up with an idea to use metal with wood for the forest scenes, to keep the conversation rolling.

Gitana fell asleep to the drone of their voices. At one point, someone placed a blanket over her. She woke later to Cade snuggling with his head on her leg. His arm curled around her thighs as if he held a pillow. Rex and Layne sat on the floor with a bottle of wine between them. They talked as if alone, huddled in a fort, as they shared deep secrets.

What a cute pair.

The next time she stirred, the morning light streamed through the windows. Layne slept on the other leather couch. He snored with his head half hanging over the edge. Cade sat on the floor near her feet. He read his Blackberry. Rex patrolled the kitchen.

The smell of coffee seeped across the room. She

inhaled the aroma and loved the mocha added to the ground beans. Rex appeared with mug in hand. "Here you go, Wild Child."

She sat up. "I guess I fell asleep."

"You were out." Cade continued working his Blackberry. He yelled to Rex, "Mrs. Pearson left me twenty messages. Make it twenty-two."

"The woman is a nut." Rex clucked. He dug out a pan from the cupboard.

The noise woke Layne. He opened his eyes and glanced around the loft, a little confused. He stretched using the full length of the couch. When seeing Gitana, he scratched his belly and asked, "What time is it?"

Cade checked the clock near the front door. "Ten. My first meeting's at noon."

Gitana threw off the blanket.

"No." He held out his hand. "You can stay as long as you want. No rush."

"I'm making breakfast, you all," Rex called from the kitchen. "How do pancakes sound? Layne?"

The devil man did not seem like the pancake type.

"You want eggs? I can switch," he said when no one spoke.

"No, no. Pancakes are fine." Gitana said, then asked Layne, "You like pancakes?"

"Love 'em." He smiled.

Gitana got up. She had to work at two and still wanted to go through the paperwork she brought home. She shuffled her way up the stairs and into Cade's suite. His bed called to her, but she resisted the temptation.

In the bathroom, she straightened her hair with her fingers. Her mascara smudged under her eyes, and she wiped the black marks until they disappeared.

Cade tapped lightly on the door. "Mind if I join you?"

"Please do," she said and licked her lips at the sight of his bare chest when he entered. She enjoyed watching the muscles tag team down his front to the white Calvin Klein underwear.

"Okay if I take a quick shower?" He leaned over to turn the water on.

Gitana wanted to grab his ass but knew he had to get ready.

"Sorry. I'm intruding." She was in his space. She headed for the door, but he blocked her. His arm came around and brought her back in.

"You can't get away from me yet," he said and planted wild kisses across her face.

"But you need to get ready." She tried to push him away.

"So do you."

He unhooked her bra, then cupped his hand around one of her breasts. Her nipple turned rock hard. She moaned. The wetness of his tongue sent waves of pleasure through her body. She bit the top of his head in a playful manner.

"I could get used to this," Cade said. He removed his Calvies.

Gitana smiled as she recalled their first time in the

shower. She had no complaints.

They made love, slow and gentle with him coming from behind. The water sprayed against their backs and rolled between them. They bathed each other. The lather built up, then ran down their peaks and valleys. Cade trailed the suds with his fingers and rubbed his hand between her legs. He rinsed with his tongue.

The less than quick shower had them running late. With rosy cheeks, they appeared for breakfast. Layne and Rex had already eaten. Upon their arrival, two plates stacked with pancakes were ready at the kitchen island. Real maple syrup was placed in front of them along with a plate of thick bacon and large glasses of orange juice.

"This looks great." Gitana leaned over her plate to smell the delicious food. Her stomach growled.

"I'm starved!" Cade rubbed his hands together.

"I bet you are." Rex snickered.

Gitana blushed. Had he heard their play in the shower? By the way Rex bit his tongue, she knew he had. Her cheeks turned redder. Cade just laughed it off. He glowed, something she had never seen before in a man. Her heart lifted. Cade had fallen for her. Truly fallen. And it made her scared.

Lesson #12
Trust your instincts.

Gitana waited for the florist to finish her order. She idled away the time by looking around at the different arrangements and let her mind drift to the last few weeks. Where in the hell did the time go? The days had flown since the night they picked up the paintings at her papa's house. Rex kept her busy with details for the show. The winery kept her busy preparing for two events, an anniversary party and a bridal shower.

On Sunday, before Cade headed to New York, she signed a contract with the gallery, which Pete's lawyer looked over. Her signature joined Cade's on the piece of paper, and she became her lover's business partner. Butterflies still fluttered in her stomach.

The florist finished the order and repeated back her request. The anniversary client wanted exotic orchids, frangipani, and hibiscus to decorate the castle. One joy she got from working as an event planner was spending someone else's money. Her budget couldn't afford the luxury of lush tropical flowers, but a little splurge on some jewelry would suffice.

Gitana decided to shop for herself. She had time to run into Nordstrom's to check the sales. She needed another pair of black earrings after losing one at work. Like socks, one goes missing while the other stays in the drawer until found. She gave up on finding the lost one.

Scouring the jewelry cases, she spotted a pair of ebony crystals reduced to $49.95. More than she wanted to spend but a deal nevertheless. Gitana made the purchase before talking herself out of it. She deserved a treat on occasion.

A woman wearing a long, navy raincoat bumped into her. "Gitana, right?"

She turned, face to face with Maddy.

"What a pleasure seeing you again," the woman said.

Not the words Gitana would use. Her back turned straight as a board. Cade deemed his ex-wife harmless. Gitana raised her guard, not so sure.

Maddy poured honey into her smile and drawled, "Out shopping?"

"How'd you guess?" she asked. The woman's hairstyle had changed since the party. The color was now copper rather than red, and the ends were curled instead of straight. White-rimmed glasses rested on top of her puffed hair.

"Listen." She fanned her hand against Gitana's shoulder. "Forgive me if I failed to mention my situation with Cade. I didn't mean to give you a wrong impression. I want to make amends."

If Cade had not explained her connections in the art district, Gitana would have walked away. Instead, she needed a cautious truce. The woman oozed power and the right friends.

Gitana opened her mouth to say how Cade explained their situation, but a shrill laugh stopped her. The high pitch with short bursts belonged to one person. Trisha, her ex's new wife.

Her day now turned to shit. First bumping into Maddy and now she had to deal with Trisha.

The woman stood in the aisle near the perfume, talking to a passing friend or one of John's distinguished acquaintances. Her head bobbed with agreement as the other person talked. The white, fake smile and the lifted face showed she was trying to impress.

She looked slim under her canary trench coat. No baby bump under her belly. Gitana figured baby number two would be on the way by now. Her long, blonde hair flowed down her back. No split ends—just shine like on the commercials.

"Is she a friend of yours?" Maddy asked and leaned against the counter.

"Not really," Gitana replied. "I know someone she knows."

Maddy pulled her glasses down for a sharper view. "I thought I recognized her. Trisha. Trisha...I can't remember her new last name. She just married. Had a baby too."

"Oh really?" Gitana turned her rabbit ears on. Cade was

right, she did get around.

"Just imagine, getting married because you're pregnant. How stock is that?" Maddy rolled her eyes, then tipped her glasses up again. She leaned forward. "He didn't want to have the child. Wanted her to abort."

"Why would he not want children?" Gitana's voice raised and she lowered it. "I mean, I thought he wanted kids."

"No, no. He doesn't like kids. Never has."

Gitana frowned. The woman lied again. Was this another one of her exaggerated stories to rile her? It had to be. But she said the words without drama. Gitana picked for more detail. "Are you sure he wasn't the one wanting a baby?"

"Not this one. According to Trisha, if it wasn't for his father, who found out about the pregnancy, she would have been stuck as a single mom."

"His father," she repeated like an idiot. Her throat balled in a knot.

Gitana pictured Mr. Sothers taking over the situation. He never hid the fact she was useless to John or the family if she could not produce an heir. He needed a grandson, and she kept him from it. Now she wondered if he had manipulated the affair.

No matter, John wanted a family. He was devastated when her test results came back negative. She still had a hard time believing what Maddy said. The woman may have heard gossip from someone else, but Gitana was there first hand. John wanted a boy to carry on the tradition. With five generations of doctors in the Sothers family, he didn't want to break the chain.

"Do you know if she had a boy or a girl?"

"A girl. Pretty sure a girl." Maddy fished in her purse as her phone rang.

Perfect timing. Gitana glanced at her watch. "I have to run. I'm late. Nice running into you."

"Ciao, darling. I'll tell Cade hi for you."

"No need." Gitana dashed off before Maddy had a chance to remember Trisha's last name and correlate it with hers.

She thought about Maddy's remarks and had to dismiss them. She knew John. He wanted kids. Maddy had her signals crossed. Now she had to focus on getting to the city. She was crunched for time, already late. She had to hurry to Ghirardelli Square for a lunch date with Layne and Rex.

A mass of people gathered in front of the famous chocolate store as they waited to get in for the delectable ice cream treats and the bars of chocolate. Her stomach turned just thinking of the sweets.

Layne waited on a bench. He stood and opened his arms for a hug. "You're looking better."

She had cancelled her date with him the night before. She needed down time. He had agreed after seeing her pale and ragged. She tried to pass it off, but he kept asking her questions. "When was the last time you ate? Anyone sick at the winery? You sleeping okay?" She promised to get a good night of sleep, and it must have worked.

"Nice to see you too." Gitana wondered whatever happened to hello.

Layne turned away from her, spun back around, and then opened his arms again. "Hello, Beautiful!"

"Nice try. Aren't you supposed to be at your rehearsal?" He had a three- or four-hour jam session with the band twice a week.

Layne's grin widened. "I talked to Jules."

Gitana's ears perked. She became suspicious when he fidgeted like a kid. So unlike him. "What's going on?"

"I'm done."

She gave him a blank stare. Once it hit, Gitana gasped. Her mouth stayed open. "*You didn't!*"

"I did! I quit." His crooked grin broke into a smile.

"Wow." Her face glazed with shock. He never liked the attention or the hours spent practicing. He struggled for the last few months. Layne wanted to quit but didn't want to hurt the band's feeling either. "Good for you. What made you finally decide?"

"Rex. He's helping me with the gym. He knows people and those people have *the* spots available for lease. Now's the time."

Rex became devoted to Layne the minute he batted his eyes in their first greeting. She never put the two of them together—Rex and Layne—but now it made sense. Life rolled together and fate drove. Fate introduced Rex to Layne through her. Rex became his watcher just like Cade was to her.

Gitana was not sure how to approach their closeness.

"You two seem to be hanging out a lot."

"He's pretty cool," Layne admitted and crossed his arms. "We've been working on the frames for your paintings."

"I thought you were framing with Cade."

"He had to finish his current piece before leaving."

Cade locked himself in his garage and stayed up three nights in a row to finish the commissioned work, a large sculpture for the front of a mall. He flew to Florida to put it in place.

"Speak of the devil," Layne said. He stood straight as Rex appeared through the crowds.

"Hello, darlings!" The devil man turned into one big smile. He gave her a hug and air kisses. He bumped fists with Layne. "Hopefully, I'm not too late. The tourists are worse than ever. And I'm *starved*."

"Then let's hit it," Layne said and took the lead as they walked the main drag. He puffed his chest and held a tight-jawed, hard-eyed stance so people walked around him. People moved over. Rex and Gitana tagged behind like wagging tails.

"I am so in the mood for crab!" Rex shook in ecstasy when they walked into the restaurant.

The host sat them at a table on the second floor. Gitana settled in. She liked the view of the water, and the afternoon sun on her chair. The waiter came with their menus. The two men ordered beer and she stuck with water.

"What you having, Gitana?" Rex asked as he buried his

head into the menu.

"I'm not sure." She leafed through the pages.

"Ohhh," Rex exclaimed, "look at the seal."

She scanned the entrees and made a face. Why would they have seal as an entree? She glanced at Layne. He had the same expression as she did.

"Asspots!" Rex laughed. "Outside. Look."

A group of seals bonded together on a small landing near the pier. One little "Sparky" fought to join them. He hopped on top of the crowded platform only to have a larger seal flip him back into the water. No matter what angle he tried, Sparky was more in the water than not.

As Layne pointed for Rex to watch the seal's antics, the devil man leaned over and placed his hand on Layne's shoulder. Both laughed and neither minded the connection.

Gitana's eyes opened a little wider to Layne's world, always alone and rarely seen with a woman. He never snapped a solid portrayal of preferring men until now. Seeing him with Rex, he shined and smiled like a charcoal drawing turning into an oil and coming to life with the addition of color. Layne deserved to be happy. Quitting the band was good for him. Rex was good for him.

The devil man leaned away from Layne when the waiter came to take their order. The scallops were on special and Gitana opted for those. The men went for the Dungeness crab.

Another waiter passed by with a tray of food. A hint of salty butter trailed behind him. The smell buckled her insides, and a wave of queasiness hit.

She picked up her glass with the lemon wedge and sipped the ice water. The cold felt good as it trickled down her throat. She wished she knew why she wasn't sleeping at night. Food wasn't appealing and her energy faded like the sun.

Rex's phone went off. Beethoven's Fifth. He excused himself to take the call.

Perfect moment. Gitana leaned forward and put her elbows on the table. She said rather than questioned, "You and Rex are hitting it off."

He witnessed her smile and knew what she meant but kept his mouth leashed. He diverted his eyes to avoid her stare. To her, Layne was either not accepting of his place or comfortable with his choice. She was not going to drill him for a response.

"Nothing wrong with creating a little happiness in your life," she advised. "If you go with the predictable, life's not always what it's cracked up to be. I sure as hell didn't get far. You know how miserable I used to be."

"And now?"

"What do you think?"

He sat back in his chair and rubbed his hands against his thighs. "I don't see those bitch hairs curling up as much as they used to."

"Ha. Ha." Gitana rolled her eyes.

Layne laughed. "Actually, it's nice to see the real Gitana has blossomed like a flower. You're looking toward the sun after years of being stuck in gray clouds."

He had a point.

"You gonna let somebody find your heart again?" He leaned forward and flicked her arm with his fingers. "You were dead-set against even talking to another male about three months ago."

How true. She remembered moving into the houseboat. Every pore in her body seethed total bitch as she unloaded her belongings. She wanted nothing to do with him or any other male in the city.

"The pain's going away," she said. "Maybe time does heal old wounds."

"And the right man," he added.

"True," she agreed. She recognized the flaws now that had pecked at her marriage with John. Ones she ignored but shouldn't have—his nights away, his whispered phone calls, and his too-tired-for-sex yawn when she offered herself in lace and chiffon. All signs they were failing.

"He loves you, you know."

Gitana jerked her head up. She then shook her head to clear her mind of John. Layne meant Cade.

A warm feeling nestled inside her. She missed him. "Why would you think that?"

"I catch on to these things," he said. "The way he gazes at you. How he protects you. He's a good guy, you know, if you let him in."

"I am letting him in."

He shook his head. "Almost. The thorns are still there so no one can penetrate your heart."

"I'm trying. I'm better."

"But what's missing?"

She clammed up. Cade's attitude on family and having kids still bugged her. Even if she couldn't have kids, there was always a chance to adopt. She stared at her silverware wrapped in the brown napkin.

"I'm not out to get you," Layne apologized. "I just don't want you to lose someone who's good for you."

Surprised by his analogy she asked, "You think he's the one for me?"

"Yeah," he nodded, "Yeah, I do."

Layne had raw insight. She experienced it before when she went for the interview at the winery. He wanted her to take the job even before Pete called with an offer. Sometimes he floored her, and today was one of those times.

Rex returned to the table and their conversation ended.

"Sorry 'bout the interruption." He slid into his chair and leaned toward Layne. "One of our exclusive customers has asked for another painting."

He squirmed, unable to contain his excitement. Layne and Gitana eyed each other and wondered if Rex would crack.

"I mentioned your work, Gitana," he sang. "He wants to view one of your paintings."

"Before the show?"

Rex nodded and clapped his hands together. "And guess who it is."

She was clueless.

"Come on, guess," he nudged her to play.

"The mayor?" she blurted.

"He was at one time." He could barely keep it in. He sang, "He's the CEO of Digimagnum."

"No way." Gitana refused to believe him, thinking back to the event she hosted at the winery.

"No, really." If Rex had a tail, it would have been wagging. "If he buys one painting, he'll buy more. Trust me."

"Here we are…" the waiter said as he came with a large tray balanced on his hand. He placed the dish of hot scallops in front of her and the air steamed. Chunks of white meat swam in a buttery sauce. Even the side of pasta and asparagus oozed with melted butter. Yellow liquid ran everywhere. Loads of it.

Layne rubbed his hands when his plate was set before him. Rex moaned with anticipated pleasure. The Dungeness crab overpowered their plates. A bucket, claws, bowls of butter, their side dish of rice and bread followed. Their table flowed with an abundance of food. Way too much food.

Gitana's stomach rose to her throat. She drank some water.

Rex and Layne grabbed their claws, then launched into snapping the legs. Her arms stayed near her sides with her hands in her lap.

"What's the matter, Wild Child?" The devil man asked. "You haven't taken a bite."

She forced her hand up like an obedient child and lifted her fork to spear one of the scallops. She dipped it into the butter. The tiny pieces would have been the first morsels to disappear from her plate. Now, the idea of popping one in her mouth curdled her stomach.

Oh, God, not here!

She dropped the fork and knocked her chair aside to get to the bathroom. She did a dance and in despair searched for the women's room. A sign in the far corner became her target. She swung the door open into the restroom and made it to a stall before her stomach heaved out a rush of mixed mush.

Gitana's face beaded with sweat. She grabbed some toilet paper and wiped her mouth. It must be the flu. A few customers at the winery had coughed. One mentioned something about recovering from a stomach bug.

In hopes nothing more would come up, she rinsed off and wobbled back to the table. Rex and Layne were hunched over as they worked the shells. They dug for the white flesh, and stuffed their mouths. They had no intention of waiting for her.

The two stared at her with guilt soaked into their faces when she stood in front of them. Or maybe it was the grease from the butter.

"We figured we better eat in case we had to leave right away," Layne explained. "Did you puke?"

Gitana nodded and wiped the edge of her lips.

"You look pale." Rex shoveled an asparagus spear into his mouth.

A hurricane had hit their side of the table. Debris of crab, spilled butter, and crumpled napkins littered their playing field. Her side stayed neat and untouched.

"You gonna sit? Eat?" Layne wiped his chin.

Gitana held her breath. Her stomach flipped again. She had to get out of the restaurant. "I'm going outside."

"We'll be right with you." Rex snapped his fingers feverishly to get the waiter's attention.

She left as he requested a box and the check from the guy. Pronto.

Outside, she leaned against the building and lifted her head to the cool, salty breeze. The restaurant boasted fresh crab and displayed the beady-eyed creatures in a tank next to the entrance. The distinct smell of seafood did not seem to worsen her ailment. It had to be the butter.

"Sorry," she apologized to Rex and Layne when they burst through the doors with two containers.

"You pregnant or something?" Rex teased. "You sure turned sour fast."

Layne cringed. He turned his back on her, gave Rex a daggered look, and made a slight cutting gesture with his hand.

Rex was beside himself, not happy with his new friend scolding him.

To spare them the awkwardness, Gitana explained to Rex, "I can't have kids. My body won't allow it."

"Oh." Rex grimaced. "I'm sorry."

"Not your fault," she said without emotion, as she had many times before, "just not in the cards for me."

Rex's suggestion had also played in her head a few days before. Gitana was more than two weeks late with her period. She blamed her sickness on the busy weeks and her terrible eating habits, for lack of a better reason.

Lesson #13
Get confirmation.

Layne kept his eyes on Gitana. Anytime she saw food, she became sick to her stomach. Only cinnamon Pop-Tarts and weak green tea managed to stay down. And like at the restaurant, butter seemed to be the worse culprit.

"What am I going to do?" she whined to Layne when he came over to check on her for the third time. "No fever, no aches, no runny nose."

She sat in the bathroom next to the toilet with the door ajar. He found a spot on the kitchen floor to sit and peeked in at her. She propped her elbow against the porcelain seat and rested her cheek on her hand.

"Maybe you're pregnant," Layne suggested, ignoring her sensitivity on the subject.

"Yeah, right." She tucked a piece of hair behind her ear.

"There's one way to find out," he said.

"Been there, done that. Hundreds of times. Always negative." She pushed away from the toilet. Ten minutes had gone by without her throwing up.

While she washed her mouth and her face, he got up from the floor and leaned against the pantry.

Gitana examined her face in the mirror. "I look like shit."

"Yes, you do," he said and reached for a towel to hand her. She had lost her sun-kissed glow and her eyes drooped. Gitana covered her mouth again.

Layne turned back to the kitchen and searched through the cupboard for Pop-Tarts.

"You need to eat," he said. No Pop-Tarts. "How about some crackers and soup?"

Gitana retched but nothing came up. She held her stomach and hobbled to the kitchen.

He grabbed his keys from the counter. "I'll run out and get you Pop-Tarts."

"You don't have to." She fell into the kitchen chair.

"Oh, yes, I do." Layne sprinted down the pier to his car.

Traffic rolled like snails crossing a field, a nightmare. Damn tourists. At the store, every parking spot was taken. He drove around until finding one tight spot. He squeezed in between a truck and a van. Layne hoped to be out of there before either left. He wanted no dents in his Falcon.

Inside, he found the Pop-Tarts and the two dozen flavors along with it. *How in the hell could anyone pick?* He decided on four boxes, two with frosting and two without. He picked up more tea, in case she was getting low. He grabbed crackers. Bread. Heading to the check-out line, he passed the pharmacy. He stepped back when he spotted the pregnancy test kits down the aisle. He glanced around to see if anyone watched. Four different brands and one said, "Pick me."

She would hate him, but oh, well.

When he stepped on her boat half an hour later, he handed her the white plastic bag. She pulled out a pack of Pop-Tarts and then the kit.

"*Arghhh!*" she cried and tossed the kit on the counter. "This is ridiculous."

"Come on, Gitana," Layne pleaded. The hurt and shame poured from her eyes, the kind that made him realize how many false hopes had destroyed her before. He persisted. "You'll get a little peace of mind."

"Never has before."

"For me?"

She stared at him with brown, penetrating eyes. He matched her bullheadedness, not giving in. Soon, the lines around her temple softened. She snatched the box off the counter and headed for the bathroom. She slammed the door shut. The results would drop the subject.

"I'll be here on the couch," he yelled through the door. He sat and drummed his hands against his thighs. He glanced at the bay. A thin blanket of fog drifted across the water. He cracked the window open to let in the breeze and planted his face next to the screen to breathe in the fresh air. He decided if she wasn't pregnant, the next logical explanation to her sickness was the stale air in the boat.

Ten minutes passed. He got up and went to the painted

white bathroom door. "How you doing?"

"Fine," she bellowed.

He paced the galley and living room. The rooms dripped vintage, which included the green and gold couch. He hated the couch. What was it? From the fifties? The wood frame had some charm but needed to be stripped, stained, and varnished. Better yet, throw it into the garbage.

Layne jumped when the bathroom door sprang open. She leaned against the frame with stick in hand. He couldn't read her. She had no expression; her eyes glazed over. He walked to her and she held it up. Too close to read the small screen, he stepped back.

Pink. A plus sign.

"Pregnant." The word smacked him in the face. He blinked and looked at it again. His almond eyes turned round as the blood started pumping through him. "Oh my god. You're pregnant!"

Gitana hyperventilated. She fell against the counter.

"Breathe, Gitana." He grabbed her by the shoulders. He made her focus on him.

She kept gasping with her eyes closed.

"Look at me," he ordered.

She did. He took in a breath, then slowly exhaled. He did it again so she would do the same. Inhale. Exhale. Inhale. Exhale.

"What the fuck," she said after catching her breath again. She wiped away a tear from her cheek.

"People do get pregnant." Layne let go of her shoulders.

"Not me."

He stared at the stick, now on the counter, without touching it. He said, "Yes, even you."

She sat on the couch. The cushion became a springboard when she bounced back up and stood. She paced and thought aloud. "I don't understand. The hormone shots John gave me never worked. All those years. Nothing. Why now?"

"Shit happens. The stress, trying too hard, working yourself up..."

"The odds are against me. I was told I *could not* have children."

"You want me to get another kit? Just to make sure?"

Gitana shook her head. She looked at the stick again, this time with a different expression. Did he catch a glimmer of hope?

He said, "Make an appointment. Let your doctor confirm the results."

She nodded. Her expression changed from blank to panicked. "Who the hell can I go to? I can't see my ex." She gripped his arm and her nails dug into his skin like sharp little burrs. "I don't want him finding out about this."

Layne removed her hand and checked for blood on his skin. Perfect crescent-shaped dents but no red.

Her eyes grew larger, and she batted her thick lashes at him for help.

He got it. After some thought he said, "I can get you a good doctor. She goes to the gym. I used to train her. I'll tell her your situation."

"What's her name?"

"Wendy Braustein. She's more of a sports-type doctor, but I think she's practiced normal, family-type stuff."

"Braustein. Braustein." Gitana repeated her name as if going through the rolling index in her head. "Name doesn't ring a bell. Are you sure she's good?"

Layne ignored the punch. He would not give her a bad name, and she should know it. "She's my doctor."

"Sorry." She realized her words stung. "I didn't mean it that way."

Layne brushed it off. "I'll ask if she knows your ex. Just go to her. Even if she does, you'll be able to trust her."

Gitana drummed her fingers on the counter. "Okay, talk to her."

"And what about Cade?"

Her mouth made a perfect 'O.' She then said, "Oh, shit!"

Yes, she had forgotten the other player. Mr. Daddy. He was going to be pissed.

"I can't tell him," she said and went to the living room. She plopped on the couch. She rubbed her hands to ring out the anxiety.

Layne followed and stood with arms crossed in front of him. "You have to."

"Not yet. Not until the doctor confirms." She gasped with another moment of panic and pleaded with him. "You can't say anything."

"Not my job to let him know."

She honed in, eyes hard and jaw firm. "I mean Rex too.

Neither one can know. I have to be sure."

Layne nodded.

"Promise?" She was on top of him.

Lesson #14
Don't procrastinate.

The morning light streamed in from the long, narrow windows. A golden cast filled the spacious hall of the winery, devoid of any customers. Gitana's heels clicked more loudly than normal as she walked to the back.

She tried remembering the medical terms thrown at her by John and the other doctor—the fertility specialist. She recalled the ultrasounds, the tests, the hormone shots. They seemed like a lifetime ago, and all of it stopped, including the injections, after their split. Why bother without a husband, a life. Not to mention the numerous bills that had piled up.

The light was on in the back. Pete was probably in the office tallying yesterday's sales. He still preferred paper and pencil to the computer. Technology could not provide the labor of love for his winery; he used his mind and hands.

Another set of heels. Gitana saw a flash of skirt in the break room near the sink. A young woman appeared, petite with short-cropped hair and a round face.

"Annabella," Pete called to her. He popped his head out to the hallway. He seemed brighter, less droop to his eyes and chin. "I thought I heard you come in. I want you to meet someone." He shuffled out to the hall. The woman in the break room joined them. Beaming, he said, "Here she is—this is my granddaughter, Jillian."

Gitana's heart stuck in her throat. The granddaughter who one day would take over the business. She smiled, shaking her hand, and the words fell from her mouth. "Nice to meet you, Jillian. Your grandfather has told me a lot about you."

Gitana had to be cheerful, but deep down she knew what this meant: her job was over. Pete made it clear when his granddaughter returned, the temporary position would end, adding a different bundle of anxiety to her list.

"Hello, Annabella." The young woman stepped sidewise to put her arm around Pete. "My grandfather hasn't stopped talking about you. He keeps me updated with the changes you've made to the place."

"Thanks," Gitana managed to say. In the back of her mind, she started a list. Dust off and update her resume with the winery job, get ass out there and find new work.

Gitana asked if Jillian was on break, if she were ready to take on the business. Little questions to find out where his granddaughter stood. Where she stood.

The perky woman rattled on about the European wineries and the way they processed their grapes. She had a few blends she would like to add to Stone Legend's bouquet of flavors. She never answered her question.

Gitana was rude to stare, but the thought of this little nymph being Pete's granddaughter had her mind boggled. She expected someone heartier with a big nose, thick hair, and big chest. This girl had ideas. She carried excitement and a passion for wine. As the young woman talked, Gitana listened to the drums play in the distance. One beat and one foot closer to the door. She wondered how long she had and guessed maybe a month or two before getting her notice.

Gitana had to excuse herself and rushed to the bathroom. Tiny beads of sweat formed above her lip. Pregnant. No job. *What next?*

***

On the outskirts of Oakland, the tan one-story medical building, past its prime by about thirty years, waited for her arrival. Gitana checked the address again. The white stick-on numbers—6667—identified the right place.

Disinfectant hit her nose when she opened the doors to the reception area. Stained tile flooring and dark wood paneling set the mood. She gave her name to the receptionist, then sat on one of the blue vinyl chairs. The one next to her had a strip of duct tape on the edge of the seat. The furniture was probably as old as the building.

Gitana was the sole patient in the waiting area and the last appointment for the day. The doctor stopped seeing patients at six but allowed her to come in after hours because of the sensitivity of her situation.

The bleached blonde receptionist came over with a clipboard, forms, and a pen. She asked Gitana to complete the insurance papers and the questionnaire for the doctor. Health issues, pregnancies, hospital stays, family history, last period. Gitana breezed through the questions, then returned the forms back to the receptionist.

A stack of *People* and *Sports Illustrated* magazines with curled and stained pages lay on the end table. John would always swear at her when she picked one up at his office to leaf through them. Germs. Patients touched those magazines with their filthy hands and left diseases for someone else—like her—to pick up. Normally, she would not care, but if she were pregnant, she did not need to take a chance.

She wagged her foot back and forth like a dog's tail. She hated waiting. But doctors were busy, and she could be with a patient or on the phone with one.

Gitana glanced to the front doors. They were a few steps away. Her hands shook. She wanted to think she was pregnant yet understood the downside, the odds not being in her favor. She eyed the *People* magazine and started for it when her name was called. She jumped to a standing position.

A woman in a white coat came out of the back offices clutching a clipboard. She moved it to one side and extended her hand in greeting.

"I'm Dr. Braustein. Wendy." A Mary Lou Retton look-alike smiled at her. She had the famous short-wedged hairstyle and big, round cheeks. She even had the same girlish smile.

"Thanks for seeing me," Gitana said and shook her hand. Nice firm grip. She liked the doctor's strength.

"Come on back."

The petite woman held the door open for her. She had Gitana step on the scale before directing her into the first of three exam rooms. The tiny area reminded Gitana of doctor visits when she was younger. She always thought the little rooms smelled like shots, a sweet, odd smell.

A picture of a runner hung against the wall; the lone piece of art in the room. The other poster was a diagram of the different muscles in the human body.

Dr. Braustein motioned for her to sit in the chair to the side of the desk. She sat in the other chair and removed two folders from the clipboard. Facing her, the doctor said, "Layne explained your situation and the need for privacy. Your confidentiality is just as important to me as it is to you."

"You were highly recommended."

She smiled. "He told me you are aware that my patients are typically those with sports related injuries?"

Gitana nodded.

"I do have experience with family practice and ob-gyn. I worked at Regions Hospital in Saint Paul delivering babies, among other things, before moving here. If I didn't feel comfortable providing you with excellent care, I would have referred you to another doctor."

Gitana nodded again. She liked the way the doctor

pinpointed her concerns right away. Get 'em out in the open before they even start.

"Now, how do you feel?" Dr. Braustein stuck a thermometer in her mouth.

After the beep and removal, Gitana said, "Tired. Sick to my stomach. Numb. I still can't believe it."

The doctor asked questions and Gitana answered as best she remembered. She thought back to when she documented the details in a notebook. She used to be able to rattle off specifics. Not anymore.

"I'd like to start with a urine sample. When you're done, come back, undress, and I'll give you a quick exam. We'll also draw some blood."

Gitana nodded. She sucked in air. *Here I go.*

During the exam, Dr. Braustein asked questions about her fertility. She was thorough with both. She laughed, joked, and kept her professionalism and courtesy when she explained, with each step, what she was doing and why.

Gitana relaxed. She had her doctor. Layne was right. Dr. Braustein cared about her patients and didn't give in to the fifteen-minute-max for the office visit. She would take as long as needed.

After the exam, Gitana dressed, then headed to Dr. Braustein's office at the end of the hall. She took a seat on the other side of the doctor's cluttered desk.

"Annabella," she said and held out her hand. "Congratulations. You're going to have a baby."

The words rang into an official announcement. This wasn't Gitana "thinking" she was pregnant, but a doctor telling her first-hand. Tears sprang from her eyes. So unbelievable. She asked, "Are you sure?"

"Yes." The doctor smiled and emphasized each word. "You are pregnant."

Gitana took a moment to let the news soak in. She grabbed a tissue from the box on the desk and dabbed her eyes. She tingled as if something new transpired in her veins. Her heart swelled.

A baby. A baby!

She started to cry.

Dr. Braustein let her have the moment. She handed Gitana a new tissue when she quieted down. "I'd like to get your medical records as soon as possible. I need to know what we're up against. Two months is good; getting over the first trimester is better."

Gitana nodded. She would give the doctor whatever she needed.

"Here's a prescription for some prenatal vitamins," she said and handed her the slip. "I suggest taking these once a day. Start right away."

Gitana nodded again and clutched the prescription in her hand.

"If you want, Sally will set up your next appointment. It'll be longer next time, and she'll go over some of the paperwork, schedules, etcetera."

"Thank you," Gitana managed to say. The shock reverberated inside her, along with the fear. Still, she was going to have a baby.

"I'm merely the messenger," Dr. Braustein said. She

handed Gitana her purse when she left without it. She then walked Gitana to the front waiting room.

Sally had the medical release form ready for her to sign. Gitana signed the paper and made the next appointment, still in a daze.

Once outside, she welcomed the breeze and let the coolness shake away the shock of what happened inside. She stood on the sidewalk with her feet half off the curb and looked around. The modest and outdated buildings on each side of the street needed repair. A forgotten part of the city as newer, taller buildings became the rage. She turned to the tan building, her new favorite place.

Gitana's purse vibrated. She found her phone. Layne was probably too excited to wait until she met him.

"You sound out of breath," Cade shouted. She tripped on the uneven cement and made a noise. "You okay?"

"A little. I'm heading to my car," she said and rebalanced. She changed the subject. "How does the sculpture look?"

Her car was about half a block away. She walked, plugging her other ear from the noise of the traffic whizzing by.

He was at the airport, waiting for a second flight to New York. The artist who was having a show at his gallery was not cooperating. This meant an additional three days before he returned home. Gitana only half listened when he rattled off the last-minute demands the artist insisted he needed. She thought how the delay helped. It would give her more time to plan. She pictured meeting him for lunch at a restaurant. No, they'd meet on her boat. She would have some cute way of telling him he was going to be a daddy. He would be shocked at first, but then his blue eyes would dance with excitement as he embraced her and swung her around.

She needed the right time, the perfect moment, to break the news. No blurting or having him find out from someone else.

"You still with me?" Cade sounded a little irritated.

Gitana apologized. She told him about the lesser of two worries, Jillian had returned to the winery, and she may lose her job. Cade laughed it off. If all went well, her art would be her career.

Gitana still had her doubts. The reality of no work or solid future became another shock to absorb. Once again, she would be out in the cold. A single, pregnant woman searching for a job in maternity clothes was not the best move on her part.

After hanging up with Cade, she drove to the bar where Layne played with the boys. She promised to stop by and tell him the news. If she hurried, she would catch him before their first set.

Gitana parked in the lot next to the bar. The last glow of the sun stretched down the street and reflected off the darkened windows along the front side. She glanced about. Her muscles tightened. She hesitated to enter the dank room as the memories from the last time came flooding back. Different area, different bar. She had to remember it was a one-time deal. Ten minutes was all she needed.

Layne spotted her coming in. He met her near the entrance.

"When's your last night with the band?" Gitana asked. She forgot what he told her before. She waved to Jake and Jules. Freddie had his back turned, deep in conversation with a large man wearing a suit and hat.

"End of the year. Sooner if they find a replacement."

The split was amicable, a big relief for him. The boys were supportive of his new adventure. They knew music came second to his gym. Layne always mentioned his concern at not wanting to leave his friends on a bad note.

"So?" He could not take it any longer. "Are you?"

She kept a poker face. Someone hit him on the shoulder in greeting. He gave the guy a nod, then turned back to her.

"Well?"

The dam broke. Gitana smiled from ear to ear.

"You are!" His almond eyes sparkled.

"I am," she blurted, then laughed as he swung her around. He did not squeeze as hard, and he made sure she landed flat on her feet.

"Let's get you out of here," he said and took her hand.

He escorted her back to her car so they had a chance to talk. "How'd it go? You like my doc?"

"Yes, I do. Thank you." She hugged his arm. "I really like her. She has to review my records, though. I'm still at risk, since I had trouble before. She wants to know what we're up against."

"How about all the puking?"

"A good sign. It should stop next month."

"Due date?"

She stalled. He gave her an impatient look. She wrinkled her nose and said, "April Fool's day."

Layne tried to keep his smirk hidden when he opened the car door for her.

"Kind of appropriate," she bubbled.

"This will be a lucky baby," Layne corrected. "And when is the dad gonna know?"

Gitana avoided the question and fixed his white bandana. She lowered one side so it was even around his face. He stared at her. She had to respond. "He won't be home for a few more days. He had to fly back to New York."

"You need to tell him," he warned her.

"I want to tell him in person. Just don't say anything to Rex. I need this time to think."

"I already gave you my promise." He kissed her on the forehead.

"I know." She frowned, worried about Cade's reaction. "I'm just afraid because he doesn't want kids."

Hugging her again, he tried being positive. "He may change."

She shook her head. "He was pretty adamant."

"Why?"

"He doesn't think he'd make a good father, based on his past."

"This is different. He'll come around."

"I hope so." She was not as optimistic.

"Just don't wait too long." Her friend repeated the warning. "Now spells honesty. Delay spells deceit."

Lesson #15
Both sides have a story.

Cade tingled from head to toe when Gitana walked through the doors of his loft with Layne by her side. Their first night together since his return, and Cade wanted to ravish her. She had on an amazing loose-fitting blouse and a pair of jeans that showed what he wanted, cleavage and ass. Her cheeks turned rosy as their eyes met. Throughout the trip, he thought about her. She had his heart and he was okay with it.

Layne had his hand protectively around Gitana's waist. A pang went through Cade. He wanted to be the one in her neighbor's place. He wanted to be her center.

The oven door slammed shut, catching all of their attention. Rex had taken a loaf of bread out of the oven and placed it on the counter.

"Thank you, Jesus, for not letting me burn my braided masterpiece!" He wiped his hands on his paisley blue and white apron then walked over to greet their guests. Cade stayed at the stove.

Layne stepped away from Gitana and slapped Rex's hand in a handshake. His assistant had other plans and grabbed him in a hug.

Cade motioned for her to come over. He couldn't leave the wok unattended. He slid his hand around her waist, just as Layne had moments before.

"I missed you," he whispered in her ear after their kiss. He wanted to drink her in, form his body around hers. He sensed her hesitancy and remembered how she said she hadn't been feeling well. "How are you doing?"

"Still a little weak," she said, "but I'm all right."

"Watch it," Rex warned Cade and nodded toward the stove.

Cade grabbed the smoking wok and removed it from the heat. He emptied a bowl of raw vegetables and hoisin sauce into the oil before he returned it to the burner.

"How was your trip to New York?" Layne asked and sidled up to the kitchen island.

"Had some issues but sold two artists' paintings and one of my larger sculptures, so can't complain," Cade said. He caught Gitana slipping away to the bathroom with her hand over her mouth. He frowned. She wasn't acting right. A little distant. He wanted to ask Layne what happened, get the scoop, but his assistant interrupted. He had the veggies for the wok.

Gitana returned and Rex stopped talking, mid-sentence. He moved his straight little hips in a samba move and came toward her with arms out. "Hello, Wild Child. You miss your daddy?"

She laughed. "How could I not?"

He kissed her on the lips. "I told Layne here how the two of you need to come with us to New York some time."

"Is that an invite?" She seemed better and a little more relaxed once she returned from the bathroom.

Back with her, Cade snuck in another kiss. He pulled on her hair so her head came back. He wanted to stare into her gypsy eyes. He smiled and her face lit up. Her hand rose to the side of his head. She tweaked his ear.

"Isn't it done yet?" Rex peeked around to see how the food was coming. "I am famished!"

Dinner came first. Cade didn't want to burn the stir fry and had to refocus on the wok. While he cooked, Rex set the table in the dining room. He dimmed the chandelier above the table for a romantic glow. He then went to the living area and turned on some Frank Sinatra for ambience.

Ready to eat, Cade seated Gitana at the table. Layne helped Rex bring the bowls of noodles, white rice, fried rice, and stir-fry to the table. Cade opened and poured the wine. Gitana covered her glass with her hand.

"Just water tonight."

He set the wine down and passed the noodles to her. She passed the bowl to Layne. She chose the white rice for the pork and vegetables. He noticed and squeezed her thigh. More rice than stir-fry. Two slices of bread, no butter. She liked his cooking, and she loved Asian food.

"You still sick?" He asked.

"Getting better," she said and stared at her food.

"My gracious heaven, Wild Child. Was it food poisoning?"

She glanced at Layne again. His head was near his plate as he shoveled a pile of noodles into his mouth.

Cade stopped eating. His chopsticks dangled between his mouth and plate. He glanced from Gitana to Layne to Rex, then back to her again. "Is it serious?"

"Not poisoning. I'm good," she assured him. "I'm a little tired. That's all."

"Rex." Layne changed the subject. "I thought about what you said the other night, having music for Gitana's opening. I'll play guitar if you want."

Rex perked. "Acoustical?"

"If you'd like."

"Something light? Not to overpower the conversations but enough to make the mood?"

"Easy to do."

"Actually, I like the idea," Cade added. "People love music. Makes the event more sociable."

The conversation turned to William Hormenster, the pain-in-the-ass artist who had the recent showing in New York. After dinner, Cade set up his computer and projector to show Gitana and Layne the pictures he'd taken so they knew what to expect for her night.

Rex brought glasses of Cognac for the men and tea for Gitana into the living room. They nestled in to watch the slide show projected on to the white brick wall above the fireplace. The first picture was the front of the gallery—impressive but not as sophisticated as his San Francisco place.

Rex found a spot on the couch next to Layne and leaned toward him. "This is the front of the gallery."

"I gathered so." Layne bit his lip to hide the smile. "I see the sign. Cade's."

Cade flipped through a set of pictures of the artist's work. Brilliant colors expanded across the canvas. The person painted in the foreground posed as if the background portrayed his mood.

"See how the bastard cocks his head?" Rex tisked as the artist stood next to one of his larger pieces. He made no pretense of liking William. "His smile?"

"Why do you keep him on?" Gitana asked.

"He's in demand," both Cade and Rex said in unison.

"He's a moneymaker," Rex added. "Otherwise, we'd drop his ass in a heartbeat."

The last set of pictures featured the show, the people milling about. Cade pointed out bits of the gallery's features to Gitana and Layne. The modern style had silver brackets, white walls, and a shiny black tile floor.

"I never realized how fancy these events were," Layne said. He straightened in his chair and stretched.

"Some are black-tie affairs, some are more casual. We base it on what we're showing and the artist." Cade powered off the projector from the couch. He didn't want to get up in case Gitana tried to slip away.

Layne yawned. The night had stretched beyond midnight.

"I agree." Rex commented on the yawn.

Cade wondered how long before he'd get his woman alone. He wasn't prepared when Layne asked if she was ready to leave. Cade held her as she stretched her legs. He whispered, "Stay with me."

"I have to work tomorrow," she whispered back.

He ran his hand down the side of her body. He wanted her naked, in bed. With his trip taking longer than expected, he needed her warmth, the silkiness of her skin. Her arched hips when he came inside her.

"I know what I can do for you," he purred in her ear.

She shivered and caught her breath. He liked the sign.

"Why don't I take Layne home," Rex offered. "Gitana, you can drive his car tomorrow."

Gitana eyed Layne. They had a conversation with no words spoken. Her neighbor shrugged and left the decision to her.

Cade held her tight. His arm went across her front in a shield. He made the decision for her. "She's staying."

Rex and Layne said their goodbyes and left.

Cade went for Gitana as the door shut. They started on the stairs going up to his bedroom. Her breasts burst from the white lace bra and dangled for playtime. Like a man crazed from drought, he devoured them when she leaned forward on the step. He was home and wanted to show her how much he missed her.

His lips touched her body like an angel's breath. His tongue tasted the sweetness of her inner thighs and the folds between them. Cade's satisfaction came when each one of her nerves layered with ecstasy. He teased her until she came with her hands gripping his head. Twice. His pleasure came second, and it didn't take long before he was nuzzled up to her warm body with his arms wrapped around her. Yes, he liked it. Loved it. Sleep came easily.

In the morning, the sun cracked through the window and shined into the bedroom. Cade woke, buried deep in the middle of his bed, but the sheets were empty and cold. Gitana had left. He remembered she had slipped out from under the covers and sprinted toward the bathroom. He flung the white fluff up and over his side as if a gust of wind took the sheets away. He rolled out of bed to go find her.

Cade used his finger to ease open the bathroom door, left ajar. He brightened. Did she tempt him with an invitation? He enjoyed the last time the water from the shower streamed down her curves and her mouth covered his shaft. He stiffened. Now was a great time for a repeat.

He was about to enter when he saw Gitana crouched on the floor with her face planted near the toilet seat. He stood at the door and watched. She wiped her mouth with a tissue and discarded it in the bowl before flushing. She used the toilet for support as she stood. He watched as Gitana then went to the sink, turned on the faucet, and swished her mouth with water. She washed her face and grabbed a thick, white cotton towel to dry off. For a minute, she held it to her mouth. She breathed in to steady herself as if she teetered on throwing up again.

Cade first thought she might still have the stomach flu. She seemed fine last night, after dinner. And he found no fault in their lovemaking. This wasn't her being sick. Those worries of not using condoms now ticked inside his gut. She had a secret. He knew when she kept her eyes on Layne last night.

He opened the door wider. With arms crossed and lips tight, a scowl darkened his face. Gitana lowered the towel away from her eyes, and his reflection stared at her in the mirror. She spun around. Her face turned a shade whiter.

"You got something to say?" His voice was cold as she held onto the towel for security.

"I'm pregnant," she said with no sugar coating, no words leading up to it, just straight.

A tense silence filled the air. Birds flew off the roof as if knowing it was time to leave.

Cade's face turned red as the heat in his belly burned upward. He shifted, then stretched his head from one side to the other, as if ready for a fight. *Stay in control. This is a woman.* One he thought he knew. "How long have you known?"

She placed the towel back on the rack. Her hand shook. Silence suffocated any redemption on her part. She squeaked, "Since going to the doctor. Umm…the day you called me, on your way to New York."

His head went down. The fire exploded within him like a pressure cooker.

"Fuck!"

He hit the wall with his open palm when reality hit.

Gitana yelped. She jumped back. She knocked the porcelain soap dish from the sink and had to save it. Cade turned away and stormed into the bedroom. He had to separate from her, too angry, too unsure of himself. *How in the hell could this happen? She fucking lied to me.*

Gitana came out of the bathroom moments later. She said, "I'm just over two months."

"And you're telling me now?" He threw on a pair of jeans and grabbed his shirt off the floor. They still had time to take care of it. She had to know of a doctor.

"I didn't believe it myself."

Cade zipped up his pants and fled the room. He headed downstairs. She followed and gathered her clothes from the steps. She tried to put them on as she reached the kitchen.

The word "pregnant" repeated in his head. Not even Maddy would stoop so low.

"I thought you said you couldn't get pregnant." He went for the fridge, opened the door. He saw nothing. He slammed it shut again.

"I can't," she cried. "I know. I am. But I can't. I thought I couldn't."

"Really? Is that how you tell everyone? Whine for attention. Poor you?" He fired the bullets and hit her directly in the heart. He had no control.

Gitana stared, now her turn to be shocked.

He found the Cognac, left out from the night before, and poured the gold liquid into one of the dirty glasses on the counter. One long, hard swallow and it was gone. Each move he made showed hostility. Short, choppy anger.

"Please don't be like this," she begged.

He laughed. He rubbed his head, then turned to face

her. A dangerous smile flashed before he pressed his lips together. He shook in disbelief. "Are you serious? You think I should just act as if everything is normal? Say it's all right and give you a big *fucking* hug?"

Nothing she had to say would matter. He turned red as the alcohol fueled the fire instead of slowing it down.

She reached for Layne's keys on the kitchen island. Cade grabbed her wrist in a tight squeeze as she snatched them into her hands. His face contorted with accusation. "You set me up."

"Why in hell would I set you up?" she shot back. She twisted herself free.

He let her go and raised his hand as if he were reading a headline. "Woman Gets Her Way—Surprise Baby equals Money."

Gitana stood, numb. Her lips trembled and her face registered disbelief. "Do you really believe I would trap you?"

His silence answered for him.

Gitana grabbed her purse and shoes. She wouldn't look at him as she raced to the door.

Lesson #16
Tomorrow does come.

Layne fumbled out of his houseboat in boxers and robe. After Rex's call, he watched for Gitana's black hair to bob up and down the pier. This was not going to be good. Rex babbled, his pitch too high. Layne's ear hurt, but he got the jest. Cade knew.

Seeing Gitana, he hopped from his boat to hers by grabbing the rail and springing over. They met at the door. She had swollen eyes, smeared with mascara. Shock written all over her face. He had his own key and fumbled with the lock, while she cowered to the side. Her arms wrapped across her chest. He stepped aside for her to enter. She stood, legs frozen. He gave her a gentle push.

Again she stopped inside the doorway. She looked around her space as if for the first time. Her voice trembled when she said, "I never asked him for anything. Not one thing."

Layne made her sit on the couch. Gitana slumped like a

rag doll. She was too pale. Her black hair contrasted against her fallen face. He crouched next to her and put his hands on her knees. He made her look at him. "Breathe. Let's get some deep breaths." He had her follow his moves as he exaggerated inhaling and exhaling.

She mimicked with some sarcasm but he ignored it. He went to get her a glass of water. She continued until the pattern of air became quieter, more normal.

"A free ride," she said, still in shock. He handed her the water. "He thinks I trapped him."

"You told him?"

"Yes, but I didn't have to. I got sick and he figured it out."

She brought her knees up to her chest and hugged them. Her head dropped and she cried. Layne grabbed the box of tissues from the end table. He handed her a new one each time she blew her nose. He stayed with her. Layne kept his hand on her back or on her arm or on her leg so she was aware of his presence. He rocked her to sleep when she leaned against him, his shirt soaked from her tears.

Once she was snoring, Layne covered her with a blanket and went outside to make a few phone calls. The fog had rolled in. The stench of fish settled in the bay—not surprising for the day.

He had cleared his calendar after the initial call from Rex as he waited for her to arrive home. Now he did the same for her. His last call was to see how the other side was doing. He called Rex.

"He's furious, Layne. More than furious."

"He's got to give her a chance," Layne said, squeezing the life out of the phone to get the point across.

"He doesn't want kids. A family scares him."

"I wish he could've seen Gitana's face when she told me. This was just as much a surprise to her. Mind-blowing." Layne said in defense. "I also saw the fear. She's scared too. This wasn't planned."

The two talked, weighing both sides and knowing this wasn't the greatest of circumstances. After a time, Layne said goodbye. Rex wasn't any help. He wanted to meet, but Layne couldn't. Gitana needed him.

He stayed on patrol and sat in the chair in the far corner of her living room, not wanting to disturb her sleep. Fitness magazines, quiet exercise, and pacing kept him busy. After finding nothing in her fridge, Layne found a Pop Tart and then stood on the deck of her boat to eat it. He stayed near the open door to make sure he heard if she woke. The fog burned away while he played with his cell phone.

The sun was heading toward the horizon when she moved. Gitana turned onto her side. She rubbed her eyes and looked about. Layne was now sitting in the chair next to her.

She asked, "What time is it?"

He pressed the button to light the dial on his watch. "Seven."

"Shit!" She jumped up, then fell back down.

Layne put his arm out to keep her from getting off the couch. "Don't worry. I called Pete. You're good."

She hesitated, not sure on what to do.

"Relax," he ordered and held out his hand to keep her in place. She relented and leaned back onto the pillow. He headed to the kitchen. "I'll make some tea."

She rubbed her face. "I slept all day?"

"You did." He filled the kettle full of water and turned on the stove. Layne came back and swooped down to sit by her. The couch cushion hissed air to protest the sudden added weight. He leaned in, "I talked to Rex."

"So he knows too, huh?" She blew her nose.

"He tagged it at the restaurant. I swear he's got some kind of sixth sense going on."

"I suppose he feels the same. Pissed."

"Not pissed, but he's protective of Cade."

She massaged her forehead as if wanting to forget. She shook her head. "I can't believe he thinks I did this on purpose. Why would I?"

"Child support," he responded. "Forced marriage."

"Thanks," she said in a flat tone.

"Hey, I'm on your side."

Gitana got up and headed for the bathroom. He turned on the TV and flipped through the channels. Her TV sucked. No cable. She moved from bathroom to bedroom. After his fourth round of surfing, she stumbled out, appearing in fuzzy blue slippers, dull green sweats, and a burgundy tank.

Layne had steeped green tea and it waited at the table.

"What am I gonna do?" Gitana saw the tea and slouched into the chair. She grabbed the cup with both hands.

"Right now, you're going to plant your face into some TV." He motioned for her to sit with him on the couch. She walked over and did as told. Layne nestled her into his arm. "Tomorrow, you're starting a new day with positive energy and a better perspective. You got a baby to take care of."

She half smiled as if remembering the other precious gift inside her. She didn't say aloud he was the greatest but her expression did. Layne had vowed to protect her, and he planned to stay with her. She had to keep busy, and he made sure of it for the next two weeks.

He forced her to go to the gym. She declined, preferring the safety of the boat, but he refused to let her wallow in self-pity. Besides, she had to keep fit for the baby.

When she wasn't working out, they did chores together. He helped clean her place, she helped with his. They waited for a phone call, a text, an email. Any word from Cade. She played with her cell phone, dialing his number, then hitting the back button. Layne had the same urge but held his ground. This wasn't his business. Cade had to man up and be responsible.

However, Layne did try calling Rex. His phone rang, but no one answered. He left no message. Like Gitana, he would have to wait.

***

At work, Gitana arrived early and left late. She used her job as an escape from the boat. From life. She wrapped herself in details. If her life was shit, then she wanted the customer's events to be successful. Seeing their happiness helped her forget her situation.

Even Pete noticed a change. He appreciated the energy she put into her work but also knew, like a parent, something was not right. He showed concern but let her be.

Each day, she listened for her phone and hoped time would correct itself. She shot Cade telepathic messages to call. His first reaction, the anger, would subside. He would call. He had to. What hurt even more was how Rex turned dry. Not one peep to ask how she was doing.

"I did nothing wrong," Gitana said to herself when she woke each morning. She was determined to move forward. Little by little, she raised her head with a restored self-confidence. She survived the death of her mother. She survived her divorce. She was tough. And now she would raise this baby, the miracle growing inside her. Something she had to look forward to.

Painting also helped. She sat in her perch with the windows open to keep the air moving. She used acrylics, safer than fumes from the oils and thinner.

In the evening, sitting in front of her canvas, with orange and purple streaks outlining the sky, she smiled to herself as a sense of renewal washed over her.

I will be okay.

She dabbed cadmium yellow paint on one of the boats.

The sun's glow reflected from the bow. The delicate strokes of light provided warmth to a flat painting. A new dawning, one she also had to take for her future.

A pencil on the counter rolled toward her when the boat rocked. She caught it before it rolled off the counter. It must be Layne. The sliding door opened.

"Gitana." His voice had a different lift to it.

"Up here," she yelled from her stool. She continued to paint by adding a small streak of red to water next to the boat. She remembered Layne had a meeting with his lawyer. He narrowed his choice to two gyms for his business and needed legal advice on which had the better contract for leasing. "How'd your meeting go?"

"We had to cancel," he shot back. Clunking noises came from the kitchen. He shoved the food around from inside the fridge. No, it sounded more like food going into the fridge. He continued to say, "It's tomorrow at ten instead."

"Can you bring me a juice?" she asked.

He came up the stairs, shaking her bottle of orange juice. A second set of footsteps echoed his.

Gitana's heart flipped. She stopped painting. The feet were too flighty for Cade. A tuft of hair circled upward. After hitting another step, Rex popped up like a Jack-in-the-box.

"Hey, Wild Child," he gave a half pout, half smile. "I couldn't wait any longer to see you."

Gitana stood when he came over to hug her.

"Rex," she said, her voice stiff.

Layne cleared his throat and sent her a fatherly look to mind her manners. Gitana somewhat ignored him. She had the right to be upset. Even if Rex's loyalty belonged to Cade, a phone call or text would have been nice.

"I'm really feeling pissy about this whole thing," Rex said. He held her tight with one arm. He hid something behind his back with in his other hand. "I so wanted to come over, but I had to fly to New York. A friend of mine died." He turned his bedroom eyes into puppy eyes.

Gitana shot daggers toward Layne. Her neighbor grimaced, not liking her accusation. In defense he said, "I just learned myself."

"He died of AIDS."

Oh, boy. She swallowed some guilt. "How awful. I'm sorry."

"Yeah," he sighed. His tune changed as if not wanting to spoil the evening. "I did buy something for you though." The hand from behind his back snapped forward. He held out a teddy bear wearing a rainbow dress, bright red lipstick, and long eyelashes.

Gitana laughed, taking the bear. Leave it to Rex to be a little crazy. She hugged him and glanced over his shoulder at Layne. He winked, then headed back down the stairs.

"My! My!" Rex spotted her new creation from over her shoulder. He sidestepped to get a better view of the painting. "Love the lighting."

Gitana pushed her stool aside to give him more room. He squeezed over and stood for a moment to drink in the colors. He looked out the window. "Perfect. You caught it, girl."

"Thanks." She set her paintbrush into a jar filled with a couple inches of water. She then sprayed the paints on her palette to keep them moist until after her break.

"Will this one be done for the show?"

"The show? Yeah, right." She snorted. Gitana caught his wince, the wrinkled skin between his eyes pressed together. "I assumed you already cancelled."

Rex shook his head, puzzled. "We have a contract."

Gitana understood the legalities, but she would not hold them to the commitment. "I'm not sure it's a good idea anymore."

"Wild Child, you have no choice. You signed the papers." He turned business-like.

"And Cade? He agrees?"

"Don't you worry about him." Rex shifted his gaze away from her.

She hated being the ball breaker. "Devil Man, this ain't gonna work."

"I won't cancel." He was adamant. "He knows you have talent. The paintings are ready, the printing is complete, the invites are in-house, and we've begun advertising. We got a month and a half until opening. You deserve this."

Gitana clicked her tongue a little louder than expected.

"Wild Child," he tilted his head and stared at her, "I mean it. You deserve this."

She deserved Cade. She deserved many things, but this one she could give or take. Gitana crossed her arms over her waist. In a lower tone she asked, "How is he?"

Rex tapped his fingers across his upper lip and rolled his eyes with frustration. "Under a bridge and in the muck."

"Is he still mad?"

"He's not talking. Everything's a little ugly right now, but we'll get through the yuck factor. He can't run from you."

"Yes, he can," she said. He already had.

She missed their connection. They fit. What they had, vanished within a matter of seconds.

"He loves you, Wild Child. The snarly bastard is like a snorting bulldog without you. He just has to work through his choices."

Gitana had her doubts. "This is a big one. He doesn't want kids. Period."

"He's in shock."

"But he thinks I got pregnant on purpose."

Rex absorbed her pain. "That does make for a touchy situation."

Lesson #17
Deceit can be blinding.

Gitana had her appointment with the doctor the next day. Rex insisted on tagging along. He fidgeted in the waiting room while Layne read a magazine. A buff man with a leg brace stood at the counter with papers in hand. A teenage girl with her mom walked from the back and out the doors.

"Where are all the pregnant women?" Rex asked, showing his disappointment in the area, the building, and the contents. "This is not making my day."

"She specializes in sports injuries more than ob-gyn," Gitana reminded him.

He pouted. "I hoped she'd at least display one of those cool-looking uteruses on her counter. You know, the one showing you how the baby grows."

Smiling with some annoyance, she asked, "Do you want me to ask if they have one in the back so you can play with it?"

"That would be good," he said. "I remember when my mom was pregnant with my sister. I'd go with her to the doc's. She'd never let me touch them. Maybe because I drooled, wanting a uterus of my own."

Gitana glanced over at Layne. Rex was dead serious. They struggled to keep from laughing. Now they knew what to get him for Christmas.

A nurse called her name. All three of them stood. Gitana held out her hand to stop them. "This is an exam, guys. Not just a discussion. Neither one of you need to see my legs spread open."

Layne and Rex slumped back to their chairs while she disappeared with the nurse.

The examination was thorough. After she dressed, Gitana waited in Dr. Braustein's office. She picked at her nails and looked at the clutter surrounding her. Pictures, papers, and books scattered about the place. A framed eight-by-ten of the doctor with Magic Johnson sat on the bookshelf. She didn't remember it being so messy the last time she was there.

"I must confess, Annabella," Dr. Braustein sprang into the room and Gitana jumped. "I'm a little confused. I find everything to be normal and healthy."

"Please, call me Gitana."

The doctor shut the door and went to her side of the desk. She had two folders labeled with Gitana's given name in her hand.

"Wait, what did you say?" Gitana caught what she said. "Nothing's wrong with me?"

Dr. Braustein smiled. "Results show a healthy baby growing inside of you. Your morning sickness should go away soon, usually at the three-month mark. I didn't find anything to be concerned about."

Gitana placed her hands on her stomach. She let out a breath. She wanted to say she was relieved, but the nagging worry of having something wrong overshadowed her words.

Her doctor continued. "I read your files three times." She held up the blue folder. "These are the records from the fertility clinic, and if I'm looking at them correctly, everything checked normal."

Gitana moved to the edge of her seat, and took the file. She shuffled through the papers. Each piece had her name typed in the upper corner. Gitana shook her head. They had limited marks and few notes, which meant no concern.

"These can't be mine." Gitana refused to believe her. "My ovaries can't produce the eggs needed. They gave me Pregnyl."

"Who gave you the shots?" Dr. Braustein peered over her readers.

"My husband."

"Did you go to the clinic or hospital?"

She had to think back. "Just once, I went to the clinic, I believe. Six months after going off the pill, when I still wasn't pregnant."

"I found one fertility test from the hospital records," she said and held up her notes. "Your husband was Dr. John Sothers, right?"

Gitana nodded.

"He ordered Depo Provera. Do you know what that is?"

She shook her head.

"Birth control. An injection will last for three months to prevent pregnancies. The drug stops the ovaries from releasing eggs."

"No," Gitana said with a slight laugh. Her blood pressure started to rise. "He gave me hormone shots so my ovaries *would* produce eggs."

"How many shots did you get?"

Gitana raised her eyes and tried to think back. "Once every three months?"

"Depo Provera is given once every three months. Pregnyl is given, depending on the patient, every month for an approximate three to six months."

"I didn't get a shot each month." Gitana tried to understand what her doctor said but couldn't comprehend. She thought back to those unpleasant days. The five minutes of tense silence when she sat on the bed as John prepared the needle. He'd give her a look as if to say, "Don't disappoint me again." She hated getting pricked, hated how the needle dug in. She said, "Those shots continued for years. I stopped when he left me."

"Nobody explained to you what they were doing? What they gave you or how the drugs worked?"

Gitana turned red, embarrassed. "Why should they? I trusted John. He's a doctor."

"Ummm," Dr. Braustein said as she wrote her notes.

"I don't get it." Gitana sat zoned out and stunned.

"According to your records, you had a prescription for Depo Provera—getting birth control in shot form." She shuffled papers around. Dr. Braustein pulled out a pale green sheet with notes. "However, a nurse on January 4, 2000, wrote in here you asked how long the shots would take before you became pregnant, and if the treatments were working. She noted Dr. Sothers' response. You were concerned about getting pregnant, not wanting a baby."

The blood drained from Gitana's face. She choked, "He said I didn't want a baby?"

Dr. Braustein frowned. She came around the desk and held Gitana's wrist to check her pulse.

Am I losing it? Is this a joke? Gitana sank into the chair.

"I found something else."

Gitana's ears perked.

Dr. Braustein clasped her hands together. She hesitated as if trying to find the right words without getting into trouble.

Gitana understood the doctor's precaution—confidentiality, protected information. John would not let her view her own records. He did not want her to go through the pain of seeing them. He would take care of her.

"Please, Doctor," Gitana said, having enough of the secrecy bull crap. "I need to understand what's going on."

Dr. Braustein agreed. "I did some research. At the same time he prescribed the birth control pills to you, Dr. Sothers wrote a prescription for Pregnyl to another patient of his." She went back to sit. "She became pregnant two months into the treatments. A medical complaint, filed against him, stated he treated her for fertility when she wanted to abstain from getting pregnant. She's now a mother of triplets, a definite sign of fertility treatments since she had no family history of multiple births."

"Why are you telling me this?" Gitana became nauseated. Just thinking of John and hospitals left a sour pit inside her.

"Did you keep any receipts or Explanation of Benefits, anything with Pregnyl or Depo Provera written down? A prescription?"

"John gave me the shots at home. He handled everything."

"He doesn't specialize in fertility does he?"

"No, neurology."

"I'm showing here, you came into the office regularly for three months to get the shots."

"Not true."

Dr. Braustein took her reading glasses off. "Do you have any proof he gave you Pregnyl?"

Gitana's hand went to her mouth. She gasped. "Why? You think he mixed up our shots?"

Dr. Braustein lifted her eyebrows but kept her lips tight.

Gitana thought about the papers she took when they split. Most she had already shredded—she wanted nothing to do with medicine or doctors ever again. "I didn't take much when I moved, but I do have a couple of boxes of papers in my closet." She had a new task to keep her busy. "I'll dig through them."

"If you find anything to help, give me a call."

Gitana's ears perked again like little radars. The doctor found this to be serious, not an oops.

After their goodbyes, she left Dr. Braustein's office and walked past the waiting room. She forgot about Rex and Layne. The boys scrambled to catch up.

"She's pale," she overheard Layne say to Rex. "This doesn't look good."

Gitana stopped. How could she explain something she did not even understand? She had been on hormone treatments. She was not some stupid delusional idiot dreaming this up. John had not given her birth control.

She replayed the memories of her ex, who wanted to spare her the office visits. She thought out of personal embarrassment. They were just as painful for him as for her. He did not want his colleagues knowing; reason enough for him to treat her at home.

Dr. Braustein's words repeated in her head. "Nobody explained to you what they were doing? What they gave you or how the drugs worked?"

She never questioned any of it. She trusted him. She did not research what she was taking or worry if it was the right stuff. He was a doctor. *A fucking doctor!*

But what if Dr. Braustein said were true? What if she had been on birth control? She stopped a year ago. Over a year ago.

Visions of her with Cade in his shop, in his loft, and her boat floated in her head. The hot, unprotected sex. He opened her up; let her emotions free for the first time since her divorce. And now she was pregnant.

Layne and Rex waited. They gave her space as she stood at the car. They glanced at each other and became anxious. They wanted to ask but must have feared she would break.

Gitana watched the cars zoom by without seeing them. What the doctor had said seemed so ridiculous. Even she had trouble believing what just went on. Any explanation would have been better than saying "according to my records, you were on the pill."

Gitana's head spun. Now she had to find some truth. She pressed her hand against her stomach.

Leaning against the hood of the car for support, she told Layne and Rex the news. She hoped by telling them, the words would make sense to her.

Lesson #18
Do your research.

Gitana stretched on her tiptoes to reach the upper shelf of the closet to grab the first box. She set it down in the living room, then went for the next box. This one was heavier. She poked her fingers at the bottom to bounce it off the shelf. She quickly grabbed the top when it tipped. The box was coming apart. She carried it to the living room just as the bottom gave out and the contents spilled. Ironic, she thought. The scattered papers symbolized their marriage, nothing she wanted to go through again.

Gitana began with the pile on the floor and grabbed for a stack of papers. She set them on her lap. Tiny particles of dust danced in the air. She sneezed twice, then blew her nose. She moved the tissue box next to her side.

Her back began to hurt as she inspected each receipt, card, document, and letter. Gitana covered the shag carpet within the reach of her arm to organize the mess. To the left were stacks for medical and household. To the right, were personal, toss, and shred.

The sun rose in the sky and made its way downward by the time she finished the first box. No prescriptions, Explanation of Benefits, or notes cried out "bingo" to help her situation. Gitana held her back, aching from sitting cross-legged too long. One box completed was an accomplishment. She hobbled to bed when the boat turned too dark to see.

In the morning, she made tea and toasted Pop Tarts. She nibbled on the cinnamon pastry until the signal came for her to hit the bathroom. She reached the woozy stage but no churning. She should have celebrated her first morning without throwing up, but the piles on the floor waited.

Gitana stepped across the mess and opened two windows in the living area enough to let in the breeze from the bay yet not enough to blow her papers about. She went back to the center of her piles and spiraled down to her spot from yesterday. The first batch she pulled out from the box was dated 1996. She had stapled some medical bills together.

If in doubt or she needed to look at anything in detail, she stuck the bill or paper in the "read more closely" pile. By ten o'clock, she had a fourth of the box completed. The backs of her knees were wet with sweat. She stretched one leg and then the other, careful not to smear the piles. This box had more receipts to go through than the first.

A light tap came from the sliding glass door. Without looking up, she said, "Come in."

The door slid open. A different, familiar smell and presence shot her head upward. Gitana's mouth dropped open when John, her ex, stepped inside. He kept the door open. His lean, tall figure towered in her little space.

"Hello, Annabella," he said and looked around at the papers scattered about. He rattled his keys in his pocket and became nosy. He tried reading a document in the pile nearest him. "Did I catch you at a bad time?"

"I'm organizing, so yes. Shut the door," she snapped, not wanting the breeze to shift her piles. "What are you doing here?"

She hoped her mission didn't show on her face. He was nosy enough to squint and focus on her stacks. She wanted to cover the papers, but he would then get suspicious.

"Why are you here?" she asked again. She wished he would leave. This was her place. Not his.

He darted his eyes from her living room to outside, then back again. "I'm completing a little cleanup myself." John didn't divulge what he meant. Instead, he changed the subject. His face turned upward. "Oh, did you hear? I have a daughter. Clara Jane."

Gitana rolled her eyes and bit her lip. She refrained from telling him her news. He had no right to know. At least, not yet.

"Pop Tart?" He caught sight of the piece still uneaten on the paper plate beside her. He turned his mouth in disgust. "You know better than to eat those things."

"My choice."

"You'll get fat."

"Probably," she agreed. She was pregnant.

He seemed thinner than before. He wore his classic Polo shirt and khaki dress pants, now sagging against his hips. His jaw stuck out with sharper definition. His sandy hair receded along the hairline. It gave her some satisfaction to see Mr. Debonair was aging.

Gitana stayed in her spot. She was not going to ask him in for a chat. He needed to spill. She waited with a hard, cold stare to make him even more uncomfortable.

The slight twitch came to his smile. She recognized the sign. He wanted something, but his ego struggled with having to ask. She cocked her head. "What do you want, John?"

He half chuckled while rattling his keys again. He avoided eye contact. "I was wondering if you have the key to the safety deposit box."

"You got everything." She was not being mean, regretful, or jealous. Simply put, he took what they had.

"Remember the one we opened in San Jose?"

"Yeah?"

"I'm looking for the key. I don't think I got yours back."

"I gave all my keys to your lawyer," she said. "Ask him."

He grabbed the handle to the door, maybe regretting he had come. He asked, "You like living on the water?"

Gitana scanned the cramped quarters. Yes, they were tight, but this was home. Her place, and she liked the quaintness. "Actually, I do."

"You take this out on the bay?"

She laughed. For once, she could size him down. "This isn't a pleasure boat. I live on a houseboat."

That irked him. The crow's feet tightened and his teeth clamped together. He jerked the door open, but stopped halfway. "If you find the key, call me."

"Very doubtful," she said.

"Yeah, thanks." He tripped on the threshold when heading out. His polished shoes were not skipper material.

"See ya." Gitana saluted him with her middle finger. She stood to stretch and saw Layne on the dock. He frowned and must have seen John at her boat.

She watched as Layne huffed to show his muscular arms and chest as the two men passed. They gave each other a hard look. John was no match for Layne's tough face. Her ex scurried for distance. Gitana chuckled. She loved her neighbor.

"Everything okay?" he asked when she met him at the door.

"Can you take me to San Jose?"

"Now?" He tried correlating the two—her ex and San Jose.

"Yes, now." She moved aside so he could enter.

He mulled it over, then shrugged. "Why not." His eyes wandered across the jumbled mess on the floor. "Any luck?"

"Not yet."

Gitana went to her bedroom on a new mission and opened the drawer under the bed where she kept her jeans.

She pulled out the small plastic container filled with junk; a place to store items she wasn't ready to give up. She dug inside and pushed away bolts, tacks, and buttons until finding the bronze key. Now she remembered what is was for.

"Where we going?" he asked when she reappeared. He helped himself to the last bottle of apple juice from the refrigerator.

She showed him the key. "We're going on a treasure hunt."

Gitana put on her sandals and waited for him at the door.

Layne cocked an eyebrow and tried not to laugh. "You want to get ready first?"

Even before he spoke, Gitana realized she had not changed out of her pajamas. Nor had she put on makeup, brush her hair or teeth. Shit. She laughed, thinking of John. He must have been disgusted by the way she looked.

"Give me a few minutes," Gitana said and disappeared to the back. She freshened up, then ran a brush through her hair before wrapping the length into a loose bun. She slipped into khaki pants, a white shirt, and grabbed orange heels from the closet. All within a record-breaking seven minutes.

Layne left for his boat while she got ready. She waited on the dock a few minutes before he joined her. She twirled around and asked, "Better?"

"Definitely." He changed the subject as they walked the dock. "That guy was your ex, right?"

They stepped aside as another boat dweller carried groceries home. "Yes and I bet it pained him to come here." She raised her hands and wiggled her fingers to quote him. "To be seen with the low-life."

"You don't seem too upset he came by." He opened the passenger door for her when they got to his Falcon.

"Not entirely true," she said. "I first thought it was you." She peeked over her sunglasses. "Wasn't I surprised."

"And his purpose?"

"He wanted this." She held up the key. "And we're going to find out why he dragged his ass all the way to my place to get it."

Layne's curiosity rose as they drove off. "What if he took your name off the box?"

"I guess we'll find out. John and I hardly went to this bank. He wanted to store our valuables with a bank other than the one we normally used. I have no idea what's in it."

The distinct beat from Dionne Warwick's "Do You Know the Way to San Jose" stopped their conversation. They both laughed at the irony and started to sing. Layne sang bass while she belted out the words in harmony with Dionne.

Their playful drive stayed upbeat until they reached the bank. They parked in front of the tan brick building with wide-paneled doors.

John and she opened the account as lovebirds— engaged, giggly, and happy. It was their first joint account. Guilt now shadowed over her. The box was no longer theirs but his legally. She imagined herself in handcuffs and in jail for trying to break into it. With losing Cade and soon her job, the stakes were high for this to turn ugly too. The color left her face.

"You don't owe him anything," Layne said, catching on to her doubt. "If you don't find out now, you probably won't have another chance. He'll be here soon. Key or no key."

Gitana nodded. Her hand went to the door handle to open the car. She let go of a breath, inhaled, then exhaled again.

Layne came around and met her. He helped her out and said, "You have a right to what's in the box."

Standing, she smoothed her pants and stood tall. Her airs of a doctor's wife began.

"Shit," she cursed, temporarily leaving her attitude.

"What?" Layne scanned the area as if he expected John or the police to rush toward them.

"We need a bag."

Layne gave her an 'are you nuts' look.

"I don't know what's inside the box. I may not be able to carry it all. You have anything?"

He popped the trunk, and she found a plastic grocery bag. She stuffed it inside her purse.

Setting the stage again, she walked into the bank with her handsome friend two steps behind. She waited at the safe deposit area. Layne sat in one of the blue upholstered chairs in the waiting area. He nodded his approval as she played the part of a confident, sophisticated doctor's wife.

A female banker walked toward her. Like a flight

attendant, she was all smiles. The woman had Gitana sign in and took the page to verify the signature.

Whatever is in the box is rightfully mine, she kept thinking, and held her purse tightly as if it would lessen the guilt. Two of the tellers liked the eye candy she brought with her and had not taken their eyes off him. Layne was scrumptious in his bandana and scruffy face. She would drool too if he weren't her friend.

The banker opened the steel gate to the secured area. She said, "I'm glad you found your key."

"Excuse me?" Gitana swore the thump in her heart echoed off the walls.

"I spoke with your husband on the phone the other day. He asked about our procedures if he lost the key." She smiled and opened the gate for Gitana to enter, but showed no sign of suspecting anything out of the ordinary.

Good.

Gitana composed again. "Yes, he forgot I had it. Thank you."

"Please, step this way," the woman said, and they entered the large vault-like room. She stopped three rows down and four over from the wall. She took the bank master key from her pocket and slid it in the slot.

Gitana looked for Layne. He was not in view. Good. Otherwise, she may have blown their purpose.

The banker waited for her. Gitana raised her key and fumbled to place it in the hole. She jiggled and pushed in, but the end stuck. She tried again. A rush of heat rose to her cheeks.

"Would you like me to try?" the woman said. "Sometimes these boxes can be tricky."

"Please do." Gitana stepped back.

The banker angled the key and pushed upward. She slid it into place, and the door clicked open.

Gitana let out her breath. Her hands shook when she slid the box out and set it on the table.

"Thank you." Gitana smiled. She waited until the woman left before she opened the lid from the top of the box. Inside, she found a bundle of papers held together with two binder clips. Not a crease or a fold marred the sheets. John's work.

Too nervous to look at them in detail—or maybe, too guilty—she shoved them into the plastic bag. So much for neatness.

Underneath the bundle were six white boxes. Three were empty. Gitana assumed he used them to keep the bottom of the box level for the papers. In two of the remaining boxes she found his grandma's jewelry. The last box contained a black velvet pouch. She opened the strings and emptied the contents. Four diamonds tumbled into her hand. Two were traditional rounds and the other two were pear-shaped. She remembered the round ones and watched as they sparkled in the light.

They had each bought a half-carat diamond from a student who needed cash. The other two John must have purchased. His loss now. She put the four diamonds back in the pouch, then dropped it into the grocery bag. She left Grandma's jewelry alone.

The diamonds she took would help pay some bills. And one was hers. She clutched the loot tightly in her hand and returned the box to the wall. She waited for Ms. Friendly to let her out.

Layne had poured himself a cup of coffee from the courtesy station in the middle of the lobby. He stood next to the chairs, deep in thought. He stared at a picture of daisies sprinkling a field. The tellers, still dreamy-eyed, whispered to each other as they continued to drool for him.

"Thank you," Gitana said when the banker returned and let her out of the gated area.

Layne spotted her and drank the last of his coffee. He dumped the cup in the wastepaper basket. She met him at the black marbled foyer, and they headed toward the door. His arm came around her shoulder to escort her out. Gitana imagined the employees wondered what she was doing with someone other than her husband.

"Any luck?" Layne asked, his arm still around her when they crossed the street.

"Four diamonds and some papers," she said.

"That's all?"

"Afraid so."

"Let's hope the papers are worth more than the diamonds." Layne's phone chirped inside his pocket. He ignored it. When they got in the car, the chirp repeated.

"Well, aren't you going to find out who called?" she asked. "Publisher's Clearinghouse may be trying to get hold of you."

"I sure would like a million bucks right now," Layne

said and dug into his pocket.

Gitana heard Rex on the other end after he dialed the number back. The devil man yapped away with some animation in his voice. When he paused, Layne pushed the phone to his cheek and asked, "Can we stop by the gallery? Rex needs you. He said no more than ten to twenty minutes."

"Is Cade there?"

Layne shook his head.

Gitana shrugged. "It's up to you. I don't want you late for work."

"Be there in a bit," he said on his cell, then snapped it shut.

***

Cade nodded to Rex when he arrived at the gallery, a detour from heading to his garage. Rex, helping a client, paled when seeing him, and stuttered halfway through his sales pitch. Cade frowned and tried to place the elderly woman who wore a feathered hat. She had to be important if Rex was nervous. Putting on the charm, he greeted both and then left them alone. His assistant seemed to have recovered.

Cade walked behind the counter. He found a red tag and stapled a business card to it. A new client had called him in the morning and bought one of his sculptures after seeing the one in Florida. Taking the tag, he went to the pillared dome room to mark the copper piece with gold and yellow glass sold.

A piece of lint hung on one of the spikes, and he picked it away after hanging the tag. Four out of six pieces now sold. Five had been there for over three years. He gave Gitana, his good luck charm, credit for selling them.

Cade stepped back. He stared at the sold sculpture and remembered how she admired the blue and gold glass spirals down the metal leaves. Ever since he found out she was pregnant, he couldn't get the image of her in the bathroom out of his mind. Her tousled hair, full lips, and wide, brown eyes had caught him off guard. Her words hit like a brick. She had been scared. Scared of his reaction, not from what she did. He should have listened to the warning signs, her obsession with family. The constant reminders how she couldn't get pregnant. He kicked himself for not using protection. He never went without it. But then she put her spell on him. Good luck charm, my ass.

Damn her!

"Hey, Cade." Rex entered the room. He had a rolled-up poster in his hand and seemed stressed. "I thought you were at the garage today."

"I got a call from Lon Jurstin. He bought this one." He pointed to the sculpture with the new sold tag. He then pointed to the poster in his assistant's hand. "What do you have there?"

"An artist came in just before you arrived. He wants us to consider his work."

Cade left the pillared room to return to the front.

"You heading out?" Rex was right behind him.

His assistant rubbed his trimmed beard as his gaze darted about. He seemed agitated. Even his foot tapped the tiled floor to relieve his nerves. Cade eyed him suspiciously. "What's going on?"

"Nothing." Rex crossed his arms across his chest.

A tense silence landed in the room. Rex remained tight-lipped.

"If this is about Gi—" Cade started to say.

"Shht!" Rex made a noise to cut him off. He lifted his finger, then glanced toward the backroom.

Cade tilted his head and his eyes narrowed. His assistant danced in place.

Laughter came from the backroom. A man's voice. Rex's smile meant he hid something. A boyfriend?

More laughter. This time a woman's soft, playful laugh. Cade's neck twitched. His muscles tightened. Gitana. Before he took his first step, they came out. Layne pushed her playfully from the back. Neither one saw him.

Rex cleared his throat. Gitana turned toward him and froze in place. Layne walked into her and grabbed her waist.

She looked good, fresh. She was dressed up, maybe heading to work. Their eyes locked. Her face became as pale as Rex's.

Cade kept silent. No hello, no sorry, no meltdown between them. She had her mouth open, lips shining with gloss. She was touchable but off limits.

His stomach flipped, then tightened. He couldn't forget what she did to him. She lied. Just like his family. His mother telling him he would never make a good father. His sister mocking him. His brother asking for money to help him find a job or get out of jail. Cade's head spun. The feelings returned, the insecurity and guilt for blocking them out of his life.

No. Their decision. He had nothing to do with it. He just stopped being the enabler.

Gitana lowered her gaze. Her face crumbled. Layne put his arm around her shoulders. She looked to Rex, and her voice faltered. "Sorry, Devil Man, we have to go. Layne's gotta work. Call me later?"

Layne pushed her along.

"I'll call, Wild Child." Rex seemed apologetic.

Gitana kept her eyes to the floor when she followed Layne out the door. Not even a backward glance.

"You idiot!" Rex snapped. He hit his boss with the rolled-up poster still in his hand.

"What did I do?" Cade ducked too late.

"Nothing. Absolutely nothing." He tossed the poster on the bar. "You missed your chance."

"To do what?" Cade tightened his back. "Why in hell are you so pissed?

"You can work this out."

"Like hell."

"She didn't do this on purpose. It's not her fault."

"And how do you know?" Cade asked with a raised voice.

Rex took a step back. He puckered his lips, hurt by the anger.

Cade didn't care.

"I went to the doctor with her. She's trying to figure it out herself."

Cade's eyes turned a darker shade of blue as he stared at Rex. "You went with her?"

"I went with Layne."

Cade raised his hands, then dropped them in exasperation. They were on her side, and he was the one having to pay for it.

Lesson #19
Be there for a friend.

Gitana woke early and grabbed her tea. She sat among her nest of papers. This was her first full weekend off in two months and a good time to sort through the box and the piles cluttering her living room.

By noon, her energy waned. Looking at the old records became tiresome fast. Her eyelids drooped. John's name was on too many of the papers; a rental agreement for their condo, some student loan statements, and medical receipts from when he broke his leg skiing in Aspen. She wondered why in hell she saved the stuff. What was she thinking? Most went into the shred or toss piles. More in the trash meant additional closet space.

Nearing the bottom of the box, a bright yellow envelope caught her eye. She opened it and pulled out the card. The front had a tapestry of blue and pink flowers. She frowned, not remembering when or if she had opened any card from John.

Annabella,

I'm sorry the results weren't as expected. Having a baby with you means the world to me. We'll do what we can, I promise. One day you will have a baby in your arms.

Yours always,
John

Gitana's heart skipped. She read the note again. He wanted a baby. He wrote it. His handwriting.

She sat with her legs crossed and held the card close to her chest. Would this be proof to help Dr. Braustein? She picked up the envelope that had fallen to the floor. He rarely gave her cards. Yet, he wrote her name on the outside of the envelope. It was for her and not someone else.

She snickered at the "yours always," and placed the card to the side in her new "important" pile. She continued to dig.

The last item in the box was a tattered blue journal with pink swirls. Gitana brushed her fingers against the worn cover. She felt the rippled stains, her tears of frustration. She opened the book and smelled a trace of Chanel No. 5. The scent she used to wear, when she could afford it. She flipped through the pages. Some days she wrote a lot and others brief sentences. The journal would give Dr. Braustein dates to research.

Gitana laid the journal on top of the card. The two items in her "important" pile might be enough information, but she went back to the "review closer" pile just in case. Nothing stood out.

With the closet boxes empty, she shredded and tossed the larger piles into a paper bag for recycling. The ones to keep, she returned to the smaller box and put it back on the upper shelf of the closet.

The papers left were from the bank. This time she sat at her little table in the kitchen. Her legs, cramped from sitting, needed to stretch. She took the bag and removed the pouch with the diamonds. She tossed the pouch on the counter, then unclipped the papers and started reading. The first few papers made no sense. They were a bunch of numbers scribbled on lined paper. She saved them for later.

Next were her bills and results for the fertility test. She squinted to read the scratched note on one of them. John's handwriting lacked professionalism with large loops and letters tilted left and right. This writing had swirls that ended each letter and looked more like a woman's handwriting. The note read the tests were normal. She was healthy. She found no signature.

Gitana sipped on her tea and stared out the window. How many papers did he have on her? She didn't remember seeing the detailed lab results, the medical terms cryptic to her. Not once did she discuss her results with anyone except John. He translated what she needed to hear and took care of everything else. He had held the papers in his hand when he told her the bad news. He waved them around, then tossed them aside as if they were full of poison. His voice, the strain, and hurt carried with each word, provided ample proof of her failing.

Gitana's neck tightened with anger. She sat with fingers pressed against her nose. Visions of John popped into her head, and she wanted them to go away.

She had cried and begged him for forgiveness. Each time he patted her back in sorrow. All the years she felt less than a woman. Gitana rubbed her head, overwhelmed and not understanding.

Back to her task, she read the second set of papers from the bag. The first one in the pile, a receipt for birth control pills, had her name and old address printed in the corner. The next paper, this one wrinkled, had been flattened out as if he had changed his mind and kept it instead of throwing it away. Gitana brought the pastel blue paper up closer to read the fine print. Pregnyl. The upper left hand corner had a different name—not hers. Alison Trechmeyer. The address claimed her to live near San Jose. Prescriptions ordered at the office, typed and hand-delivered by the doctor. Gitana could understand if the receipts belonged to Trisha, his new wife, but not a stranger. Or did he have another mistress?

Gitana's head hurt. Dr. Braustein mentioned something about a switch. Someone filed a lawsuit against John when she became pregnant under his care. Didn't she say it was a mix-up with prescriptions?

A loud rap on her door cracked the air. Gitana jumped. She thought of John. He had gone to the bank. She swallowed hard.

The person banged on the frame of the sliding glass

door. She leaned over to get a better view. A man's hand knocked again. A ring, handmade and steel with blue glass, caught the sun's reflection. Cade.

She popped up from her spot too fast. Her legs tingled from sitting too long. She hobbled to the door as he leaned in with his face plastered against the glass. Gitana unlocked and opened the door to the ferocious wolf staring back at her. His jaw was set, his brows chiseled. Not like him.

No hi or how are you. His voice cracked when he said, "Layne and Rex were in a car accident. Layne's in surgery."

Gitana's face fell. She grabbed her purse, and they ran to his car.

"Rex phoned me. He went with Layne last night to watch him play. A drunk hit 'em."

She thought of Layne. Visions played in her head of his car rolling and then smashing against a cement wall or into a tree, or down a cliff. Layne dangling in his seat with blood on his face, with glass shattered all over. *Not Layne. Not Layne.*

Cade opened her door, then raced around to the driver's side. He burned out of the parking lot. Gitana gripped the seat cushion for balance. They weaved in and out of traffic, and passed cars like Mario Andretti. She stared out the side window, her tears falling freely.

Cade concentrated on the road, not her. He spoke after they crossed the bridge. "I guess they stayed at the bar longer than expected. The guitarist had some problem with a groupie." Cade stopped to look in the side mirror as he merged into traffic. "It was around three or four this morning; I can't remember what Rex said. A car in the other lane swerved into them. He tried…I mean the drunk tried regaining control and slammed into them. Not head on but close. Layne flipped his car. The Falcon's totaled."

"How's Rex?"

"A babbling nutcase. Physically, I guess some bruises and a cut on his forehead. Layne took the brunt of the hit. Before surgery, they had to stabilize him. They were concerned with internal bleeding. That's when Rex called. All I know, he knocked his head on the side window and crushed his arm as the car rolled."

Gitana bit her knuckle. She should've known he hadn't come home. Her full attention was on those fucking papers. He always stopped in or sat on the deck. *They* sat on the deck.

The cars and trucks whirled by. She wiped her nose with her hand. Gitana searched for a tissue in her purse, then looked around the car. She sniffed enough for Cade to reach in the back and find a used napkin. She took it and smelled ketchup. She blew her nose anyway.

Cade pulled into the emergency entrance. Gitana had the car door open before the Charger came to a complete stop. She jumped out of the car and rushed through the doors. She froze once in the admittance area. People milled about, some in chairs while others sat near the windows, trying to get cell service. For a second, she wondered if she had shut the car door.

A room off to the side had zombie-like patients waiting. No Rex. A gurney brought in a woman splattered with blood. Gitana overheard a nurse telling another, "Get ready. Accident coming in. Six-car collision. She's the first."

In the midst of their rush, Gitana grabbed a different nurse and asked about Layne. She pointed to a man behind a desk. He said Layne was still in surgery. She knew the hospital layout and power-walked the corridors as Cade caught up and followed close behind.

Rex sat in the waiting room at the end of the hall. He was not the crisp, tidy devil man who always sparked with energy. He rocked back and forth on the edge of his chair. His arms crossed around his waist.

"Rex!" Gitana cried out.

He shot up to his feet. His arms flew around her neck as he sobbed, "Oh, Wild Child, I'm so sorry. They won't tell me anything. I'm not related."

"Who's the doctor?" she asked and grabbed his arms in a hug. When he did not respond, she backed up and looked in his eyes. She repeated the question.

"I don't know," he said in complete disgust. He waved a tissue in the air before crumpling it again in his hand. The side of his face had swelled like a curved bar. Stitches held together a nasty cut in the center of the bruise.

"Ohhh, Rex!" She hated seeing him so broken. So typical of the situation, she asked, "Are you okay?"

"I'm okay." He matched her sad face. "A drunk driver crashed into us. We flipped and Layne's arm got pinned by the steering wheel."

Gitana kept her focus on him. She knew about people who passed off their pain, only to rush back to the hospital because their injury became ten times worse. "Did you get a full exam?"

"They checked me in the ambulance and when we got here. Two doctors checked me out, I had x-rays done, and they stitched me up." He pointed to the cut on his face.

Satisfied, she gave him a light squeeze. Gitana left him with Cade while she went to find a nurse.

"Who can tell me about Layne Jaroul?" she asked a short chubby woman with spiked hair.

"Are you related?"

"I'm his sister," she lied. They would not check.

She followed the nurse to her station and waited as she found Layne's latest report. "He's still in surgery."

"Who's his doctor?" Gitana asked.

"Dr. Fishwander. Jerry Fishwander."

The name sounded familiar. Maybe she remembered him from a guest list or a donation but not someone her ex spoke about.

"Annabella...Gitana," a woman's voice called out.

She turned around to see Dr. Braustein head toward her. The woman wore scrubs and a mask hung from her neck.

"Can you tell me how Layne's doing?" Gitana clutched the doctor's arm.

"He's fine. He's in recovery. We had to remove the bone chips, set two pins in his arm, and reattach a nerve."

Gitana let out her breath. "Thank, God!" She had to sit in a chair, her knees weak. "Did you see him?"

She nodded. "I performed the surgery. Layne insisted

they call me." She smiled and a few of her freckles disappeared.

Even rattled, Gitana smiled too. Layne must have been conscious and stubborn enough to insist on Dr. Braustein. He would wait, no matter how long, to make sure she took care of him.

Dr. Braustein placed her hand on Gitana's shoulder. She sat next to her and turned her head, away from the nurse's station, to talk in private. "How are you doing?"

"I...I'm okay." Gitana had to think about it.

"How's your search coming? Any luck?"

Search? Oh yes, the papers piled on the floor in her living room. "I may have a few things for you to look at. I kept my journal, which should give you some dates. I also have a card from John...I mean Dr. Sothers. A personal one to me. Proof he wanted a baby." She tapped her finger to her lips. "There was something else." Gitana put her head down until she remembered. She raised her head. "Yes...you were right. I found the receipts for the birth control with my name on them." She paused, then said a little lower, "I also found receipts for Pregnyl with someone else's name. Not mine."

Dr. Braustein raised her eyes. "What name?"

"Alison. Alison Trechmeyer."

The doctor went over to the nurse's station and asked for a piece of paper and pen. She returned to the chairs. "Can you repeat the name?"

She wrote it down after Gitana repeated the name. "I'll do some checking." She glanced at the white, plain clock on the wall. "It'll still be awhile before you can see Layne. I'll make sure they let you in. Okay?"

"Thanks," Gitana said and watched as Dr. Braustein darted off to the Staff Only doors at the end of the hall.

Cade stood against the wall, within earshot of their conversation. He played with his phone.

"I need coffee." Rex came from the men's room. He asked Cade, "You want one?"

Cade shook his head.

Rex turned to Gitana. "You?"

"Let me get you a coffee," she replied to Rex. He held his hand out and jutted his hip in a protective move. She relented. "Okay, decaf."

He gave her the thumbs up, spun around, and then turned the wrong way down the hall. She should have stopped him, but he disappeared.

Left alone with Cade, she sat a few chairs away from him. Neither of them spoke. He put his phone away and paced the floor. Gitana closed her eyes and rested her head against the wall.

She smelled his aftershave, his sexiness. An untouchable wall kept her at a distance. He had to take it down. She would not beg.

The drone of the hospital took over as people walked by. Soothing music piped from the ceiling to calm those waiting. Gitana concentrated on Neil Diamond's voice. As she tried to remember the name of the song, a rough half growl, half sigh brought her back.

Gitana opened her eyes when she realized it was Cade

who now sat a few chairs over from her. He glanced down the hall and then up at the ceiling. He looked over at the nurse's station and at the doctor who stopped by to use the phone. His gaze roamed everywhere but at her.

Cade cleared his throat, shifted in his chair, and then rubbed his hands together. He looked like he wanted to talk, but no words came out. She waited.

Gitana watched the clock. Another five minutes went by when he cleared his throat again. He said, "The other morning, I didn't mean to snap like I did."

The other morning? What timeframe was he on? They were talking days. Days of no phone calls or coming over.

"Yes, you did," she shot back. "You snapped loud and clear." The hurt rang in her voice. She was not about to accept his apology.

His tone hardened to match hers. "I can't pretend to be happy. Being a parent isn't part of my plan."

"And what is your plan?" Curiosity got the better part of her. One answer she knew; his ignoring their relationship.

"My plan," he said with a pause, "is to be a successful gallery owner and a successful artist."

"Mission accomplished. Now what?"

He shook his head. "That's it. I'm not making another mistake like before."

Gitana frowned and snorted in disbelief. He let his past rule him, stuck somewhere between happiness and loneliness. He made the choice to leave his family and made the mistake of marrying Maddy. Both were in the past.

His faults made her think of her own. She let hers control the bitterness in her heart like he did. Her pain and anger overruled and kept her from moving forward. She fed on the divorce. And Papa became another one of her faults for trying too hard to please him. She loved John because Papa adored John. She turned into a puppet for both of them. They pulled her strings. Now she had to pull back, live for herself. Her future was not their choice. Nor Cade's.

"You know," Gitana said, unsure if she told him for his sake or for her own, "you have the power to control your destiny. You have to think about what you want, make a decision, and then go for it. Everything is there for you. But the choice is yours, not mine. Remember the little lecture of yours…about driving?"

His foot curled in and out from the chair. He scratched his ear. "What I wanted turned out to be a lie."

She caught the past tense. The lie part made her seethe.

"I'm not looking for your money," she said. His accusation still stung inside her. "Nor do I want to get married. Do you think I'm ready? You saw me at the park. At the café. And don't tell me I framed you. I'm as shocked about the pregnancy as you are."

She had to stand and release the balled-up nerves inside her stomach. She walked toward the window but turned back around. The hurt stuck in her throat. "And do you know what's really sad? My one wish, to have a child, is causing more pain than anything else. I should be feeling total joy and happiness, but how can I under these circumstances? I would never wish this on anyone. Not you. Not me."

Gitana spun around again and walked to the window as the tears rolled down her cheeks. She wiped them away and looked outside at the parked cars. A middle-aged man got out of his Buick and raced toward the building. He disappeared into the emergency entrance.

Coffee sounded good and Rex was MIA. She went to find her own cup. A lone vending machine stood at the end of another hall. She pushed a dollar in and pressed the button for black coffee, no sugar or cream.

The cup was hot. She grabbed a couple of tissues from a table as she walked back to the waiting room. One tissue went into her pocket, the other around her cup.

Rex and Cade were having a moment. The two men hugged in an odd, close way. Cade reached down and found the devil man's hand. He squeezed it while his other hand patted his back. Gitana became jealous of their shared moment.

She stopped at the nurse's station to check on Layne's progress. Cade walked by as she talked with the nurse. She refused to look at him. His strong presence rocked her as he slowed down when he passed. His footsteps didn't stop. He walked on and the air turned cold.

Rex sat alone when she returned to the waiting area. He cradled a Styrofoam cup with another one stacked underneath it. Maybe the one intended for her. She slid into the chair next to him and put her arm around his shoulder. "How you doing?"

The devil man sipped on his coffee. "Any word yet?"

"He's in recovery. The nurse thought another half hour."

Rex's face twisted in anguish. He said, "I should be the one in there. Not him."

"Accidents happen." She patted his back as Cade had done minutes before.

"But he's a good guy."

"Layne says the same thing about you." Gitana pressed her finger under his chin and raised it. She smiled. "You're a good guy. Don't be hard on yourself."

"You know, Cade's a good guy too."

"Maybe," she said with a shrug.

"He is good." Rex defended him. He blew his nose. "Even when we stopped…he behaved like a gentleman."

Gitana straightened.

"Oh!" The devil man realized what he said. "Don't worry; my fling with him was short-lived. He's not into…into what I do."

Cade into men? She could have gone through life without knowing Cade flipped sides.

She hit the back of her head a couple of times against the wall to rid herself of the image. Cade and Rex dabbling in naked play around his loft was not what she wanted ingrained in her head.

"He's not," Rex said after seeing her face flush. "Only once. He explored. Didn't like it. He needed to find himself."

"Stop!" Gitana held out her hand. "I don't need to hear

anymore."

Rex slouched forward and covered his face as more tears sprang from his eyes. "It's all my fault. I got bold. We got into the accident because of me."

"A drunk swerved in front of you. How could it have been your fault?"

He moved his hands up to rub the top of his head. "We were driving to my place. You know, having some fun."

Gitana didn't know.

He bobbed his head like a chicken and added a little attitude. Gitana watched, confused. He was trying to tell her something without saying it. She backed off, charades not being her game nor was this the right time for it.

"He was driving...I was bent over."

Her cheeks paled.

"My face in his lap...my mouth on his..."

"Got it," Gitana said a little too loud and stood up to pace.

Lesson #20
Value what you have.

Layne refused to talk about the night of the accident. His feelings, already mixed, were closed shut. His mind, however, burned for Rex. He dreamed about the way his wet, soft tongue covered his shaft...pure heaven. He replayed the night, before the accident. How Rex's hand massaged his balls and stirred more arousal than he ever imagined. A new world opened to him, one no woman had ever satisfied.

Gitana knew what happened, and she accepted his life direction even before he had. Not that he needed her approval. As Rex told him, he could now relax. There would be no more hiding their attraction for each other.

For the next few weeks, Rex and Gitana took care of him as he recovered at home. They cleaned, entertained, and ran errands. The three of them became a tight-knit unit, working together to heal wounds and appreciate each other.

One link, however, was missing. Gitana's need for Cade. Her pregnancy meant the world to her, but without him, she had no one to share her joy. He and Rex would always be a part of her family and give her their support. The first time Rex called him Uncle Layne, a sense of pride burst in his heart. He would be the favorite uncle, but the baby needed a father.

His boat swayed. He checked his watch. Either she worked later than usual, which seemed the norm lately with the Halloween parties she had to prepare for, or the traffic bogged her down.

"Hey, Git," he said as she walked in with a bag of fresh vegetables.

"Hey, you," she said. "Are you behaving?"

He had his weights lined up on the floor. The twenty-pound one was in his hand. He counted out his arm curls, his right bicep pumped thick and hard. Dr. Braustein ordered no exercise until the bones in his bad arm healed. Gitana made sure he obeyed her orders.

"I'm behaving. You're a little late," he said between grunts. Five more to go. His arm flexed as he came up. He gripped the steel and wanted to change hands, feeling unbalanced. The cast got in his way.

"I had a talk with Pete."

Layne stopped. He set down the weight and joined her in the galley. His boat had more room than hers. He had a small island in the center with a sink and prep area. He picked up a tomato and washed the fruit.

"Is he finally helping you out?" He didn't like how her

boss stuck the entire month's events on her. Gitana gave him an excuse, something about Pete's granddaughter, and a new wine blend they were creating.

"In a different way," she said. Gitana shredded the lettuce, then tossed it into a colander. Her dark lashes batted more heavily than usual. A smile curled on her lips. She held her head higher, her shoulders straighter.

He had to ask, "What'd you do?"

"I saved my job," she said with a proud air. "At least for a while I did."

"Spill it." Layne leaned against the counter top and gave her his full attention.

"He called me into his office and said, 'you're like family.'" She did a good job mimicking Pete by tucking her head back to create a double chin.

Layne imagined Pete as he leaned across his desk with piles of papers in front of him but spread out enough to tunnel through and grab her hand, tapping the topside.

"You would've been proud of me, Layne." She shoved a carrot in his mouth. "I used some negotiation skills and got him to extend my stay."

"And?" Layne asked when she stopped talking to find a knife to cut the cucumber.

"I gave him the stats. Sales are up by 26 percent since I came on. I offered to help market the wine Jillian is now creating for the winery."

"Did you tell him how his grapes would shrivel up and the castle would be gloom and doom without you?"

Gitana rolled her eyes. She continued. "I asked him to

keep me on for another eight months or until I found suitable insurance to cover me and the baby once he or she is born. He knew something was up, so I told him."

"What did you tell him?" Layne wanted to hear her say the words.

Gitana's eyes lit up and a broader smile creased her face. "I'm gonna be a mama."

Layne gave her an all-encompassing hug to share her joy. Even more so, he appreciated how she took care of and made him a part of her family.

She continued without noticing his sappiness. "I get to work twenty hours at the winery and then twenty hours at home when I'm making my calls. He agreed to eight months but would consider extending it based on sales and being able to afford the expense."

"I'm proud of you, Git. Now you don't have to worry about a job for a while." Even if she had lost the job, Layne would have taken care of her. Rex would too.

Her smile disappeared as she became a little more serious. "I also told him about John, the papers, and what the doctor said." The confident, happy Gitana put on her worried face. "I still don't get all of it."

"Your ex was mean to you, Gitana," Layne said plain out. "You were a puppet on his strings."

"I'm at fault too. I didn't check, Layne. I looked up everything on fertility. I researched. I followed their tips, ways to get pregnant. I never thought about the shots. Never did it occur to me the dosages were wrong."

"Why should you have thought anything different?

Your husband was a doctor."

She shook her head. Layne stepped forward to put his hand to her mouth, not wanting her to go to the unhappy place. She batted his hand away, and he used his bad arm to poke her in the stomach.

"Don't you give me any trouble," she warned and poked back. She turned back to the cucumber and cut it.

Layne glanced out the window. He saw a shadow walk across the dock near Gitana's. He turned from her and stretched his neck to get a better view. The gait, the broad shoulders, and the masculine presence led to one person. Straightening back up, he said, "Cade's heading toward your boat."

She held the knife, a little too high in the air for his liking when she turned to the window. He took the sharp blade away from her.

"Yeah, right." She looked, seeing nothing.

Layne made her go to the living room window. He opened the blinds for her, and they saw her boat rock more than usual. Cade then appeared at the front deck as he peaked around the side.

Gitana jumped back, away from the window as if afraid he'd spot her.

"Go!" Layne hit her leg with his good hand. "Go!"

***

The moon's glow sharpened against the night sky when Gitana hopped from Layne's boat to hers. She tried being quiet to either surprise him or to change her mind if needed.

Her nerves shot like fireworks underneath her skin. She inhaled the salty air and took in a deep breath. This was her boat, her territory, her life.

"Hey," she said and headed for her door and not him.

When did she fall in love with him? Why did it hurt so much to see him?

Cade tipped his head toward Layne's boat, then waved as if he knew her friend was watching them from behind the blinds. "How's he doing?"

"Still bruised and in a cast, but good." Her hands shook as she pulled her keys from her purse. She tried unlocking the door. The key refused to turn. She pulled the handle in, pulled it up, but the damn thing stuck.

"Here," Cade said and held out his hand to help.

Gitana stepped back and allowed him to try. For him, the key worked.

"Thanks," she said as he moved aside for her to enter first. She flicked on the light above the counter, then set her purse down. The air intensified and suffocated the small room. "You want something to drink?"

Cade shook his head. He stayed in the doorway. He watched her fumble for a glass. She needed water. Her mouth and throat were dry. He waited as she drank. Finished, she faced him. She stared into crystal blue eyes and wondered if he was as miserable as she was.

"I miss you," he said as if he read her mind.

She set the glass in the sink. Words she wanted to hear

now had no meaning. Unable to control herself, the sarcasm spilled. "You miss the plotting gold-digger?"

"I didn't say that."

Gitana shrugged. "Pretty damn close."

She crossed her arms close to her stomach. He crossed his arms near his chest. "I am sorry I exploded. As I said before, the news hit me hard. Seeing you throw up and hearing you say you were pregnant…it was quite the blow."

"Tell me about it." Gitana needed fresh air. She grabbed her shawl from the top of the chair and headed out the side door to the deck. She flipped the knit fabric around her shoulders, clutched the ends together like a shield, and then leaned against the rail. The oily water below danced in ripples toward the boat. A few lights sprinkled the bay as the night settled in. Soft music caressed the air.

Cade followed but kept his distance. He placed his hands on the rail. A different ring—simple steel band with a layer of red glass adorned his index finger. She wanted to smash his hand into the boat, let him feel the pain in her heart. She refrained.

"Has the morning sickness stopped?" The concern in his voice rang true.

"I'm better. I can eat again."

He stepped a little closer and turned his eyes from the bay to her. "I'd like to be around."

He took one step closer. No more.

Not yet committed. Her shoulders tensed. She coaxed him along. "For me? The baby?"

He tightened his jaw.

She smelled his nerves mixed with cologne.

He stressed, "For you. I want to be there for you"

"You know what I want?" Gitana straightened her back. She put her hands on the rail as if she spoke from behind a podium. She swallowed first to control the tight ball of anger. She looked out at the bay to address the water, the sky, the boats, and to the man who listened beside her. "First, I would like to have a healthy, happy baby. Second, I really want to know how this happened. Why I got pregnant. And I mean medical-wise." Her voice softened. "Third, I want this baby to have a father who will love and be there when needed. I don't want to second-guess whether or not the father is going to blame me for trapping him. Nor do I want to worry if he's gonna run off with another woman or *a man*. I need trust."

Cade's head came up on her words "a man." He expanded his chest to defend his masculinity. He was about to explain when she held up her hand. Details were not important. He only needed to know she knew of his little tryst with Rex.

Gitana forced herself to push away from the rail. "You need to decide what you want out of life, Cade. At the very least, become a father. This is about the baby now. Not me."

He looked at the water. He raised his eyes to the fading sky and then toward a sailboat leaving the bay. An otter barked and he found its baby swimming under the neighboring dock.

His silence killed her. His deep stare into the black

water and beyond seemed hollow. He had to want it. She could not be the one who told him what to do.

Gitana was done. She stepped back inside the boat and closed the door behind her. For added measure, she shut the blinds.

Lesson #21
Reevaluate your plan.

His stomach muscles twitched when Cade entered Gallery One.

My own goddamn gallery.

Each time, he wondered if Gitana would be there. He had a flight to New York in two days. He needed a break from Rex's anger, his own anger. He was tempted to stay longer than the scheduled three days. Create a new outlook. Run away.

The rift between Gitana and him caused turmoil, more than he wanted to face. All the issues from his past and the issues with his family caused him restless sleep. He had been fine to brush them off his shoulders. Pretend they didn't exist. Could he do the same with a baby?

"I see we're in a foul mood today," Rex drawled and brought Cade to the present.

Rex dropped his briefcase onto the drafting table. He opened the main compartment and found his appointment book. He leafed through the pages as if agitated.

"What?" Cade tossed his pen down and it bounced from the desk to the floor. He had enough of his assistant's bitchiness toward him. Layne and Rex chatted like little chickadees, animated and gay. The minute he'd walk into the room, they'd turn up their noses. The two worked on Gitana's artwork together, something he would have done on his own. This time, his assistant took over.

"The brochures are here for Gitana's show," Rex said in short, crisp words. "Do you want to proof them or should I?"

"I can."

"Then do it now." Rex spun around like a soldier and headed to the gallery floor.

Cade threw his hands up. This was his gallery and his rules. He followed Rex to the front and said, "I talked to her."

"Two weeks ago."

"I need time to think."

"Tick. Tock. Maybe she's made up her mind she doesn't want you. Then what?"

"What do you mean?" Cade frowned. "What did she tell you?

Rex shrugged. He went behind the counter and straightened brochures, business cards, note pads, pens.

Anything to keep him busy, Cade thought.

Rex turned his nose upward. "She doesn't need you. Gitana has a heart as pure as an angel's. And she also has a lot on her plate—the show, her job, the baby. Now she's even strung into a potentially criminal action against her ex. She doesn't have time for you, Mr. Whiney."

"Criminal action?" Cade ignored the slam. He wanted to hear more about her ex. He remembered the conversation she had with the doctor at the hospital. He overheard something about switching records and birth control.

"She's innocent, Cade. Get it through your head. She's turning her heart around. Focus on baby, not Cade."

"Ouch," Cade said and put his hand to his chest.

"Don't cover the thing, it's already black." Rex sniffed. He left and disappeared into the backroom.

Cade rested his hands on the counter, his head down. Yes, his heart was black.

Rex's head peaked out from the door. "For God's sake, man. Think of the new life you can have."

He disappeared again. The light switches in the back clicked on. The gallery lit up. The doors opened in ten minutes. Rex's black polished shoes pattered against the tile floor as he carried a painting to place on the easel next to the counter.

He continued, "People lose direction. They can be closed-minded and not see two feet in front of them." He held a stack of business cards to enter into the mailing list on the computer. He ruffled them like a deck of cards. "You can't control your past, Cade. I had to leave my parents. Age seventeen. They didn't want a faggot living in their house. You remember how I struggled?"

Cade did. One night, after the gallery in New York

opened, they ran into his parents at a restaurant. Rex braved his fear and walked to their table. His mother's eyes welled with tears, happy to see her son. His father threatened to take him out if he didn't leave.

"You vowed to watch over me," Rex choked. "You told me they were the ones missing out. You renewed my belief in myself. Not once did you close the door on me. You took a chance. Together we succeeded in this business. We became family. And now my family is torn once again."

Cade bit his lip. Rex's face was haggard and weary from the tension, the pain of having to split his life in two. His assistant wouldn't give up Gitana as a friend. She had him pinned to her heart the minute she walked into the gallery with his jacket. Layne was another story. Rex was in love, infatuated with him.

"Here's my ride," Rex said.

Layne stood at the front doors. Rex motioned for him to come in.

The bell jingled. The Philippino had a document in his hand. He sauntered toward them, his stare on Cade. They passed with exchanged nods but no warmth. Neither one had anger for the other. The air stayed neutral.

Layne set the document on the counter with his good hand. He slid it toward Cade. "Here's your proof."

"Come on, Sugar." Rex grabbed his jacket. "Gitana waiting?"

Layne nodded. "She's in the car."

The two men left. Cade rubbed his smooth head and stared at the document. He saw the words "Medical Board of Review," "Dr. John Sothers," and "Professional misconduct" when he scanned the front page. He leafed through the rest of the document. The same scenario flashed through his head, the night of the party when he showed Gitana his divorce papers and pleaded for a chance to explain.

Cade never gave Gitana the same chance.

Lesson #22
Have faith.

Gitana walked with Rex and Layne to Billy Friedman's townhouse. Coit Tower rose to the left, a great view for the area, especially on a clear night with the moon looking down on them.

The men refused to let her stay home and drown in sorrow. They insisted she attend Billy's Halloween party. Rex wanted her to promote herself and lure potential customers to the show.

"You coat some sugar on all these people," the devil man ordered as he took her arm to help her up the stairs to the porch. He had transformed himself into Peter Pan with green tights and sequins.

Layne refreshed Captain Hook with a fake parrot adorning his shoulder. "Remember, this is your night to shine."

"I think you have that one covered," she teased and noted the shine from his outfit. She decided on a tamer costume, a white layered skirt, peasant blouse, and scarf adorning her head.

Billy Friedman opened the door and welcomed them into his home before they had a chance to knock. They stood in the hallway as Rex talked with their host, who was dressed as one of the gold-specked fishes from his paintings. The devil man's pixie dust sparkled on his cheeks as he flirted with the artist. He batted his eyes and flashed long, black eyelashes.

Gitana glanced over to Layne as they waited. He enjoyed watching his partner's openness. Not his version of gay but maybe it was okay. He wanted different and Rex was it.

"I'll go get drinks," Layne offered. He left with an amused smile and a little more wiggle in his walk.

Rex gave him a wave, then spotted Gitana still next to him. He pushed her toward the guests. "I'm not a shadow. Go network, darling!"

Gitana wanted to give him the finger but smiled instead. She walked into the living room, now transformed into a ballroom from a fantasy story. Surrounded in lace, sparkles, and black, she found the theme to be as flamboyant as the night of the birthday party at the hotel— with less splash of color.

Her first wave of insecurity hit when a man bumped her and spilled a little of his drink on her blouse. Luckily, it was clear and not red. Mr. Rogers regained control, nodded, and then moved on as if she had been the one in his way. She brushed at the wet spot.

"Turn and leave," Gitana thought. "Walk out the door." She took a step forward but Goldfish blocked her. She would have a hell of a time getting around him and his fins.

Gitana let out a deep breath and her face sagged. She missed Cade. He should be with them, and his absence weighed heavily on her heart.

Rex found her again, hiding behind a mummified cat with a sinister face. He frowned. "Shoo!"

Gitana's shoulders slumped. Her eyes went down.

He caught on and his eyes warned her not to go there. "This is about you. Not Cade. You. Go have fun."

He placed his hands around her waist and helped her forward, until she was in the midst of the group. She dragged her way through the partygoers and was the sole female without a mini or slit skirt to show off bare legs. Most wore flashy bling while she wore gold chains and hooped earrings.

Having nothing else to do but stand and watch, she noted the orange and black bulbs in every light fixture, the stretched cobwebs from wall to wall, and the bubbling dry ice in buckets in the corners of the room. A misty fog rolled at their feet. She loved the haunted organ-type music played in the background to keep with the theme and her mood.

"My, my, here she is again," Maddy smiled with a martini in hand. She appeared at Gitana's side. Her light green outfit said roaring twenties but the glittery wings on her back spoke faerie. She'd covered her eyes with glittery green glasses and pink lenses.

"Maddy." Gitana greeted Cade's ex with a smile. At least she was a familiar face in a sea of strangers.

"Aren't you the gypsy," she said while appraising her outfit. "Are you having a lovely time?"

"We just got here."

"Where's Cade? I haven't seen him yet."

"He's in New York."

"Not by your side?" She seemed amused.

Gitana curled her toes. What does this woman have up her sleeve now? Did Cade run to her after their fight and tell her about the baby? How she was ruining his life?

"Not tonight," Gitana said and believed that striking a conversation with a stranger sounded better.

"He does keep busy. He likes his independence."

Maddy appeared to know something about Cade and her fighting. This was none of her business. Gitana scanned the room. She spotted Layne and raised her hand.

He maneuvered his way around an evil princess and a hobbit without spilling their drinks. Gitana forgot Cade's ex had not met Layne before, until her green eyes grew round. She raked him over like a big juicy steak and wetted her lips at the taste.

Gitana stepped forward when Layne handed her a tall glass of water. His black vest loosened as he removed the bottle of beer tucked under his arm. Maddy drooled at the size of his chest. She noticed his cast.

"Hello, Captain." She greeted him with sultry lips.

"Layne, this is Maddy." Gitana introduced them.

He nodded politely but kept his attention on her. He said, "I added a lemon. I hope you're okay with it."

"Perfect." Gitana smiled.

"This is your friend?" Maddy meowed.

"Rex's too," she hinted.

Maddy got it but seemed determined to change his mind by the end of the evening. A man dressed as Shrek called her name and she smiled. Maddy excused herself. "You two enjoy tonight." She looked at Layne. "I'll catch you later."

"She's Cade's ex?" Layne asked when she left. He seemed amused by her interest in him.

"Be careful around her," Gitana warned. "She's a handful so watch what you say and what you do."

"I can handle her," he said with a snort.

"So you think."

He refocused. "What are you doing standing here? Go mingle."

"It wouldn't be fair, leaving you alone." She made up her first excuse since arriving. His eyebrow went up, reaching the tip of his bandana.

Gitana wrinkled her nose. "Okay, okay."

She set her smile and worked the room. She remembered faces, even behind the costumes, from previous gatherings or seeing them at the gallery. Everyone asked about Cade, and why he was not there. The man was popular; but then, it was his circle. She learned a little more about him as his friends dished pleasantries. In one way, she confirmed his reputation as a well-liked man. On the other hand, she wondered how it fit with the persistent prick who tackled her in the park.

Prick and all, she had fallen for him. Gitana fell into Cade's spell, just as his friends had. But for her, it was deeper. She found his heart. A heart now lost.

With her head high, Gitana changed her strategy for Rex's sake and went for the potential customers instead of mingling with the artists. She kept the conversation focused on the discovery of who they were without offering tidbits about herself or answering questions on Cade. She set a goal to meet ten new people, and she met twenty. Hercules, Cleopatra, and Snow White hooked her in with their friends. Their friends introduced her to more.

Rex said the party would be good for networking. He was right. She did her piece and enjoyed the mingling until finding herself alone. Three hours into the party and she wanted to replace her costume with soft, wispy pajamas and a cozy bed. Pregnancy tired her more than she anticipated.

She took a break and found an empty chair in the dining room to sit and rest her feet. She spotted Layne and Rex in the kitchen, and they hovered over each other in a private moment. The devil man's face lit up and soon both giggled like little kids. They seemed happy. She liked seeing their eyes sparkle. Layne saw something in Rex, a magnetism that Cade had seen in her.

Gitana took a sip of her lemon water to soothe the hard lump in her throat. Her thoughts clicked to Cade. She wished to find him across the room. He'd give her a wink and a smile as they shared a moment.

She would have reacted the same way Cade did about the pregnancy. Unlike him, she would have come back to listen and work it out.

The room became too stuffy. Rex spotted her. She ducked out before he could reach her and found solace in the night air versus him scolding her to mingle.

The porch, bare of any place to sit, seemed awkward. People flowed in and out to have cigarettes. The smoke and smell nauseated her. She walked down the hill about a block to Rex's car, a black Audi with chrome everywhere. She leaned against the hood. He would kill her if he found out.

She looked up. White, wispy clouds layered the night sky. A few stars twinkled but most hid as the city lights took over. A couple, dressed as Barney and Betty Rubble, waved to her as they passed and headed toward the glowing house.

She had done what she could. Done what was right.

Gitana scooted toward the middle of the hood, raised her legs up and leaned against the front windshield. She stared skyward. Maybe marriage and a family lacked unity for her. She could have one or the other but not both. A choice already made for her. She placed her hands on her stomach, the bump growing outward yet contained within her skirt.

"Mind if I join you?"

Gitana jumped and one of her heels hit the black hood. She quickly felt for damage, relieved to find no dent or scratch. It was too hard to see in the dark. But that was nothing to who she faced.

Cade stood with his hands in his pockets. He wore jeans and a white tank. His chest molded to the fabric and showed the tips of his nipples. He checked out her gypsy-style outfit and nodded his approval.

"Where's your costume?" she asked, not knowing what else to say. Dumb, but better than silence.

He looked at his clothes and then at her again. "No costume tonight."

He instilled a deeper meaning. He spoke with his eyes. "Billy will be glad you're here."

A truck passed and they watched it turn the corner.

"I didn't come for Billy or the party," he said and leaned his elbows against Rex's car. "I came to see you."

"To apologize again for your anger?" She'd heard it one too many times.

"No, to tell you I'm scared, Gitana." His eyes showed his heart. No pretense. No toughness.

"Scared of what?"

"Making it right? Becoming the man I need to be?"

His fears were different from hers but fears all the same. She had to respect him. She said, "I remember a guy who once told me to keep moving forward. Don't let the past bring me down. I get your fears, why you reacted the way you did."

"My past," he agreed. He glanced up when hearing laughter. Mr. Rogers headed out of the house and pulled along a bumblebee with long, black legs. They walked the other way. He turned back to her. "I'm sorry it blocked you out."

Gitana let out a short laugh. If only he realized the turmoil and waves of emotion that rocked her inside because he feared failure. Mainly it was because she lacked confidence in herself. She sat up and slid off the hood and planted her feet on the street with the car between them.

"Listen, I know how you feel and it's okay. Life's not fair. I guess this is one of those times. I won't demand anything from you." She walked around the car and stood in front of him. She wanted a truce. The fight over, but one thing still gnawed at her. "I'm not a gold-digger."

Cade's head went up; his hands came out of his pockets. She turned to walk toward the party, and he moved to block her, grabbing her arm.

"Gitana…" His voice quavered.

"Everyone makes mistakes, Cade. It's learning from them and growing stronger. A good heart with the best intentions is what's important."

"The mistake I made was not giving you a chance to explain." He brought her toward him. He secured his hands around her upper arms.

The intensity of his touch made her shake. Her knees weakened.

"I'm sorry."

"And now?" she asked as her lip trembled. "How do you feel now?"

He squeezed her shoulders in a firm grip. "I believe you. I'm begging you to let me in your life again."

"No," she cried. How could he do this to her? He

played with her. He wanted her, not the baby.

"I love you. I will do anything to keep you in my arms for the rest of my life."

Words she longed to hear pierced her heart, made her ache. Her heart pounded. Tears streamed down her face.

Cade pulled her into his arms. He squeezed her tight so she could not back away. "I want this. I want us. I want to be the father I need to be."

"No, you can't!"

"I can," he said in her ear. "With you."

Lesson #23
Plans change for a reason.

Cade, Rex, Layne, and Gitana gathered at the loft to eat Chinese food before the show. The little white containers spread out across the island as they dug in with chopsticks. They took portions from each one. Gitana stuffed herself, more from nerves than hunger. Rex, the timekeeper, tidied up when they had fifteen minutes to be out the door.

Gitana went to the large mirror in the dining room and grumbled. The dress clung to her belly, and she cringed in discomfort. Her reflection showed a frump instead of a sexy artist. She should have picked the Empress dress a few months ago, not the molded number she now wore. The piece lacked style with an expanding middle.

"You're beautiful, Wild Child. Don't you worry," Rex commented as he put the leftovers in the fridge.

She glared at the devil man. "I need to impress. You've been drilling me to remember for the last couple of weeks."

"Let's go!" Cade had his hand in the air. He pointed at

his watch.

Gitana leaned closer to the mirror and fixed her hair. She picked at the long strands with her fingers. The hair looked good but the dress puckered. She swore under her breath.

"Here," Layne grabbed the dark purple shawl from the chair. "Try wrapping this at your waist."

She did as told. The frump still reflected back in the mirror. She ripped the shawl off her.

"For chrissake," Rex cursed with impatience. "Come here."

Gitana moved to the kitchen and raised her arms. He wiped his hands clean and grabbed the purple shawl from her. He angled the fabric until the layers fell across her hips. He held the ends together with a black rubber band.

"Voilà" He tapped her butt.

Returning to the mirror, Gitana swayed from one side to the other and admired his work. Perfect. She grinned. "Thank you, Devil Man."

"You're more than welcome, Wild Child," he said and fixed his cufflinks.

Cade grabbed his keys from the living room. "I'll get the truck." He stopped to give her a squeeze.

Gitana smiled and thought back to the party when he held her and confessed his love. The night they became inseparable once again.

"Five minutes." Cade held up his hand and spread his fingers. "Street side."

"Yes, sir!" Rex saluted. He grabbed his wallet, keys, and

her purse.

"How's my scarf?" Layne asked. He leaned down to look in the mirror.

Gitana helped him fix the back by tucking in the corner. She liked the skull-designed scarf wrapped around his head and how it complimented his slate-blue suit.

He was handsome and Rex had no fear in telling him. He smacked his lips together and said, "You are my gorgeous one. How'd I get so lucky?"

Layne coughed to cover his embarrassment as if coming out wasn't as comfortable for him as it was for the devil man.

"Guard your little tushy from me, big guy," Rex waved his finger in a fun warning. "You may get more than a slap tonight."

"Stop!" Gitana laughed, unused to the talk. Too much information. She struggled into her black two-inch heels. Not designer wear but comfortable, and they went with the dress.

"Did Layne tell you the news?" Rex asked and held the door open for her.

Gitana glanced toward Layne. He shook his head at Rex not to spill. She would have none of it. "What's up?"

"He's moving in with me," the devil man announced with a hint of annoyance that his lover did not bother to tell her.

Gitana stared at Layne, floored he would move. He loved sitting on the deck of his boat with beer in hand. He loved watching the night dissipate to morning. The place was his sanctuary. "Really?"

"I'm not giving her up." He made it clear as they trotted down the stairs. "I figured I'd try a change in scenery."

"Are you sure about this?" She lowered her voice to him.

"I'm good," Layne squeaked. He cleared his throat and said with confidence, "I'm ready."

His submission made the tears start again. She swallowed hard. "I'm happy for you, Layne. I'm truly happy." Gitana realized how much she would miss him.

They were breaking apart from a hug when Cade flung the outside door open.

"Come on! Let's move it!"

The flurry of getting in the truck began. Doors opened, doors slammed shut. Rex, sitting in front, removed a list from the breast pocket of his suit. They went over the remaining To Do items as they sped off through the streets. They arrived at the gallery at the same time the caterer pulled up. Cade and Layne helped unload the boxes of food, while Rex and Gitana turned on the lights and music.

She removed the champagne glasses from a plastic bin and set them on a white linen table in the front of the gallery. Layne came up behind her.

"Sorry I can't play tonight," he said and rested his chin on her shoulder.

"Maybe another time." She squeezed his arm. She thought of him moving. "I'm gonna miss you, you know. Watching the stars…our beers on the deck."

"You can't have beer now."

"I know. However we can still sit and enjoy you and me time."

"What? You think you're getting away from me?" He squeezed harder and put his uninjured arm around her. "Not in this lifetime."

Gitana smiled, afraid if she said anymore she would burst into tears. He stepped to her side and grabbed one of the chilled bottles of champagne. He held the base between his chest and casted arm.

"Besides," he said and peeled back the green foil, "you won't be staying at your place either. When's the lease up?"

"End of December. Maybe I'll hop to your boat and live there."

Layne shook his head. "Not a chance."

"Why not?"

"You don't need to stay in Sausalito by yourself. Cade's got a large place here."

"But it's his."

Granted, she stayed at his loft more than her boat. Cade confessed he wanted her to move in, but they avoided discussing their future after the night of the party. They focused on reconnecting their love. They allowed their emotions to dance together without walls or history.

Layne turned away from her to pop the cork. He squeezed his eyes shut and waited for the burst. As it popped, he caught the plastic top in his good hand. He placed the cork and the bottle on the table and grabbed the next one to open.

He said, "You have to think about the baby and yourself." He worked on the wrapper. "Of course, the baby can always live with Cade and you can fend for yourself."

"Prick." Gitana laughed and hit his arm.

"At your service." Layne smiled from ear to ear.

"Fifteen minutes until we open!" Rex flew past them toward the main doors. Snapping his fingers, he said, "Gitana, Cade wants you."

She left Layne in charge of the champagne and headed to the dome room. A soft evening hue glowed downward from the skylight. Little lights dangled from the ceiling to make the place starry and serene. She found him turning on the lights above her paintings. He adjusted one of them until it lit the woods on the canvas.

A week ago, Cade had removed his sculptures from the room to give her paintings, according to him, the attention they deserved. Gitana thought differently. The twisted metal complimented her work and added ambience to the room, like having trees planted in the woods. She wanted them back, and together they chose his pieces, made of copper and green glass, to accent her forest scenes. Her strongest paintings hung on the walls while Cade's sculptures displayed in the middle platform.

"I'm nervous." Gitana shook her hands out to loosen them up.

"Just remember to breathe and have fun." He came to give her a hug.

"What if I babble like an idiot?"

"You'll be fine. Any questions, direct them to Rex or

me. We'll do the selling." His smile lit his eyes as he reached into his suit coat. He handed her a black velvet box. "This is for you."

Why was he showering her with another gift? He already made her dangling earrings and a square stud for her nose. Both matched the purple in her dress. He motioned for her to continue. Inside the box was a necklace, three pieces of purple, shard glass wrapped around silver ribbon.

"You, me, and the baby," he explained and pointed to each piece.

"It's beautiful." Gitana choked. She cherished the way he spoke the words more than the actual necklace. He included their baby.

"Just like you."

She pulled her hair back and let him put the necklace on her. He stepped away to admire how the glass piece fell between her swollen breasts. Cade looked as if he were about to dive in with his lips when the bells jingled in the front.

Gitana's eyes grew large. The main doors opened to her show.

Cade raised his head. He smiled. "We're on."

Inhale. Exhale. Stay calm.

Her family had arrived first. Maria and Jane came without their husbands, and her brothers brought Papa. Rex gave them a tour of the gallery and was proud to show off the paintings, now matted and framed.

"To think they were made into Barbie houses." Maria

laughed.

"Mansions," Tony corrected after seeing the prices they planned to catch.

Rex and Layne kept her brothers and Papa occupied, which gave Gitana a chance to visit with her sisters. They commented on the roundness of her belly but kept their chatter to whispers, still under oath to keep her pregnancy quiet. Next Friday, when they gathered for dinner at Papa's place, she would announce the news to the rest of the family with Cade at her side.

The gallery began to fill, and Gitana lost sight of Maria and Jane as a cluster of people arrived all at once. Rex instructed her to stay in the back and let the guests come to her, the newest artist on view. He assured her they would find her.

And they did. She enjoyed meeting people excited about art. Her work. Cade's work. The scene was so different from the charities she pushed for the hospital or the bottles of wine she sold at the vineyard.

"Gitana." Rex placed his hand on her arm. "I have someone here I'd like you to meet."

The tall man with dark, tousled hair was handsome, but the woman beside him was stunning. Gitana wanted to touch her perfect skin and long, silky hair.

The devil man raised his voice, and he strained to keep in control. "This is Walt Arbol and Jessie Woods. Walt is from Arbol publishing. Jessie is a freelance writer and photographer. She'd like to interview you for an article."

Gitana recognized the Arbol name, a respected

publishing company. Their magazines were light yet insightful. He was big time and she caught on.

"I'm honored." She shook his hand and then Jessie's.

"We love your work," Jessie said. "In fact, we bought the one titled *Serenity*."

"One of my favorite pieces." Gitana was thrilled.

"May I call to arrange for an interview?" Jessie asked and looked from her to Rex.

"You can call me," the devil man offered. "We'll set up a time within the next few days."

Rex high-fived Gitana after the couple left. His excitement bubbled over as he did a little dance.

One by one, the white titled plaques placed next to the paintings were stickered—red dots for sold and yellow for pending. Her success meant Cade's success. This would pay for the framing.

Gitana greeted her guests until the last possible minute before her bladder would burst. She motioned to Rex her intent and he winked. He would cover until she returned.

Back on the floor, she spotted Maddy, who was dressed in plaid. She had her arm curled around Cade's, and they were deep in conversation. Surprise. Surprise. Not wanting to disturb him or deal with her, she moved to the front for a minute to see who might be at the bar.

She grabbed one of the sparkling juices off the counter and heard a distinct laugh above the chatter. The hairs on her arm straightened. She knew of only one person who had that shrill pitch.

Gitana had to be mistaken. Trisha wasn't on the list, but

Gitana found her standing next to the old man painting. John's new wife had hair piled on top of her head like a bird's nest. She wore a speckled, light-blue halter dress with a rhinestone belt accenting her tiny waist. She had a great body for just having a baby.

Gitana wondered if John made her diet and work out to get back in shape. Those would have been the rules if they were still married.

Trisha stepped back. *Speak of the devil.* John put his arm around his wife and laughed at something she said.

Why in hell were they at her show?

Gitana saw Layne across the room. He looked up from his conversation with Billy Friedman as if knowing she needed him. She tilted her head toward Trisha and John. He followed with his eyes. At first, he didn't recognize who she pointed to and then it clicked. He seemed just as surprised.

"Annabella!"

Gitana jumped. Pete, in his normal tweed suit, walked toward her with his arms open.

"Hi, boss!" She smiled. "I'm glad you could make it." She then remembered. "Hey, weren't you in charge of the wedding tonight?"

"The reason why I have Jillian." He chuckled as if he got away with something. He pointed to her paintings. "Uff! I didn't realize how much for your talent."

Gitana laughed. "Art isn't cheap."

"But the paintings at the winery..." He shook his head.

"They belong to the winery," she insisted. The least she

could do for him, she thought. Keeping her on for the insurance meant more than he could imagine.

A broad grin showed his good fortune. He thanked and hugged her for the originals before she changed her mind.

"Have you been through the gallery?" she asked. Layne made his way toward them.

"I've only seen what's before me here." He motioned toward the front.

"Please, look around and tell me what you think." One of the servers passed by, carrying a tray of little treats, and she stopped him. "Here, try the spinach pastries. You'll like them."

Pete went for the food.

She excused herself to meet Layne. "Any word?"

"Rex isn't sure how they got in," he said low enough for only her to hear. "He thinks maybe through an association. You want me to ask them to leave?"

"No." Gitana decided, against her better judgment. John never stayed long at these events. She hoped they would get bored and disappear on their own.

Gitana laughed. Layne looked confused, so she shared. "I don't think he realizes who the artist is. He calls me Annabella. He never liked my nickname. I believe he called me Gitana once, before we started dating."

"I get the feeling he's going to find out." Layne nudged her to look.

John was talking to Rex, and he pulled Cade into the conversation.

"Shit." Gitana covered her mouth. She swore louder

than she expected. No one was staring. Good.

"Stay low," Layne told her. "I have to get more champagne from the back."

Gitana ducked to the corner of the gallery. She finished her drink and set the glass on the table.

"Annabella."

She cringed.

"I thought it was you."

"John." She acted surprised.

He still had Trisha by the waist. Her ex smirked. He noticed she had put on weight. "You're enjoying those Pop Tarts I see. Your nose infected yet?"

Keep cool. Keep cool.

He added, "What brings you here tonight?"

Gitana counted to three and smiled. "I majored in art. Remember?"

"Oh, yes," he said without interest. "I forgot."

"Who did you come with?" She smiled with a sweet demeanor. "I know your name wasn't on the invite list."

Burn. She knew who was invited.

"Harry—Harry Renford," he coughed.

"The interior designer. Interesting." She remembered Rex mentioning him. "Are you remodeling the house?"

"Yes, we are," Trisha piped in.

Irritated, John turned to his wife. "Darling, could you please find us more of the Shiraz?"

His words were not a question but an order. Gitana felt sorry for Trisha. Poor woman had no idea what she was getting into.

John changed his expression after his wife left. He moved closer to Gitana and snarled. "I want my papers back."

"What papers?" Gitana kept her composure.

"San Jose. The safety deposit box." His forehead wrinkled and the lines around his mouth tightened.

"You found your key?"

"I had it drilled. Amazing how a few days earlier a Mrs. Annabella Sothers paid a visit to the bank. *With a key.*"

She nodded to a couple passing by, then asked, "Is that my problem?"

"You had no right. The divorce gave me all our accounts, including the safety deposit boxes."

"So you knew what was in the box."

Lucky for her, he was not into scenes. Otherwise, he was ready to blow his stack. "Those documents are mine."

"Yes, unless my name is on them. My name was on *most* of them." She wanted to see his reaction. A flick of anger shot through his eyes as if he knew she was on to him. "You were supposed to hand those over to me. You kept them."

His lip twitched.

If John was so upset about her having the papers, they had some value to him. His reaction convinced her of his guilt. She pushed. "Why do you need the documents?"

He tugged at his collar as if the shirt was too tight around his neck. "Confidential information. You aren't supposed to have them."

She cocked her eyebrow. "Is that why they were in a

bank and not the hospital?"

"Still, my business and not yours."

"I wanted the diamonds," she confessed as if she had no interest in the rest. "If I get the papers back, I'll let you know."

"What?" His head cocked and the wrinkles around his eyes folded like an accordion.

Oh, this was sweet. She saw...maybe fear? "I gave them to my doctor. She needed my medical records."

A loud swish of air escaped his mouth. "Who's your doctor?"

"John, right?" Cade broke in and handed him a glass of wine. "I insisted on helping your wife."

"Cade," Gitana said to cover her sigh of relief. He had perfect timing.

John reset his face into the debonair doctor. He raised his glass to thank him.

Cade nodded, then slid his arm around Gitana's waist. "I see you've met my fiancée."

"Your fiancée?" John's voice cracked into a laugh.

Gitana ignored her ex's remark. Cade's surprised her more. She liked how the words rolled from his tongue. She tingled inside.

Gitana introduced them, "Cade, this is my ex and his wife. John and Trisha."

"Oh, Sothers. Right. I didn't think of putting the two together." He sounded so nonchalant. "Did you tell them our joyous news?"

"You tell them." She let him take the honors.

He beamed. "We're expecting. The baby's due this April."

John choked on his wine. Trisha's face twisted like the Screamer from Edvard Munch's famous painting. She stared at her husband. Did he tell her all about their troubles? How she couldn't conceive? No, but she bet his parents did.

"Simply a miracle, isn't it, John?" Gitana noticed her ex was starting to sweat.

"How wonderful!" Trisha, of course, didn't want to be rude. She smiled but shot glances at her husband.

"Congratulations," her ex muttered. His lip twitched.

"The other good news," Cade said to Gitana, "John and Trisha bought one of your paintings. The *Old Man*."

John froze, then paled when he connected the name of the artist to her. Trisha gasped and coughed to cover her surprise.

"I love the painting." Gitana rubbed it in even more. "It's one of my favorites."

The night shined brighter than she expected. Her ex bought her painting, and the most expensive one in the gallery.

"You're Gitana?" Trisha stammered.

"Yes, my nickname. I'm surprised John didn't tell you. He knew."

Trisha's face turned beet red. She glared at her husband.

Gitana said, "The painting will look perfect above the fireplace in the living room, or the upstairs hall next to the balcony rail."

Everything in their house had her stamp. She doubted if they replaced or changed any of the furniture or decorations. John liked the way it looked but maybe not so much anymore.

"Please, excuse us." Gitana spotted Pete with his lawyer coming toward her. She grabbed Cade's arm to follow.

"Your paintings are remarkable, Gitana. Stunning," Carl shook her hand with vigor. "Who's the sculptor?"

"You're looking at him," Cade stuck out his hand and introduced himself.

"I bought the *Twilight Moon* piece for my office."

"Good choice," Cade said, pleased. As they continued their conversation, Pete pulled Gitana aside.

His voice lowered. "I told Carl about the situation with your ex. He's willing to represent you. He thinks you have a strong case."

"A case?" Her voice quavered. In a funny way, she thought the events were more like a blessing. If they had not taken place, she might still be with John in her Stepford wife role. She would not be pregnant or have become friends with Layne and Rex.

"Think about it." Pete patted her shoulder. "We'll talk later."

Cade put his hand on Gitana's back and tapped his fingers to get her attention. Dr. Braustein was heading toward them.

"I appreciate your coming," Gitana said to Carl.

"You have my number." The lawyer winked. "Call if you need anything."

She nodded.

Cade eased the two men into another direction to give Gitana time alone with her doctor. They walked over to the champagne.

Gitana warned, "John is here with his wife. You will need to be careful. If he gets wind that you're my doctor, he'll hound you."

Dr. Braustein's eyebrows came up and browsed the room, curious. Tonight, she did not look like a doctor. She wore a simple black pantsuit with her hair slicked back.

"I could say the same for you. Be careful," Dr. Braustein said. "The Medical Board of California started an investigation on Dr. Sothers approximately six months ago. He's had numerous complaints filed against him. Yours is enough to revoke his license."

"Yes, I've heard." Gitana's head buzzed. Layne had done some research. He showed her the documents.

Dr. Braustein grabbed her arm when she lost her balance.

"Sorry," Gitana apologized. Even now, she had a hard time knowing John could be stripped of his doctor status. His downfall was not her gain. She wanted him to face what he had done to her, but she did not want his life ruined.

"These are serious charges, Gitana. Others have complained as well."

"Do you think he knows?" She remembered how the veins popped in his neck when he asked for the papers at her boat.

The doctor shrugged. "Does it matter?"

"It's hard to be responsible for destroying someone's life, their career."

"His life versus other patients who trusted him? You? All the pain you went through? This has to stop."

Gitana nodded with acceptance. This was not all about her. He played God on others as well. The downward turn had already started. Just as he had wiped his hands of her, she had to do the same with him. His fate.

She found a chair before her legs gave out. Dr. Braustein handed her a glass of water and said, "You look tired, Gitana. You need some rest."

She agreed. "It's been a stressful day."

"Come see me tomorrow. The clinic's not open, but I'll be at the office. Just for a quick checkup. You've had a lot on your plate."

"I will," Gitana promised. The storm had begun. She looked around but didn't see John or Trisha.

"They left," Cade said.

His support and the glass of water refreshed her enough to finish the show. As the guests faded, she stayed near the entrance to thank them for coming. Her feet pulsed in her shoes by the time the last guests said their goodbyes. She sat on one of the chairs and kicked them off.

"You, Wild Child, should smile," the devil man said.

"I am. My toes are free." She raised her foot to massage the bottom of it.

"No, silly." He locked the doors to the front. "You were amazing. Ten sold. Five pending. Out of thirty—that's half."

"And one bought by my ex," Gitana added.

"If Dr. Bunghole doesn't pull through with the sale, I have two more clients who are interested."

Cade and Layne joined them from the back. They brought beer for them and sparkling juice for her. They toasted the night and the success of the show.

Gitana raised her glass to Cade. "You were good." She thanked him with her eyes. "I wasn't sure if you knew who John and Trisha were."

"Layne clued me in."

"Did you see his face? Both their expressions were priceless when you told them I was your fiancée and pregnant."

Layne and Rex perked their ears at the word fiancée. They glanced toward each other and then back to them.

"Here's to a great evening." Cade raised his beer. "And, here's to my gorgeous artist."

"To all of us." Gitana toasted. "I wouldn't be here today without my wonderful friends, my watchers."

"What's with…" Rex was still perplexed. "Did you say…fiancée?"

Cade stood behind Gitana and wrapped his arms around her. He kissed the top of her head, the tip of her ear, her nose. "I like the sound of those words."

Gitana's hand came up to cradle him in a hug. She smiled with eyes closed. Her life, her plans now changed.

Author's Biography

Beth M James has never known life without pen and paper, or a life without lessons learned. But raising a family and career came before her role as an author. She lives in the St. Croix Valley between Wisconsin and Minnesota. Now that her children are adults and she's established in her daytime career, Beth's next step is to write about women and lessons learned. Her mind is full of different story ideas that she can't wait to write about and for her readers to enjoy... or maybe for some to become enlightened. She also likes camping, hiking, and jigsaw puzzles. You can find her at:

www.bethmjames.com
https://www.facebook.com/BethMJamesAuthor

Made in the USA
Charleston, SC
08 December 2013